JOY IN MUDVILLE

JOY IN MUDVILLE

Gordon McAlpine

E. P. DUTTON · NEW YORK

Published in the United States by E. P. Dutton,
a division of NAL Penguin Inc.,
2 Park Avenue, New York, N.Y. 10016.

Published simultaneously in Canada by Fitzhenry and Whiteside, Limited, Toronto.

Library of Congress Cataloging-in-Publication Data

McAlpine, Gordon.
Joy in Mudville.
I. Title.
PS3563.C274J69   1989   813'.54   88-30996

ISBN: 0-525-24748-3

Designed by Margo D. Barooshian

1 3 5 7 9 10 8 6 4 2

First Edition

Grateful acknowledgment is given for permission to quote lyrics from the following songs:

"Einstein Theme Song," words and music by Woody Guthrie. TRO copyright © 1965 by Ludlow Music, Inc., New York, N.Y. Used by permission.

"This Train Is Bound for Glory," adapted by Woody Guthrie. Copyright © 1958 (renewed) by Woody Guthrie Publications Inc. All rights reserved. Used by permission.

"So Long, It's Been Good to Know Yuh (Dusty Old Dust)." TRO copyright © 1940 (renewed 1968), 1950 (renewed 1978), and 1963 by Folkways Music Publishers, Inc., New York, N.Y. Used by permission.

"Worried Man Blues," adapted by Woody Guthrie. Copyright © 1987 by Woody Guthrie Publications Inc. All rights reserved. Used by permission.

For my son, Jonathan

PROLOGUE

As the clock atop the Wrigley Building struck 2:30 on the afternoon of October 1, all was still bright and boisterous in Chicago, Illinois. For in that last moment the most exuberant hopes of Al Capone, who sat in a box seat, Carl Sandburg, who sat in the bleachers, and every other citizen of the Windy City still burned brightly. Indeed, not *one* of the 38,143 who had jammed Wrigley Field might even have imagined the awesome and disheartening force that awaited their hometown Cubs in the fire-hardened wood grain of Babe Ruth's Louisville Slugger. Surviving Chicagoans refer even now to that moment as the last sixty seconds of their unblemished and innocent youth—when nights might still be spent without the recollection of Ruth's swing, the crack of the bat, the sight of the baseball soaring over and beyond the bleachers in center field, over the Paradise Theatre on Crawford Avenue, over the tenements and town houses and stockyards, hooking gently like a tiny star answering the pull of an inscrutable gravity; over the Wrigley Building and the Lindbergh Light on a course that would ultimately lead over the city limits and the state line, over the Great Plains, the

Rocky Mountains, and west to the very edge of the American continent. Two thousand miles on the dead fly.

"Guess I got all of it," Ruth would later comment.

It was the visitors' half of the fifth inning, game three of the World Series. Records indicate that meteorological conditions were routine throughout the Midwest; the University of Chicago School of Astronomy (alma mater of Loren Woodville) reported no unusual solar activity; and the tree surgeon at Louisville Slugger, whose job it was to select the particular hardwood that went into the manufacturing of baseball bats, reported nothing unusual about the Bambino's slice of wood. In all, not even Professor Marvel of Omaha, Nebraska, balloonist and soothsayer, could have predicted that Ruth would send one into the stratosphere. It was like this:

Sixteen brightly colored pennants, one for each team in the major leagues, flapped from atop the buzzing ballpark. Old Man Wrigley, owner of the Chicago Cubs and greatest chewing gum magnate in the history of the world, sat unsteadily in a box seat behind home plate with a plaid blanket spread over his shaky legs. In his monogrammed shirt pocket was a folded scorecard upon which was scrawled in his own hand, *Dear God—I will donate five million dollars and the island of Santa Catalina to the charity of your choice if you will but allow us to win.*

Young vendors with strained, cracking voices moved up and down the aisles hawking peanuts and Cracker Jack; businessmen in tailored suits and fedoras shifted nervously and loosened to the frontier of respectability their Windsor knots. While on the field the Cubs and the powerful New York Yankees were tied 4–4.

Then Babe Ruth, the Sultan of Swat, stepped out of the visitors' dugout. A low, unsuspecting murmur arose from the stands as Ruth squinted up into the bright sun. After a moment, he looked away, spitting into the palms of his hands and rubbing them together. The first vicious catcalls drifted toward Ruth from across the green playing field—from the direction of the distant bleachers in center field. Ruth took a deep breath and, with his customary hulking, spindle-legged grace, moved forward to the empty on-deck circle.

He picked up two thick bats, swung them back and forth across his shoulders, loosening up, swatting at imaginary fastballs, stretching the muscles in his back and arms. Then he smiled and knelt on one knee as though solemnly engaged in a warrior's prayer before entering the field of battle—the sublime peace before the sublime violence. But Ruth was not praying. He was, at just that moment, considering the romantic possibilities of a nubile waitress he had met that morning at breakfast. He was considering the way her flesh pressed against her jelly-stained white-linen uniform in just the right places and with just the right proportion.

All around him the Cub fans were considering murder and eternal damnation. "Drop dead, Ruth!" a small woman in a box seat yelled. "Go to hell, Fat Ass!" another called, hurling the words at the Bambino like rotten eggs. "You stink!" Old Man Wrigley screamed, the veins in his wrinkled neck standing out as clear and red as the laces on a baseball.

Ruth disengaged himself from the brief waitress reverie and glanced into the stands. "What's eating them?" he asked himself, sneering at every obscene gesture that greeted his attention.

"Go to hell, Yankee Fat Ass!"

"Strike the bum out!"

"Kill the bastard!"

So what else is new? Ruth thought. He cleared his throat and turned around in a slow circle. The Chicagoans clapped their rolled-up scorecards into the palms of their hands, not as homage but rather as a policeman claps his nightstick into the calloused palm of the law. Ruth wiped his forehead with the back of his wrist. He smiled at a pretty young Chicago girl, who responded with an obscene phrase which, in a different context and with a slight rewording, Ruth might have welcomed as an unusual but enormously appealing invitation. Before 38,143 strangers, however, he turned away and swallowed hard to keep from responding with an obscenity of his own.

"Hey, Yankee baboon! You can't hit!"

"Get out of town, bum!"

"You stink, Ruth!"

Once, the Bambino recalled, on a barnstorming tour through Florida, he had absentmindedly rushed out of the clubhouse, through the dugout, and onto the playing field without having zipped up his baseball trousers. Because Ruth never wore undergarments, his plate appearance provided the fans with more of a look at the slugger's prowess than they had bargained for when they bought a ticket. The Floridians had responded with jeers that were not unlike the catcalls that surrounded the Babe now. It was an idea. With as much subtlety as he could muster (not much), he checked his fly. "Well, I'll be damned," he said to himself. To his bewilderment, it was zipped. He reached around to the seat of his pin-striped trousers. They were untorn.

Hm-m-m, Ruth thought as he took another practice swing. He looked into the screaming, frenzied crowd, into the angry thousands. "Maybe it's just the whole goddamn world," he whispered to himself.*

The Bambino, loosened up now, tossed away one of the bats and started toward the batter's box. Alone. Babe Ruth alone against the nine Cub fielders, whose muscles tensed in determined anticipation as he neared the plate; alone against the 38,143 jammed screaming into Wrigley Field; alone against the accumulated psychic energy of the winos and bank presidents who stood indistinguishable from one another in bread lines throughout the Windy City, the prostitutes who entertained in plush Cicero houses of hospitality, the boys who played in jazz bands and the ship captains who sailed the lake, the skinny man who fed the lions at the zoo and the doctors, lawyers, and local politicians who had gathered around Philco radio sets throughout the city; alone against the lucky few Chicagoans who still had jobs in the stockyards and the gangsters who still had work in the rackets. Alone against an entire city.

*Noted psychologist Carl Jung, in his *Baseball and the Unconscious,* wrote that the Cub fans' passionate demonstration of October 1 represented "misplaced aggressions in the city's collective unconscious resulting from the adversarial relationship between the economic and social strains of the Great Depression and the heroic archetype represented by the 'invader,' Ruth."

"Lordy, lordy," Ruth said to himself as he stopped to tap, with the end of his bat, the dirt clods from his spikes.

Alone against the very soil of Chicago.

An NBC radio survey would indicate that *all human beings* then living in Chicago were pulling for the hometown Cubbies as if their very lives depended on the victory. Unsuspecting, they screamed, "Fan the Fat Ass!" as Ruth stepped into the box. Every man, woman, and child in the entire city. Except three.

Our heroes.

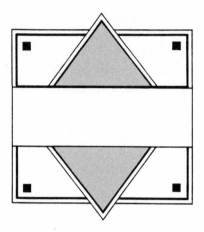

Originally, Buddy Easter knew almost nothing of Abner Doubleday—whose birthday was one hundred years (to the day) before Buddy's own—except of course that Doubleday invented baseball, fired the North's first defensive shot in the Civil War, became a hero at Gettysburg, and died roughly forty years before the day Babe Ruth approached home plate at Wrigley Field with the score tied 4–4 in the fifth inning. Everything else that Buddy knew about Abner Doubleday he learned in conversation with long-deceased Abner himself. For example, he learned that it is not improper to buy a chocolate soda for a friend even when one's friend is as insubstantial as the ether and altogether unable to partake of the physical world. He learned that Abner actually never intended, when he first invented baseball, for pitchers to come to bat; rather, Abner conceived a doomed and complex plan called the "designated hitter" that was quickly written out of the first rule book. And he learned from Abner, and Abner alone, that nowhere in the universe is there complete solitude, complete isolation, complete loneliness. The very presence of his invisible friend had taught Buddy this.

Aside from Abner Doubleday, however, Buddy Easter had no friends. After all, he was fourteen years old—long past the age when "imaginary" companions are regarded by others as charming or even imaginative. Though Buddy was tall for his age, he was frail and awkward, his perfect skin as smooth and white as a baseball fresh out of the box. When he stood beside his roommates at the Chicago Home for Boys, some of whom had gone with girls behind woodsheds or into dark garages to practice God-only-knows what dabblings upon one another, he appeared a pale and unfit product of America's most infamous city of shootouts and screeching tires.

Abner was little more impressive in appearance (though *any* animate appearance is, for the deceased, impressive in its way). He was tall, like Buddy, but was composed more obviously of sharp angles—everywhere elbows and knees. His nose was long, and his chin jutted from his face at an angle that suggested the incongruous independence of a separate organism rather than the humility of another facial feature. He wore a weather-beaten Union Army coat and trousers, heavy black boots that, naturally, made no sound upon the pavement when he walked, and a baseball cap with an embroidered insignia forgotten by all but the most devoted of baseball aficionados—the Cooperstown Roosters. In addition, Abner Doubleday was vaguely transparent. Particularly when he was in a blue mood.

It mattered not at all to Buddy Easter that when he described his friend's appearance to others—his teacher, doctor, or dormitory matron—they each responded by leading him to the public library to dismantle his delusion the way a short-order cook dismantles fowl. Here, thinking the idea original and conclusive, each would crack for Buddy's edification Volume IV of the *Columbia Encyclopedia*—glowing with omnipotence as if cracking nothing less than the famous first egg itself (the one that came either before or after the world's first chicken). There, under DOUBLEDAY, is a photograph of the Civil War hero and national pastime inventor snapped by Mathew Brady which, they believed, proved that the *real* Abner Doubleday looked nothing like the "vision" Buddy claimed to enjoy and that Buddy was therefore as cracked as that first egg. But Buddy remained unmoved, time and again, in his conviction. After all, of the myriad photographs Brady snapped on battlefields across the South, wasn't it conceivable that a few might have become confused? A mistaken caption here, an inaccurate photograph there? Indeed, Abner himself explained the discrepancy in this way. Though, ultimately, Buddy Easter knew that verisimilitude was not the issue—for he understood, though he never spoke it, that Truth may exist altogether independent from fact.

"Jeepers," Buddy said as he watched Babe Ruth move toward the batter's box.

"Jeepers," Abner agreed.

Being best friends with Abner Doubleday, Buddy had naturally developed an understanding of baseball that grew with each whispered midnight conversation he and Abner shared in the boy's darkened dormitory—an understanding grown to such heights that it had at last arrived at the place where all great understanding eventually arrives: love. Buddy loved baseball. Of course, he and Abner discussed other things on those nights as well. War, or family (Abner had been an orphan too), or school, or the dozen boys snoring peacefully around them. But always there was baseball. And with it both the reassuring certainty of a batting average figured to the thousandth place and the glorious uncertainty of next year's figures.

"Come on," Buddy whispered from the rooftop of the Parkview apartment building as the jeers aimed at Ruth drifted over the ivy-covered outfield wall at Wrigley Field and up to Buddy's perch.

"What's Ruth done today?" Abner asked, moving nearer Buddy on the otherwise unoccupied rooftop to glance at the boy's scorecard.

"Nothing," Buddy answered evenly.

"Hm-m-m," Abner said. "He's due."

Scores of boisterous street urchins jammed other rooftops that offered views, as unobstructed as that which Buddy and Abner enjoyed, of the diamond far below. Everywhere: rooftops crowded with frantic boys bobbing and bumping into one another like bubbles risen to the top of so many tall, brick cauldrons. With each inning, the heat of baseball in October grew more intense atop the roofs until it seemed the most antic boys would either ascend from the apartment buildings like lighter-than-air bubbles or pop into nothingness.

"Strike the bum out!"

"Give him a shave, Root!"

"Kill him!" they cried.

Buddy Easter envied the other boys their directness of thought and expression—even if he rarely shared their sentiment. There were many times when he wished he were different, when he wished he were more like them. Sometimes he tried.

"Go, team!" he shouted toward the ballpark as he had heard the distant boys shout. But he was dissatisfied with the timbre of his voice. Worse, he was appalled that truths unutterably beautiful and simple proved always just that—*unutterable*. What seemed rugged and expressive from the lips of the other boys seemed to Buddy merely inarticulate when pronounced upon his own. "Go, team," he repeated upon the quiet rooftop. And the simple sentiment, formless and vaguely unsatisfying if left unspoken, seemed nonetheless lost altogether when burdened by words. His most recent fear: that whatever truths he might one day find would not be simple ones. That whatever truths he might one day express would not be shared easily.

"What?" Abner asked.

"I said, 'Go, team,' " Buddy answered.

"Oh, right," Abner said.

A doctor once told Buddy not to think so much. But asking a boy not to think is like asking him not to listen for his own heartbeat in the stillness of night. Once one is conscious of such a miracle, it becomes insufferably intriguing. Thinking, thinking. Buddy discovered that there is nothing so complex as simplicity, nothing so fascinating, so thought-worthy. He spent most of one summer thinking about not thinking.

"Just watch the ball game," Abner said, as if he knew Buddy's thoughts.

Buddy nodded. "Okay, pal," he said. And this sounded right.

It was simple, it was wonderful. Buddy Easter was a lot of things (his schoolmates had a whole catalog of names for him), but he was not *alone*. Sitting cross-legged on the roof of the Parkview apartment building, Buddy moved his knee just enough that it brushed against the electric other-dimensional knee of his best friend.

"Just watch the ball game," Abner said, as if some great truth waited there.

Buddy and Abner were alone atop the Parkview apartment building not because the neighborhood boys refused to watch the ball game with them (though an invitation *was* slow in coming) but because Buddy and Abner wanted to be alone—indeed, *needed* to be alone—atop the roof. It was in answer to the basest of instincts, survival, that they had chosen the lonely Parkview as their vantage point. After all, one of them was composed of living tissue, making him vulnerable to the neighborhood boys' sticks and stones, which, unlike mere words, break bones. And though there was much that the neighborhood boys might forgive, there was one sin they believed must surely be answered with terrible violence.

Buddy and Abner breathed this sin with their every breath, sang of it with their every heartbeat. . . .

They were Yankee fans.

The deserted Parkview was the only place in Chicago from which Buddy might watch the first home game of the World Series without being beaten to a pulp. True, he might have pretended to hate the Yankees (the other boys couldn't see Abner pulling for the Bronx Bombers, so *his* sympathies presented no problem). But ultimately Buddy's inability to conceal his true colors, to contain the joy that escaped from between his tightened lips whenever a Bronx Bomber knocked a base hit, made futile any such effort. The Parkview was the only answer.

It was not the location of the building that kept the other boys away. Nor was it the rooftop itself. Potted plants and chaise lounges were spaced evenly about (though the aged tenants fancied themselves too frail to risk the October chill). Indeed, the Parkview had been the *favorite* rooftop of the neighborhood boys until the week before, when Mr. Loch arrived—the new superintendent. Now, a plague would not be more effective in keeping the boys from slipping up the dark stairwells and onto the roof.

Mr. Loch hated trespassers.

Every neighborhood boy knew that the new superintendent was a short, thick man with a mustache that had grown straight down over his mouth, like the whiskers of a walrus, until his lips were completely concealed. The boys knew that Mr. Loch's black hair sat like a mop atop his head and that his bulging muscles pulled his gray work shirt tight enough to his shoulders that the matted outline of thick body hairs pressed through. Most fearsome, however, was the genuine Texas bullwhip he carried in his toolbox. Mr. Loch was an artist with the whip, and it was through this medium that he communicated his mortal hatred of trespassers. The boys knew Mr. Loch was their darkest nightmare, yet not one of them had ever actually seen him. Only Buddy Easter had laid eyes upon Mr. Loch—and lived to tell about it.

Buddy saw the whole thing: the superintendent, the toolbox, the bullwhip, the rage, the murder. Indeed, Buddy had been *with* Frankie Pilaretti (the victim) when the murder occurred. There was, however, nothing he could do but hide behind a potted plant atop the roof of the Parkview and pray that his bulging, frightened eyes might be mistaken for blueberries growing among the half-concealing leaves. It was terrible. There was next to nothing left of poor Frankie—a neighborhood bully who had invited Buddy to the roof of the Parkview to trade baseball cards (the neighborhood boys, however, considered it more likely that Frankie had actually *lured* Buddy to the roof to playfully throw him over the edge; this more neatly fit both their remembrance of Frankie as arch-bully and their own darkest desires). In any case, fate intervened when Mr. Loch appeared on the rooftop, bullwhip in hand, at the moment Buddy happened to bend behind the blessed plant to retrieve a baseball card blown by the swirling wind. Frankie alone remained exposed upon the roof, his red hair a flame to the tinder of terrible destiny. It was all very fast. Even Frankie's baseball cards were shredded.

The most frightful measure of Mr. Loch's terrible competence, however, was that the adults of the neighborhood—including the beat cop, Frankie's teacher, and the parish priest—believed that Frankie had simply moved with his family to Decatur. After all, there had been a truck filled with battered family furniture; the Pilarettis had talked for weeks of moving; no one had ever actually *seen* this terrible new superintendent. Indeed, there was for a time nothing to support Buddy's violent story but his own resolve to set the matter straight and the fervency with which he told it to all the neighborhood boys. This was not enough. For even Buddy understood that his long friendship with Abner Doubleday had done nothing to lend credence to his report. Buddy needed evidence. The boys had to believe.

On the day before the first Chicago game of the World Series, Buddy Easter gained the evidence he required: the shredded, blood-stained Cubs cap that had once belonged to poor Frankie Pilaretti. The authenticity was beyond question. Scribbled in pen on the underside of the bill was Frankie's nickname, "Barrel" (which referred to his relative girth). In addition, the cap smelled vaguely of beer—which the whole Pilaretti family used as shampoo—and was crisscrossed inside by strands of red hair left behind like sad, greasy legacies. The blood was authentic too. Thick, knotted, dark-brown terror. Lots of it. Some of the boys were sickened by the cap. A few cried. Others managed an admirably dispassionate attitude. But all were convinced that next time it could be *their* blood flooding the alley outside the Parkview if they failed to heed Buddy Easter's somber warning. The Parkview apartment building was off-limits to any boy who valued his hide.

Which is why Buddy Easter and Abner Doubleday were alone atop the Parkview as Babe Ruth came to bat in the top of the fifth inning; why Buddy and Abner cheered for the hated Yankees without fearing a violent rebuke from the neighborhood boys; why Buddy and Abner reveled in the American practice of dissent (Thomas Jefferson would be pleased, Abner assured his friend, that in all of partisan Chicago there sat atop the Parkview two Yankee fans—except, of course, that Jefferson was a Cubs fan like everybody else). None of this, however, came about through disregard on

Buddy's part for his own hide. Buddy was as self-concerned as any of the boys, as conscious of his own mortality and of the way his skin too might split beneath the prodding of a genuine Texas bullwhip. Rather, Buddy and Abner accomplished all this because they knew the truth.

There was no Mr. Loch. No bullwhip. No murder.

The lie was actually Abner's idea and, as his invisible friend had already been judged at the Pearly Gates, it seemed to Buddy of no real moral consequence that Abner should commit another minor indiscretion. The Pilarettis were all in Decatur, the regular superintendent of the Parkview was on vacation in Florida, and the boys of the neighborhood were ripe for a violent romance—what could be more perfect? Besides, there was no other way to secure a private rooftop during the World Series.

The difficult part of the scheme was gaining the evidence. Rather, not the evidence itself—a Cubs cap is easily enough bought at one of the stalls outside Wrigley Field, strands of red hair are easily enough pulled from the head of any Irishman sleeping one off on a park bench, every boy knew that Frankie had scribbled his nickname on the underside of his bill, and a razor blade shreds a cap as cruelly as any bullwhip. The difficulty was in obtaining the blood to prove the cap not only authentic but terrifying. And not just any blood would do.

In a city like Chicago, with its shootouts and screeching automobile chases, with its St. Valentine's Day massacres and milelong funeral processions, one might have routinely found bleeding gangsters left like morning newspapers in the street. Surely there were plenty of dead and dying animals—dogs run over by the screeching automobiles in which the doomed gangsters rode, cats impaled upon flagpoles as a warning from one gang to another. And the stockyards! After sixty days on the job, a butcher's hands can never be scrubbed clean of the scent of blood. Dogs will always lick his fingers. Buddy might have dipped his recently bought and shredded Cubs cap into any one of the multitudinous wounds in Chicago. But gangster blood was impure. And animal blood was too innocent to be used for deceit, he believed. And Abner had no blood.

In the end, it had seemed right to Buddy that if his plan was to work it should be his own blood that finally made it true. Not just misleading, convincing, successful. *True.* This is the miracle of blood. Abner had explained long before that the dead most envy the living not for their consciousness—for Abner was as conscious (sometimes painfully self-conscious) as any birthday celebrant or twittering young lover—or for their blessed ignorance, but for the blood coursing through their veins. Not a lustful envy and not vampiric, Abner explained. But an envy much like awe for the prospect that this blood represented, at any moment, mortal commitment. That the living might *lose so much* is what the dead envy. Buddy believed that there was power and truth in this blessed capacity for loss.

Which is why he and Abner Doubleday had silently climbed to the roof of the Parkview apartment building two nights ago. Why they took with them the Cubs cap that by morning would be the talk of the neighborhood and the razor blade which that afternoon they had already used to shred the cap. Why, by the light of a million stars, Buddy Easter slashed the back of his hand with the blade and let his own warm blood run true over the baseball cap. Why all that would happen, would happen.

Outside the ballpark a crowd of Chicagoans who had neither tickets to the game nor a radio at home paced the sidewalk, listening to the squeals and shouts and curses from within, gauging the course of events on the diamond by the pleas and recriminations that slipped over Wrigley's brick walls. Top of the fifth, something monumental. . . . The Chicagoans wandered the intersection of Clark and Addison (listening, listening) as oblivious to the traffic as so many monks engaged in silent reverie. The men wore baggy-legged trousers, white shirts, ties, sport coats; the women wore drab skirts that hugged their hips. As one, they cheered and moaned not in response to the ball game itself but to the cheering and moaning of the 38,143 inside. They wrung their hands. On their faces were brow-furrowed looks of deep concentration. Listening, listening.

Except one.

Alice de Minuette had run all night to reach the corner of Clark and Addison, fueled by a fear that had given her graceful frame the stamina of Babe Didrikson. In the wee hours she had moved with self-conscious calm past O'Banion's Flower Shop, where Al Capone spent three thousand dollars a month on funeral wreaths for enemies who (unlike Alice) moved just a step too slow. As the sun rose she drifted past ashen women bundled in scarves who held their babies close the way girls from the Gold Coast carry gift-wrapped packages from Marshall Field's. As lunchtime passed, she glided by sunken-eyed men who sold apples on street corners and made lewd propositions of produce for passion. She had run from Cicero to the North Side, past a hundred corner markets and a thousand quiet lawns, to Wrigley Field. Not because she was a fan of the Cubs. Rather, because she was a rabbit in a world of foxes.

She might have taken a cab. But Al Capone owned the cabs— and the buses and the elevated trains. If he owned the vehicle then surely, Alice feared, he held some claim to the contents as well—if only by virtue of the savage axiom that possession is nine tenths of the law. Alice would not be possessed. This was why she ran.

"Please," she said to no one in particular.

The Cub fans who milled about her (listening, listening) ignored her plea. They thought that, like themselves, she was merely imploring God to help the hometown team.

"I need to get inside the ballpark," she continued. "But I don't have a ticket."

Such a remark would have been met with ridicule and scorn, perhaps even violence, by the men around her had she not been so beautiful. After all, *everyone* wanted inside the ballpark. The naïveté with which she had spoken was precisely that which, in similar moments, identifies for the strong their victims: the simplicity of expression that is at once universally praised and brutally exploited. But because she was beautiful, only one woman among the immediate crowd snapped at her. "We all need to get inside, lady!"

"But I *really* need to get in," Alice continued.

"Just listen to the ball game, ma'am," said an old man in a derby and bow tie.

The noise from within the ballpark grew louder. Alice took a short breath. There was a familiar passion in the voices of the fans inside—youthful, fearless, vulnerable—that momentarily distracted her and made her wonder if this game might actually speak as clearly to the hearts of the vocal thousands as it had once spoken to her own. When she too was stirred by the pageantry, the color—outfield grass the shade of new money—the graceful movements of the ballplayers, the shameless romantic gleam in their eyes. When the umpire's call to "Play ball!" conjured, devilishly in her mind, images of amorous evenings spent with the young pitching star whose team came to Chicago every few weeks. Evenings with George Herman Ruth. The Babe. Fifteen years past, now. . . . Is it possible, she wondered, to feel real passion for this game without first falling tragically (youthfully) in love with its greatest star?

No matter now.

"I *really* need to get in," Alice continued. "I need to see the Babe. He can help me. There's nobody else in this whole town. Al Capone is—" She stopped.

She could not explain.

Until the night before, Alice de Minuette had never seen Al Capone in person. Nonetheless, she was familiar with his round, scarred face. Capone's was an image found as routinely in the dreams and nightmares of the hungry city as it was upon the front pages of its newspapers. Alice knew now, however, that Capone had *indeed seen her* (somewhere, sometime) and since that secret moment had nightly recalled her image in dreams unmentionable by their nature. More, he had conceived a plan to make her his: flowers, *Sonnets from the Portuguese,* anonymity. A plan to possess her. It had almost worked.

Each night for the past six months Alice de Minuette had received at her home a dozen roses delivered by a deaf-mute who accepted no tips—roses as soft and red as the low-cut dress Alice wore to the dance hall on nights near the end of each month when she needed a little extra in tips. Alice eventually owned more empty vases than a barker at a dime-toss concession. The cards enclosed were unsigned but included exquisite poems, which asked, *How do I love thee?* Subsequent deliveries sought, to the depth and breadth and height to which one's soul can reach, to answer the question. By the time Alice learned that the poems had not actually been written by the secret admirer, it was too late. Perseverance (and the subtle aromatic spell worked by ten thousand rose petals enclosed within a one-room apartment) finally persuaded Alice to meet this secret friend—she hoped he would be tall and gentle—the night before the first home game of the Series. . . .

Capone proved short and cruel.

"Does anyone have a ticket to sell?" Alice asked.

"Drop dead, lady!"

It had been fifteen years since Alice had embraced a real friendship with a man. She was not afraid of men, and she did not dislike them. Indeed, as she moved about the dance floor each night—feeling the muscle in a workman's back, the tension in an accountant's shoulder, the quivering knot in a husband's spine which spoke of fear or lust or, perhaps, some tragedy deeper than the dim light of the dance hall might ever reveal—she understood that in the places where their bodies touched (where their hips brushed, their hands clasped, their hair mingled) was given the electric order that commands stars to shine and single cells to split. How could Alice know this and not like the men with whom she was paid to dance? It was this very liking that kept her from knowing them, from befriending them; this liking that might so easily have become loving.

Alice *had* once loved. She had been mad, she had been happy, she had been drunk with schoolgirl irreverence. Yet born of her union with joy was a glimpse of the infinite, a glimpse of the darkness at the end of the dizzying light. In the eyes of the men with whom she danced and from whom she ultimately turned away was the same light. She yearned. Yet she reminded herself that the child of her one great love had been *real* (she had named him George Herman Ruth, Jr.), more tangible than electricity, and yet now he was gone—all fifteen years removed, all as immediate as whatever song the orchestra played as she whirled about the floor for a dime a dance.

"I can pay good money for a ticket," Alice announced.

"Shut up, willya?" snapped a toothless old man who paced nearby. "Can't ya see we're trying to listen to the ball game?"

Alice knew that among the thousands gathered on the sidewalk listening to the news from within there moved some who were *looking* as well. Looking for her. She knew that Capone had agents everywhere and that, after the debacle of the night before, these agents were surely employed in seeking her out. Any one of the Cub fans might be an assassin. The gray-haired man who stood on the corner beside a sign that read May God Damn the Yankees to the Everlasting Fires of Hell!; the dour, bald man in business suit and baseball spikes; the fat woman who held a Cubs pennant before her with a silent reverence previously reserved for religious icons; the policeman with the pink, bulbous nose; the crippled pencil salesman, half torso, half wooden cart. Any one of them. Yet coming here seemed her only hope.

Babe Ruth, she recalled, was tall and gentle.

She pushed her way through the crowd toward the guarded gates of the ballpark.

"Wait!" someone called.

She stopped. She swallowed hard. She thought of the Derringer she carried in her purse. She had never fired the tiny pistol (a gift from another admirer). She had never held it. She had not even *seen* the gun since it was given to her. It had remained at the bottom of her purse among a half-dozen lipstick cases, a compact, three matchbooks, a picture of Tahiti clipped from a magazine, and two lucky Russian pennies said to have been taken off the eyes of Catherine the Great. She had pushed away a thousand men whose pawing hands sought to gain more in the dark than their dime for a dance entitled them to, without once drawing the gun. But this was different. This was not honor, this was not pinches that left bruises in the morning—this was her life.

"Wait!"

Turning toward the voice, Alice de Minuette discovered that choosing to *draw* a weapon is not nearly as simple a decision as it appears in the movies. Real life is too filled by doubt. Besides, she wasn't sure the gun was loaded.

"May I be of help, miss?" asked the policeman with the pink nose.

She shook her head no.

"Miss?" he asked, pushing past Cub fans in a crooked path toward her. "Are you all right?"

Alice pressed her purse nearer her body.

"Miss?" the policeman repeated as he stepped around a priest in a Cubs cap whose fingers and lips worked in frantic perfection upon a rosary.

Alice brushed back a strand of hair that had fallen in her eyes. She took a deep breath. She steadied herself.

The policeman smiled. "Miss?"

"Yes," she said at last. "I suppose you may be of help."

No Derringer. No flight. She had run far enough. Most of the policemen in Chicago were on Capone's payroll as well as the city's. This was a good part of Alice's problem. But not all the policemen. Alice had to trust *someone*. The lumbering movements of the approaching officer gave Alice reassurance.

She smiled.

"Christ, miss," the policeman said, stopping an arm's length away. "Jesus H. Christ."

"What is it?"

"You're very pretty," he answered.

Alice shook her head. "I'm a mess," she said. Then she looked away as she had looked away a thousand times at the ballroom when gentlemen made similar compliments. Looked at nothing; looked at anything but the eyes that just then looked upon *her* with such bold desire.

"No," the policeman said.

She was not a mess. Even after hours of flight through the back alleys and crowded avenues of America's sooty second city, she remained beautiful. With cheeks flushed and chest still lightly heaving, she grew only more alluring—more impossibly perfect for these very reminders of her imperfection. A sprinkle of perspiration on her brow served, like dew on a rose, to illustrate that real flowers exist not under glass but in a world of damp nights and spurned admirers grown mortally hateful.

"I need to see somebody in there," she said.

"Do you have a ticket?"

She shook her head no.

"Then we have a problem," he concluded.

"It's very important," she said.

"Your hair!"

"What?" she asked.

"Very nice," the policeman explained.

The gentlemen at Marnie's Dance Hall reported that Alice's long hair radiated in the half darkness a golden light of its own that lingered even after Alice had moved on to the next dancing partner. She rarely wore hats.

"It's just hair," she said.

"Who do you need to meet in there?" the policeman asked. "Your husband?"

"No."

"I guess you're not married then?"

"I need to meet Babe Ruth," she answered.

The policeman smiled. "Goddamn Yankee," he muttered. He removed his hat, scratched his head, replaced the hat, and stepped nearer Alice. "I think he's kinda busy right now, miss. Maybe I can show you around until after the ball game."

"I used to know him," she explained. "I used to—" She stopped, suddenly breathless. She raised her hand to her eyes for a moment to regain composure, startled by her own words, by a sense of profound understatement that seemed in its simplicity more frightful than any confession. "I used to know him well."

"He's playing ball, miss."

"He'll remember me," she said. "It's been a long time, but there are some things you don't forget. Like I remember that there are three outs to an inning, nine men to a side, three strikes to every batter. There are some things you can't forget."

The policeman held his palms up. "Okay, miss, I believe you. But that don't change a thing. You can't get into the ballpark without a ticket."

"But *you* can," Alice said.

She removed from her purse a sealed white envelope. Across the front she had scribbled:

Dear George,

There were reasons I never said goodbye. You'll understand. For now, I need your help. I'm outside the ballpark. Please hurry! I'll explain later. I'm sorry. There is no place else for me to turn.

Alice

The policeman glanced at the envelope, flipping from one side to the other—pretending not to read what Alice had written. His lips, however, moved with each silent syllable.

"Do you have a problem, miss?" the policeman asked at last. "The Chicago Police Department is at your service. Anything we can do—"

"Thank you," Alice said. "But all I need you to do is give this to Babe Ruth."

"What are you to Ruth?" he asked.

This was not a simple question. Had Alice ever really known the answer, she might just now be standing someplace other than outside a ballpark in mortal danger.

"I mean, are you his girl or something?" he continued.

She shook her head. "No, not his girl."

"You an actress?" he asked.

"Please," she answered, touching his shoulder with her fingers. She felt his arm tighten, watched him stand straighter, shoulders back. She felt a shudder run through his body. It was not fair. But then, as far as Alice had seen, neither was any other aspect of real life. "Just take the envelope inside," she continued. "Then you and I can get to know each other."

"You a painter's model?" he managed, gulping a breath of air.

"Please?"

"A singer?"

She shook her head. "I work in a dance hall," she answered at last.

"You what?"

"A dime a dance," she continued. "Six nights a week. Nothing funny."

"Oh," he said. "I see."

But she knew he didn't see. Alice knew from his change of expression that she was suddenly no longer a candidate to meet his saintly mother or ever to wash his police-issue blue socks. Not a dance hall girl; perhaps an actress—but never a dance hall girl. The policeman, his cynicism a habit, a conceit, which left him more ill-prepared for truth than even the most debilitating naïveté, could never conceive that Alice might *not* sleep with every paying customer. After all, she was a *dance hall girl*. It didn't matter to Alice. Contradiction and confusion and misconception seemed the natural order. These days Alice herself thought only of survival (and sometimes of the child, lost as an infant during the influenza epidemic).

At last the policeman nodded. "You wait here." He slipped the envelope into his shirt pocket. "I'll be back. Maybe you can owe me a dance lesson or something for this favor. Right? Maybe you can make it something real nice."

"I'll be here," Alice said.

She watched him pick his way through the crowd, shuffling through pockets of burly men, sauntering past clutches of silent women. At last he arrived at the main gate. She watched him gesture to the attendant. After a moment, he passed inside the ballpark and Alice allowed herself a single premature sigh of relief.

Then something happened.

It began with a buzzing from within the ballpark—as if the myriad human voices had blended into a chorus as simultaneously meaningful and unintelligible as the humming of bees in a hive. Alice didn't know what to think but only what to feel: fear. Something terrible inside. The hum lowered until it scraped the bottom of some aural pit and became at last intelligible. "Boo!" the Cub fans sang, losing themselves in the long vowel as dervishes lose themselves in the dance. Then a frantic pulse of voices gradually rose above the terrible minor chord and screamed in atonal fervor for blood. Alice recalled once hearing a lion roar at the Lincoln Park Zoo. She remembered sensing that what she heard was the voice of Death itself. She had felt the adrenaline race in her veins in unconscious answer to the lion's primal reminder that *she* was prey— that the world was not so civilized as to have altogether turned away from the consumption of human flesh. The song from within the ballpark held the same reminder.

This is not baseball, she thought.

She turned in a slow circle. The crowd jeered and screamed *outside* the ballpark now as well. On the faces of the fans was a viciousness that Alice had never seen in such number. She knew the expression (the cold furor in the lines around the eyes) from the faces of doped sailors fresh off the lake who fought with knives in the alley outside Marnie's Dance Hall—but in the eyes of children, their mothers, their fathers? This was something new and terrible to Alice.

It brought Capone to mind.

"What is it?" she asked a man standing beside her.

He merely turned to her and snarled, literally baring his teeth.

"What *is* it?" she repeated.

A round, talcum-powdered teenage girl turned toward Alice. She wore upon her face a mad grin outlined by lipstick a shade too red to be respectable, too pale to be profitable. "It's Ruth," she explained.

"What's he done?" Alice asked.

"He stepped into the on-deck circle," the girl answered. "He's up next, the bastard."

Alice stopped. The hatred thickened, like a swarm of mosquitoes, around her. Engulfed, she understood (in a single, complete flash, an epiphany as she imagined must come to saints) the great danger of her plan to escape Capone's vengeance. She could get Babe Ruth killed. It had not occurred to Alice before. Only now, as she listened to the threats made upon Ruth's life, did she understand that the Bambino was as human as she—he had merely dared the lion's den and emerged a thousand times triumphant. She understood now, however, that these triumphs were defined as much by the fact that at any moment he might have been consumed as by the fact that he never had been. And Alice believed that Ruth *would* come to her aid against Capone—in Chicago, in the very jaws of the beast. *Against* Capone.

"I can't do this to him," she whispered. It didn't matter that she had no other plan.

The teenage girl who stood before Alice turned, her mad grin leveled to a precarious self-control, and announced, "I'd like to kill him real slow."

"Ruth?" Alice asked.

The teenager nodded.

"Really?" Alice continued.

The teenager grinned once more. "Really," she answered.

"I believe you," Alice said.

She moved away from the girl. Away from the ballpark. Once more, she moved away (without a goodbye) from the only man she had ever loved. She pushed her way toward Clark Street, finally moving away from the terrible crowd—just *away,* altogether heedless that one is always moving *toward* something at the same time.

From the narrow metal railing of the Addison Street Bridge, Loren Woodville found it difficult to believe that the river flowing beneath him, violent and dark, was the same he had crossed so many times before without ever so much as a second thought. Now, the distant water looked infinitely deep and Loren couldn't help but wonder (his ever-questioning mind active till the very end) whether he would maintain consciousness down to the muddy bottom. Or would he expire before coming to rest among the sunken tires and cement-shod gangsters? The Chicago River would be cold in October. Interesting possibilities, he thought. He tied a rope to his ankle.

The other end of the rope was tied to an old trunk that had previously stood in a dusty corner of Loren Woodville's tiny apartment. Today—the day of the first home game of the World Series—the trunk would accompany its owner over the railing of the bridge. Loren had rented a mover's dolly to bring it with him. Nearly two hundred pounds, the trunk would serve not only as ballast for this permanent expedition, but also as a coffin for the complex scientific formulations and theorems that had driven Loren Woodville to the bridge and that rested now within the trunk on thousands of carefully typed pages.

A steady line of cars cruised past him on the bridge. Each car slowed, drivers glancing toward the lean young man, but none stopped because no one believed that a sincere leaper would jump in broad daylight and with such theatrical gestures. It seemed too *simple* to stop. Besides, there are few creatures deemed less deserving of help than insincere suicides. And the World Series was under way. Who could end it all before the winner was decided? Most passersby reasoned that Loren Woodville was a tourist (the trunk contributed to this opinion) who had climbed the railing for a better view of the city. In this way, Loren's leap was viewed with the same disinterested disbelief as had been the Woodville Theory itself—the scientific passion that rested otherwise forgotten in Loren's heart and trunk.

"Ladies and gentlemen of the Academy," Loren shouted over the sounds of the river, car horns, and the suburban hum of the North Side. "Your Swedish hospitality touches, but I cannot accept your Nobel Prize."

Loren Woodville was a scientist. Since the private publication of his Woodville Theory, however, members of the scientific community had taken to calling him a "raving maniac." His areas of expertise were astronomy, physics, and mathematics, and he had become—just three years before, at the age of twenty-six—the youngest man in the history of the University of Chicago to earn a doctorate in each of these disciplines. At that time there were articles about him in newspapers and journals across the country and countless invitations to join respected faculties from universities all over the world. But times changed.

Loren Woodville had come to believe that Earth was being visited by tiny Martians who traveled across the sky in speeding white spaceships. Worked out in meticulous detail, this was the Woodville Theory. Times indeed changed.

"To sleep: perchance to dream: ay, there's the rub."

In all of Chicago, Loren alone was ignorant of the fact that a ball game was being played at Wrigley Field. His research had been so intense that he had not attended a public event of any kind for over two years. He had lived apart from other men, not to mention women. After Edwin Hubble's daughter Astra angrily broke off their engagement in shame and humiliation over the publication of his theory, Loren concluded that the whole gender was about as conducive to real scientific inquiry as had been the Spanish Inquisition. Which is why he walked the crowded streets that led from his apartment to the university library every day without once stopping to speak to another pedestrian. He did not need friends anymore. He could not afford the spiritual debt their doubt demanded.

Loren Woodville had long ago resolved to live alone with his ideas. All else was distraction, discouragement. It was not that he would have others misunderstand him. Rather, he had simply given up hope that they might ever see what seemed to Loren so clear: the truth. His truth. Indeed, he had forgotten the time when such hope even existed, though it was not so far removed. The days before the Woodville Theory had been days of simple understanding, connection. On a warm spring afternoon at Comiskey Park on the South Side of Chicago, however, there had arrived the illumination (as Loren imagined must come to saints), and nothing was ever the same. The Woodville Theory. It had come in a single, complete flash, burning brain cells like Barney Oldfield burned gasoline—the result of an accident that nearly took his life. It had happened like this.

Loren's friends from the university (there were many then) had persuaded him to attend a decidedly uncivilized afternoon at Comiskey Park. Baseball. Loren, who was then completing a book on thermodynamics, thought the change of environment might provide inspiration for the chapter concerning properties of friction. He knew that fieldwork was as essential to research as library study. Indeed, Loren had made startling discoveries about the very subject while entertaining Astra Hubble at his apartment the night before. Comiskey Park, field study. He never dreamed that the afternoon would provide inspiration for a whole new life.

Loren and his friends sat in a box seat at field level behind the visitors' dugout. Astra sat beside him, her red hair gathered in a startling ponytail that rested on the place where their shoulders touched as they leaned together. Though Loren was not a fan of baseball, he nonetheless enjoyed the geometric arcs of the fly balls, the pitchers' use of friction and momentum to curve the flight of the speeding ball, the long waves of sound that swept over the ballpark when a White Sox player came to bat, and the awesome jumbling of molecules that occurred each time the wood of the baseball bat collided with the horsehide of the ball.

He was deep in thought, contemplating the properties of the human wrist, as he watched the pitcher deliver the ball to home plate. He watched the rhythmic motions, the windup, the rocking back, the delivery, the graceful follow-through. The *real* physical activity, however, was taking place at home plate, where a rotund batter from the New York ball club stepped into the pitch, connected, jumbling the molecules of the pitcher's best effort, and sent the ball on a screaming line drive past the first base coach, over the visitors' dugout, and into the crowded field boxes. *Crack!*

Acoustics, Loren thought. His academic friends, responding to decidedly nonacademic impulses, ducked all around him.

The next thing Loren remembered was waking up at Wesley Memorial Hospital with a thick bandage around his head. When the doctor asked the young scientist how he felt, Loren answered, "I feel we're being visited." In the next few hours, in a hospital ward shared only by a feverish actor incoherently reciting lines from *Hamlet,* the essential concepts of the Woodville Theory were developed. The great notions, which in two years would lead to Loren's despairing moment on the Addison Street Bridge, had been formed essentially complete in the reverie of unconsciousness. Born like a healthy child with fingers and toes intact.

The child had not developed as Loren hoped. During these last months, he had found it difficult to concentrate on anything but the possibility that his theory was flawed. Perhaps Martians *weren't* visiting the planet. His laundry had gone for so long unwashed that it had grown stiff in many places. His rent was months late. He had lost nearly twenty pounds from an already lanky frame simply because he had forgotten to eat. Standing on the edge of the Addison Street Bridge, however, it all seemed to wash away in the distant splashing of the hard, dark water below.

Loren Woodville looked over the city from his perch on the bridge railing. He saw De Paul University, gray slate walls, shiny windows, foolish young physicists of great respectability and promise; to the north was Horner Park, where children flew kites heedless of the tiny Martians who somewhere shared the same sky; to the west was the Avondale railroad yard, where the cumbersome rhythm of the massive steam engines must, he believed, overwhelm and conceal the mouselike heartbeats of the Martian visitors; and directly before him, three or four miles distant, was the shimmering blue of Lake Michigan, into which might well have crashed the very spacecraft he longed so to see—perhaps centuries before the red man gazed upon the shores, perhaps an hour before Loren himself had taken up the search.

His heart was as blue and empty as the sky above.

Loren Woodville had been unable to gain the simple piece of empirical evidence that would justify his faith and finally prove his complex theorems: a sighting. The mathematical computations were correct (he'd been over them a thousand times), the logic was flawless, his conviction bordered on the religious, but without the sighting it was ultimately empty. For Loren was finally subject to the loneliness that shakes even the confidence of stars, moving them to quiver and flicker in the clearest night skies. The recriminations had not moved him to doubt. The rejections had not moved him to doubt. The silence had.

"I could be bound in a nutshell and count myself king of infinite space," Loren shouted as the steady stream of cars continued past him on the bridge, "were it not I have bad dreams!"

These days the bad dreams were not of professional rejection and abandonment but of personal dissolution. If Loren Woodville and his theory were one, and if the theory proved false . . . ? Doubt had driven Loren to the bridge, his own doubt; without the righteousness that had sustained him he was a lonely man without meaning or purpose. Deluded. It seemed to Loren that no vision existed so cruel as that which allowed a man to finally understand his own folly without once offering even a glimpse of the Truth, the longing for which drives him to delusion in the first place.

If but once he had *seen* his Martian spaceship. . . .

He raised his eyes slowly to the familiar blue sky while balancing himself precariously on one foot upon the metal railing. Hoping, perhaps, that he might slip and fall before focusing on the great blue void and thereby spare himself the labor of finding once again nothing but birds and clouds and conventional heavenly objects. His resolution to look into the sky was born of the same strange mixture of resignation and senseless hope with which broken-hearted lovers resolve to gaze once more at a photograph tossed in the trash. Birds, clouds, conventional heavenly objects. Nothing more.

Then one of the passing cars, perhaps as a joke, perhaps out of real distress, perhaps distracted by news over the car radio that Babe Ruth was coming to bat for the Yankees in the top of the fifth, swerved toward Loren's perch on the bridge. The driver, for whatever reason, leaned on his steering wheel to expel a shrill blast of his car horn not three feet from Loren that ignited the scientist's synapses, awakening the unconscious, and sent startled Loren Woodville straight into the air.

"No!" Loren shouted.

He came down atop the railing, his face pale, his palms damp, his heart thumping like a snare drum—all this in half a second. No balance. For a moment, he danced on the thin metal railing like a marionette worked by a drunken puppeteer: hips this way, arms out, one foot in the air, bent, slipping. . . .

Then he tumbled over the side of the Addison Street Bridge.

It was the visitors' half of the fifth inning and the ball game was tied. Buddy Easter watched the Bambino step into the batter's box, heard the jeers drift over from across the street, whispered, "Knock it outta there, Babe"—slapping his hands together—"show them!" Buddy marveled that the brick ballpark could contain within its chalked dimensions a soul of such grandeur as that which burned within the wide frame of the Babe (who looked into the sky for a moment before digging in). Buddy thought the Grand Canyon would be a suitable ballpark for such a man.

"We been a lot of places together," Abner Doubleday said from beside Buddy atop the Parkview.

"You and the Babe?" Buddy asked.

"You and me," Abner answered.

Buddy nodded. "He's due," he said, pointing toward the Babe.

"And we've done lots of things."

Buddy nodded.

"And you got lots more things to do," Abner said.

Buddy continued nodding, still watching the game. "Got to get FDR into office," he said. "Got to pass those buttons around the school. Talk to the voters."

"Damn right," Abner said.

Charlie Root reared back for the Cubs, kicked his foot, and delivered a screaming fastball to the Bambino that split the plate for a perfect strike. Ruth watched the pitch pass with a half-interested nod. He stepped out of the box and raised his right hand as if he were the umpire calling the strike. His gestures were as broad as those of a clown—he was playing to the cheap seats (the free seats). The jovial spring to his posture, so incongruous among all the loathing, was unmistakable even from the roof of the Parkview.

"What's he doing?" Buddy asked.

Abner shrugged his transparent shoulders.

"Did you see it, Abner?"

"There's something I've been meaning to ask you," Abner said. "I've been putting it off for some time now. But I can't put it off any longer. I need to know."

"What's he doing?" Buddy repeated.

"He's the Babe. Who knows?"

"What do you want to know?" Buddy asked.

Abner cleared his throat. "If we'd been friends back when I invented baseball," he began, "I'd have asked for your suggestions. Your ideas. I mean, starting only with cricket as a model is about the same as starting with nothing, right? There are so many places you can go wrong when you're inventing a national pastime."

Buddy nodded.

"So I'm asking now," Abner said.

"Suggestions?" Buddy asked. "About the game? The rules? Everything?"

"Everything."

Abner was quite transparent today. When Buddy looked into Abner's eyes he saw flying behind them the great American flag atop the distant Wrigley Building—a tiny fluttering of red, white, and blue within the black of one pupil. Transparency was not a happy sign. But why would Abner be sad, Buddy wondered, on the very day they had taken the high ground, conquered the Parkview? On the day of the first home game of the World Series?

"I wouldn't change a thing," Buddy said.

Abner smiled. He stood up. As he moved between Buddy and the sun he blocked no light, cast no shadow. As he passed a potted palm he fluttered its leaves not an inch. He turned to Buddy. "I know the truth about Mr. Loch and the bullwhip," he said. "And I know about other things too. Remember? I'm not so easily deceived."

"Heck, Mr. Loch was your idea," Buddy said.

"That's not the point," Abner answered.

Buddy nodded. He could not lie to his friend. "There is one

thing I'd change about baseball. Just one. And it's not really a change. It's an addition."

Abner was once more at Buddy's side. He didn't *move* to Buddy's side. He was just, instantaneously, there. Here, there, gone, back again. This is how the dead move—as magical as fireflies in a lightning storm. Abner smiled, not a foot away from Buddy's face. He closed his eyes for a moment, as if bracing himself, and then sat down beside Buddy.

"Well?" Abner asked.

"I'd play winter ball," Buddy answered.

"Like in Puerto Rico?" Abner asked, vaguely disappointed.

Buddy shook his head no. "Not like that at all," he said. "It would have to be played in the northern latitudes. On the coldest, clearest day of the year. When the snow's six feet thick and as hard as ice. When even an old man's breath comes out as hot and steamy as Walter Johnson's best fastball. And the ballpark would be made of ice. And the scoreboard in center field would be operated by Eskimos who shape numbers out of hard-packed snow—" Buddy stopped.

"Well?" Abner asked.

Buddy held one finger to his lips and pointed to the ballpark across the street (the one made of brick, not ice). There, Charlie Root kicked and delivered: another fastball right down the pipe. Babe Ruth smiled as he watched the pitch go by—*Thud!*—into the catcher's mitt. The Bambino raised two fingers and called out in his booming voice, "Stee-rike two!" The stands erupted in raucous delight.

"What's he doing?" Buddy said. "Why doesn't he take a cut?"

"Why winter?" Abner asked.

"I'd play in summer too," Buddy said. "Spring training, Fourth of July, Labor Day, the October Classic—it's great as it is. I'd just add one game to the schedule. The Winter Game. It wouldn't have to count in the standings. But all the greatest stars would play. Ruth and Gehrig and Lazzeri. Their uniforms would be white and the field would be white and the sky would be as blue as a damn Cubs cap. And do you know who would be watching from the ice grandstands?"

Abner shook his head no.

"All the people who *need* to be watching," Buddy said. "The people who don't have anything else. The kids and the old people and everybody in-between who don't have friends or family to give them things at Christmas or their birthdays. Not the people who can afford to buy a ticket. Our people would be out there on the coldest, clearest day in January or February, just because they belong. And they belong in the ice ballpark because they don't belong anywhere else. You know there are people like that?"

Abner nodded.

"And the game would be theirs," Buddy said. "And both teams in uniforms as white as the snow."

"Why winter?" Abner asked.

Buddy smiled. "Because we'd use a baseball made of solid ice. Perfectly round. Like the planet Neptune. And the Bambino would come to bat in the last inning. Lefty Grove on the mound. And everybody in the stands would be pulling for the Babe because they'd know he was their man. And he'd smack it. *Whack!* And the ice baseball would explode into a million pieces, each sailing up into the winter sky until they all disappeared. And though the umpires, who would also be wearing white, wouldn't know how to call it—an out or a home run—everybody would go home feeling like a winner. And that night when our people were alone again and forgotten, they would each look into the clear, cold sky and know that among the countless stars were twinkling some tiny pieces of ice that belonged as much to each one of them as to anyone or anything in the universe. That's why I'd play the game in winter."

"Winter baseball," Abner said. "It's a good idea."

Buddy nodded.

"So what's the count?" Abner asked.

"No balls, two strikes," Buddy answered.

The Bambino had stepped out of the batter's box. He took a deep breath, rolling his head in a circle, stretching the neck muscles and the tight places in his shoulders. He bent at the knees to a crouched position. The ballpark waited. He held the bat in two hands behind his head, stretching his thick arms. The fans screamed their impatience. At last, the Babe stepped back into the batter's box, digging with the toe of one shoe into the hard dirt. Red dust flew up around his knees. He brought the bat to a vertical position behind his left ear, arranging his body in such a way that he became a graceful, coiled spring of pinstripes, and stared out toward the mound.

"Smack it, Babe," Buddy said.

Before Root could deliver the ball, however, the Bambino smiled and backed once more out of the box. The crowd screamed and howled in loathing. Root shook his head and stepped off the mound. The Bambino picked up a handful of dirt and rubbed it in his hands. He spit into his palms. Then he rolled his head in a circle, bent at the knees, and started the whole process once more.

"Why?" Buddy asked.

"Because he's the Babe," Abner answered. "He wants to get under the pitcher's skin."

"No," Buddy said. "Why'd you say you couldn't wait anymore to ask me what I'd change about baseball?"

"Oh," Abner said. He stood. He was barely visible to Buddy. He moved to the edge of the building. He looked out over Chicago. Because Abner was so transparent, Buddy was able to see at once both his friend and the vision before him: Lake Michigan to one side of Wrigley, the Chicago River to the other, the whole world beyond. Yet Abner seemed focused on some place even farther away than all that.

"What is it?" Buddy asked. Though Abner was transparent, his thoughts were not. Indeed, Buddy would never have guessed and had never imagined—

"I have to leave," Abner said without turning around.

"What?"

"It's time I went away."

"But the game's not over," Buddy said.

"I mean for good," Abner explained.

"What?"

"It's time," Abner said.

"What?"

Abner merely nodded his head.

"No," Buddy said. "You can't leave." He stood and moved beside his friend at the edge of the building. Abner turned to him. He was smiling, but his eyes were sad. Buddy shook his head no. "You can't leave," he repeated. "There's too much left undone. Too much still to talk about."

"There are other things," Abner said. "For you."

"You can't leave."

"I'll miss you," Abner said.

"Why?" Buddy asked.

"Why will I miss you?"

"Why do you have to leave?"

"Because it's time," Abner said. "Believe me. There are other things."

"It's cruel," Buddy answered. He turned away from his friend, closing his eyes and swallowing hard. "I don't understand any of it. It's nothing but cruel. That's all it is."

"Nothing's so simple as that."

"Do you want to leave?" Buddy asked, his eyes still closed. "If you do, then it's all right to go."

"I don't want to leave you," Abner said.

"Then don't."

"I have to."

"You can't!" Buddy said. When he opened his eyes he discovered Abner standing before him. The color had literally gone from his friend's face. He was little more than a shadow. Or a dream. "I made you up," Buddy continued. "I imagined you. You can't leave if I don't want you to. I'll just imagine you staying."

Abner shook his head. "It doesn't work that way."

"Then how the hell does it work?"

"It's like this," Abner said. He fidgeted with the fading brass buttons of his Union Army coat as he spoke. "The moment you imagine something, the moment you give it life, it ceases to belong to you. It becomes real, in a way. Right? And everything real has a measure of independence. And also responsibility. You can give life, Buddy, but you can't keep it."

"Then what about your responsibility to me as a friend?" Buddy asked. "I need you."

"It's because of my responsibility to you that I have to go," Abner answered.

"I don't understand," Buddy said, sitting down once more on the rooftop. Across the street there was pandemonium. But Buddy didn't care about it anymore. He couldn't imagine life without Abner. He swallowed hard, took a deep, quivering breath, and spoke with great care to keep his voice from cracking. "Why like this, Abner? So sudden?"

"I thought it would be best," Abner answered. He was barely more than a voice now.

"But if I had known," Buddy said, "I could have planned something. Something special. We could have done it together. Something we would never forget. Something perfect."

"Stand up and look around," Abner answered.

Buddy stood. He looked.

Babe Ruth stood outside the batter's box (heedless of the fans' obscene entreaties to swing the goddamn bat) and stared not at the pitcher, the third base coach, the dugout, the bleachers, or the scoreboard. Rather, the Bambino stared at a spot far above the ivy-covered wall that seemed to the thousands gathered at Wrigley Field empty of all relevance. They thought it merely another of Ruth's ploys to unnerve the pitcher, to compensate for his beer belly and advancing years. They booed louder. To Buddy Easter, however, it seemed the Bambino was staring directly at *him*.

Buddy moved nearer the edge of the building until one foot rested against the ledge. He considered his position—alone with Abner atop the finest apartment building for baseball in all of Chicago on the day of the first home game of the World Series. So superior a position that the Sultan of Swat took notice some five hundred feet away! Buddy looked beyond the Babe, beyond Wrigley Field, and toward the west. The whole city lay before him. Beyond that, a whole country. In this moment, it all seemed his. As much his as the brick ballpark across the street (for Buddy realized that he and Abner owned the park more surely today than even Old Man Wrigley himself). As much his as Charlie Root, the ill-fated Cubs pitcher, *belonged* to Babe Ruth.

"It is perfect," Buddy said. He turned to Abner. But his friend was gone.

"Oh," Buddy said.

He sat down once more on the roof. The joy of a moment before drained from his heart as, in those last seconds, the color had drained from Abner Doubleday's face. Buddy took a deep breath and rested his crossed arms upon his knees, his head upon his arms. He closed his eyes. Across the street, the screaming of the fans rose to an angry crescendo—something was happening. But Buddy didn't look up. As Wrigley Field rocked with agitation, Buddy was imagining his friend's return. He pictured in his mind Abner walking across the roof of the Parkview, smiling, explaining that it was all a joke. Buddy imagined to make it real. But nothing happened. Abner was right. It didn't work like this.

Then Buddy heard footsteps behind him.

For an irrational moment, he considered that his experiment had indeed brought his friend back. But he shortly remembered that Abner's boots made no sound when he walked. This was someone in whose veins flowed warm blood. Buddy turned. He gasped.

"You believe in ghosts, right?"

It was Frankie Pilaretti. The boy Buddy and Abner had advertised throughout the neighborhood as having been murdered—the boy they had shredded like so many voting rosters in Chicago's shadier precincts, *rip, rip, rip*—whole once more (as always). Angry. Frankie the broad-chested, red-haired bully. Yet he smiled. His hands were clasped behind his back. He smiled even more broadly. In all, his peaceful manner was more frightful than any tirade Buddy could imagine.

"What are you doing here?" Buddy asked, standing up. Only

when he gained his feet did he realize how violently his knees were shaking.

"Come back to haunt you," Frankie replied.

From out of the dark stairwell behind Frankie a score of the toughest neighborhood boys emerged, all laughing and slapping one another on the back with a frightening predatory glee. Buddy moved backward. One step and he was at the edge of the rooftop. He glanced down. It was four stories to the ground. The jump seemed to Buddy one story too high to risk.

"Good joke, huh, guys?" Buddy said.

The neighborhood boys formed a half circle extending from the edge of the building around Buddy and Frankie. There was no escape. The elegant plan had gone wrong. Still, Buddy couldn't help but believe that if Abner were here they might together think of something to salvage the moment. But Abner was gone.

"You really thought I'd stay away from the Series?" Frankie asked, stepping toward Buddy. The smile disappeared from his face. "Can you imagine how surprised I was to hear I had been murdered—huh, Yankee fan?"

"Yankee fan?" Buddy asked. "What do you mean?"

Frankie removed from behind his back a genuine Texas bull-whip—shiny leather more terrible than even Buddy had described to the boys of the neighborhood. Frankie's knuckles were white around the handle of the bullwhip, fingernails blue and bruised from his angry grip upon the weapon. The veins in his thick neck stood out like red highways on a road map. He moved nearer. A trace of blood appeared on his lower lip where he had bitten his tongue in rage. "The whip's your idea, kid," he said. He raised the bullwhip above his head. "Not mine."

Buddy nodded. "Abner and I saw it in a Gene Autry movie."

"Why don't you jump, kid?" the neighborhood boys suggested "Jump! Or he'll make shoelaces out of you."

Buddy shook his head. He turned his back on them, facing the ballpark, and closed his eyes. His knees were shaking so badly he could barely stand. Yet, he knew he mustn't fall forward, for the prospect of being found broken upon the pavement by strangers who would probe and prod his body was too much to bear. And he mustn't fall backward because that would allow the boys behind him to see his face, to see the fear in his eyes. And he mustn't fall to his knees because he *mustn't* fall to his knees. So he closed his eyes more tightly and concentrated more completely on maintaining his balance. Nothing else. Which is why—though he faced the ballpark—he never saw Babe Ruth (as did the 38,143) point with his bat to the same spot far above the ivy-covered wall that moments before had seemed to engage the slugger's attention.

ANNOUNCER: Top of the fifth. Tie score. The noise in this ballpark is deafening! If it gets much louder you'll have to turn your radios down, ladies and gentlemen. I hate to imagine our broadcast shattering windows all over town.

Ruth steps out of the box. I don't know how much more stalling Charlie Root'll take. Or the umpire, for that matter. The count's at two balls, two strikes. Babe Ruth has certainly stoked a fire in the hearts of these fans. What's this? Ruth is pointing with his bat toward a spot in the outfield. No, he's looking beyond the outfield. Out toward the bleachers, maybe even beyond that. Ruth is holding his bat in the air, pointing like a bird dog. What is it? What's he see? He gestures now. Of course! He's pointing with his bat toward the bleachers as if to say that's where he'll put Root's next pitch. The audacity! I'll tell you this, the fans don't like it one bit. I'll bet Charlie Root doesn't like it either. Ruth gestures with his bat, pointing toward the sky, the distance. He stops. He steps into the box. Nobody can fault the Bambino's confidence. The son of a gun. The damn Yankee! Sorry, folks. Root marches up to the rubber. He stares in for a signal. It's a madhouse here, folks. You can hardly hear yourself think! Who but Ruth would call his own shot? The cocky son of a . . . gun. Root winds and delivers. (*Crack!*) It's a long fly ball to deep center. It's going. . . . My God! My God! He did it! Good Lord! I've never seen anything like it. A home run! I don't believe it! Ruth did it! The goddamn sonofabitch! I can't watch anymore.

Buddy Easter heard a loud *crack!* and grimaced, pulling his arms in close to his body and tightening his muscles to better ward off the first blow of the vicious bullwhip. He felt a sob welling up from his chest but managed to hold it down. He waited for the pain, but he felt nothing. He turned and opened his eyes to discover that Frankie Pilaretti had *lowered* the cruel whip and stood now with his head turned toward the ballpark across the street. Frankie's mouth was open and his eyes moved from street level to a spot high above the flagpole at Wrigley Field and then continued up until his head was tilted back so far that Buddy Easter could see spots of dried blood on Frankie's neck where he had cut himself shaving that morning. The bullwhip slipped from his hand and fell to the rooftop. Buddy followed Frankie's eyes into the sky.

He gasped.

The crack he had heard was not the expertly wielded bullwhip but the collision of Babe Ruth's three pounds of seasoned ash with a baseball whose direction of travel had been thereby changed forever. High over their heads the white sphere of horsehide and wound string floated upward, propelled by the powerful (if unlikely) combination of sheer animal strength, courage, sunlight, and a residue of mustard that the Babe had accidentally smeared on his hands while eating a hot dog in the dugout. The combination had created a chemical, physical, and psychic reaction that propelled the baseball into the Chicago sky with a force matched only by the fiery experiments of a scientist named Goddard, working then in New Mexico with rocketry.

"Wow," Buddy Easter said.

Buddy could make out the red laces rotating end over end. He looked toward Wrigley Field where Babe Ruth, his dignity and hulking grace never more in evidence, rounded the bases. The hometown Club fans sat silently in the grandstands looking at one another, too angry to watch the Babe, too dejected to lift their heads and watch the flight of the baseball.

"Shit," Frankie said, gazing almost straight up.

"Goddammit," the neighborhood boys grumbled, equally distracted by the soaring baseball.

"Abner," Buddy whispered, looking once more into the sky. He watched the baseball. He smiled, as distracted as the other boys. "Look at the goddamn baseball, will ya? Look what he did, Abner. Look at it go."

The baseball rose like a bubble at the bottom of a ginger ale.

"The thing's never gonna come down," Frankie said.

"Goddammit," the neighborhood boys repeated.

"The Yankees lead," Buddy whispered.

"The thing's never gonna come down," Frankie repeated.

"Sure it is," Buddy answered, taking a step toward his red-haired enemy. "It'll come down *somewhere*."

Buddy picked up the discarded bullwhip and tossed it over the side of the building. None of the boys even noticed. Indeed, Frankie's mouth hung open so wide that if the ball had come straight down it might have passed between his lips and down his throat without so much as the slightest brush against his teeth.

Then Buddy's words echoed in his own head. "It'll come down somewhere!" he shouted.

Frankie turned to Buddy, his eyes red and teary from having stared so long into the bright sky. "What did you say?" he asked. "Are you *happy* about this, asshole?"

"The ball!" Buddy answered. "The ball that Babe Ruth just hit clean out of the ballpark. *That* ball." He pointed once more into the sky. "That ball's gotta come down somewhere." There was a spot on the shelf above Buddy's bed that would be perfect. The morning light, as it shone through the dormitory window, would illuminate the baseball as though it were the centerpiece of a museum exhibition. Perhaps the schoolmaster would allow him to convert the glass case that presently stood in the lobby and housed Civil War medals into a display case for the baseball. The Babe's baseball. *The* baseball. Shiny trophies littered the dormitories like hood ornaments in a parking lot. But no boy had a trophy like this. Not a baseball hit for a home run in the World Series by Babe Ruth.

Not *this* ball. No one owned anything like it. And better—to catch the ball! To shag it to the ends of the Earth and then snag it on the dead fly. Buddy was not a good center fielder in physical education class. But this was different. This was real life. A circus catch! One-handed!

"I can do it," Buddy said.

"You can do what, shithead?" Frankie asked, turning his gaze once more toward the sky.

"*It,*" Buddy said.

"Goddammit," the neighborhood boys murmured, transfixed by this product of unimaginable power, awed by the majesty of flight, distracted by hatred and fear.

"It," Buddy repeated. He believed that if he caught the baseball, if he gripped it in his own hand, if he held it up to the moonlight on the clearest, coldest night of the year, he might bring his friend Abner back. This was *it*. This was everything. After all, if stars shine and beckon to earth, why wouldn't a round white horsehide star held on the ground beckon back to the heavens? Abner surely would not resist such a relic—such a feat of courage and coordination inherent in the catching.

"It ain't coming down," Frankie observed.

"Sure it is," Buddy whispered. "Everything comes down." He set his jaw, steadied his feet, and removed his gray cap. He spun like a discus thrower and tossed the cap far out over the street toward Wrigley Field. He didn't know why. He only knew that there seemed nothing more appropriate. Except to catch the baseball.

"Hey, asshole!" Frankie said, turning to Buddy with renewed rage in his eyes. "You're happy about this, huh?"

Buddy nodded. He smiled. There would be no more lying.

Frankie clapped his hands to gain the other boys' attention. He looked about the rooftop. He clenched his fists. "Where the hell's my bullwhip?"

Buddy glanced once more at the tiny white speck far above. It seemed to be hooking toward the Chicago River. Rising, rising. Into the western skies.

"Where the hell's my whip?" Frankie shouted.

Buddy Easter slipped past the neighborhood boys, each still slack-jawed and weak-kneed from the impact of bat on ball, and ran for the stairs. " 'Bye, guys," he said, emboldened by the great possibilities. He crashed through the doorway that led down to the street. The stairwell was dark. He dived blindly down the first flight, pulling himself by the handrails. Then he stopped. Listening, listening. To his surprise, silence. No pursuers. No shouted threats, no obscenities, no echo of footsteps. Perhaps the boys had given up on him. Perhaps they had decided to watch the rest of the ball game from the rooftop. Things were looking up. Silence. Then the pounding of Buddy's feet as he descended the last flights.

"Great things," he said aloud.

He rushed through the quiet lobby on the ground floor, where the aged tenants sat in bathrobes, pushed his way through the revolving door, and burst onto the sidewalk, where he immediately collided with a woman who had been moving along her own path with equal speed and disregard. They both went sprawling—he into a pile of garbage and she into the street, where she skinned her knee.

"You all right?" Buddy asked, standing up from among the rotting vegetable scraps and empty boxes of corn flakes.

She stood up slowly.

"You all right?" Buddy asked. She was better than all right. She was beautiful.

"You work for Capone?" Alice de Minuette asked.

"I'm real sorry, miss," Buddy said.

"Are you one of his street gangsters?" Alice continued.

Buddy laughed. "I'm no gangster, miss."

When she brushed away the wrinkles in her dress, Buddy caught sight of some perfect curves the likes of which even Lefty Grove had never thrown. When she raised her hands to her head to straighten the golden hair that had fallen before her eyes, he saw her smile. She shook her head. He swallowed hard. Her face was beautiful. "It's familiar," he said.

"What?"

Buddy shook his head. "Uh, your perfume, miss," he answered. "Your perfume. I know it."

"I'm not wearing perfume," she said. She pointed to the rotting vegetables at his feet. "Perhaps that's what you're smelling."

Had he seen her in a magazine? Was she an artist's model? Or had he seen her someplace else? Buddy never remembered his dreams (though Abner somehow knew of them and retold them to Buddy each morning). Yet he suspected that this face might have come from just such a dark, beautiful place. "I'm chasing a baseball," he said. "I didn't mean to knock you down."

She stepped toward him, holding out one hand—as fine and white as porcelain—and touched Buddy's smooth chin with her fingertips. With the slightest pressure she raised his head until their blue eyes met and washed together like river tributaries spilling into a single sea. Buddy inhaled quickly, startled but not frightened, holding his breath. It was as if he were looking into his own eyes.

"Miss?" he asked.

She said nothing.

Buddy was attracted to this woman in ways he didn't understand. She affected him altogether differently from the girls on the French postcards passed around the dormitory. He didn't know how much time passed in silence. A second, a minute? As long as she touched him he felt removed from considerations like time and place. No bullwhip, no baseball, no Buddy at all. Just this strange, silent understanding. He was terrified.

At last she stepped away from him. "I'm all right," she said.

"Me too," he answered. He swallowed hard and cleared his throat. Perhaps, he considered, the terrifying moment had been nothing more than his imagination. He put his hands in his pockets and nodded casually. "See the baseball?" he asked, pointing heavenward. The ball was a tiny white speck in the vast blue. "See? It's very special. I'm going to catch it."

"What's your name?" she asked.

"Buddy."

"Buddy," she repeated. "That's your real name?"

He nodded. "It's as real as I've got."

"My name is Alice," she said.

"His *real* name is mud," said a voice from the direction of the Parkview. "You know, mud. Like blood."

Buddy recognized the voice. He turned.

"Hi, Buddy," Frankie said.

The neighborhood boys had slipped down the stairs and out of the building. They moved onto the street. They were not happy. Once more, they encircled Buddy Easter. ("A goddamn regular drill team," Buddy thought.) Frankie held no bullwhip. Rather, his fists were clenched and his jaw was set in so hard and straight a line that Buddy suspected one might use this feature as a straight-edge or T-square to draft plans for the reform school into which Buddy wished he might magically cast his rival.

"You pay now," Frankie said, stepping into the circle.

Buddy shrugged his shoulders.

"You sonofabitch," Frankie said.

"Goddamn Yankee fan," the other boys added.

"You pay," Frankie repeated, squaring his shoulders.

Alice de Minuette pushed into the circle of boys. "No," she said. "You leave him alone."

Frankie turned. He spit. He smiled and shook his head.

"You boys go home," Alice continued. "Or else."

"Or else?" Frankie asked.

"Yeah," Alice said. Her bleeding knee dripped on her blue patent-leather shoe.

"This ain't your fight," Frankie said.

"Get away from him," Alice continued.

"Nice ass," Frankie said. "Too bad you don't have no brains." He clapped his hands and doubled over with laughter, stomping his foot on the pavement. "Too bad you don't have no brains," he repeated.

The neighborhood boys slapped one another on the back.

Alice remained steadfast.

"It's all right, miss," Buddy said. "I'll be all right. One way or the other. Don't worry." It was one thing to be abused by neighborhood bullies. This happened to boys all over the country on every day of the year. It was quite another, however, when the humiliating spectacle was witnessed by the most beautiful woman Buddy Easter had ever met. *This* was more terrifying than either the bullwhip or Frankie's fists. "I can handle these cream puffs," Buddy continued. "Don't worry."

"Get the hell out of here, lady," Frankie said, smiling no more.

"I won't warn you again," Alice answered. "I'm tired of this. All of it."

Frankie laughed. "You want us to leave him alone?" he asked. "Then just give me a little kiss. Right here on my cheek. That's not so much to ask. Hardly nothing for a woman like you, right?"

Buddy wasn't altogether sure what happened next. Quick as a dream, a lifetime passed in the turn of a cheek against one's pillow. Alice reached into her purse. Or perhaps she was holding the gun all along. Buddy wasn't sure. In any case, she fired a tiny pistol into the air. *Crack!*

The boys in the circle jumped as one, startled and pale.

She lowered the gun at Frankie. "I know how to use this," she said. She was not smiling.

Frankie froze, his mouth wide, his fists unclenched. He said nothing. It seemed he had forgotten how to speak. A line of spittle slithered over his bottom lip.

Alice pulled back the hammer on the gun.

Frankie broke first. The neighborhood boys followed, scattering in every direction, knocking into one another like turkeys at a Thanksgiving Pilgrim convention. Cursing, crying. It was over in a moment. They were gone.

"Alice?" Buddy said, turning in a circle.

But she was gone too. Slipped into a crowd gathered on the sidewalk before the Biograph Movie Theatre. Buddy caught a glimpse of her golden hair as she dodged through a line of Chicagoans awaiting the matinee showing of *Scarface,* starring Paul Muni. The Chicagoans seemed as unaware of the delicate, blond miracle passing among them as they were of the soaring, round miracle above. Gone.

Buddy smiled secretly.

"Great things," he said to himself.

He turned once more to the sky, closing one eye to better gauge the soaring baseball's direction. "Great things," he repeated, starting west down the sidewalk.

Loren Woodville dangled upside down beneath the Addison Street Bridge, tied at the ankle to the trunk above. He swayed in the swirling breeze like a side of beef in a stockyard freezer. His arms hung in answer to gravity. It seemed he beckoned to the churning water below. His coat hung down over his head. From top to bottom: legs, torso, coat, hands.

"Great things," he muttered to himself, his cloaked head heavy with blood, his ankle aching where the rope strained. "Just great, great, great."

It was the *crack!* that brought Loren at last to action. He might have simply dangled and swayed until the rope frayed and finally snapped like a guitar string tuned too high, had he not been distracted in his despair by the strange sound in the Chicago sky. Loren believed it too resonant, too rich to have been gunfire—too musical. Almost like a baseball struck by a bat, except that Loren could not conceive that such force might be generated by such frivolity (yet it *did* remind him of the afternoon at Comiskey Park). Almost like the pop of a soap bubble must sound to a gnat.

Otherworldly? Loren thought. No, can't be.

He struggled with his coat, dangling, straining, Harry Houdini-ing above the river until at last his arms came free. The coat fell like a wool leaf into the water. He could see once more. He raised his chin to his chest, sighted straight up the taut rope, and looked into the sky. He was frightened of what he would find there. Frightened of the sun and clouds and birds—not as objects, but as terrible reminders that his fruitless pursuit of "other" truths had corrupted his once keen sense of wonder for the natural world above (sun and clouds and birds). Now disillusioned in the Woodville

Theory, he was left altogether empty of wonder. For Loren, this was to be altogether empty. Conventional heavenly objects reminded him of what he had lost. He was deathly tired of conventional heavenly objects. Still, he looked.

Conventional heavenly objects are all one might have expected to find that afternoon by gazing into the bright sky. Years of diligent observation, however, had sharpened Loren's vision. He was an experienced sky-gazer. His eyes were as finely tuned as his mind (and less damaged by screaming foul balls). He could read the fine print of a newspaper at a dozen paces—though he generally found the content altogether without interest at any distance. He spotted a tiny white speck against the blue. Perhaps a zeppelin coming to Chicago for a meat packers' convention, he thought. He knew in his heart, however, that this was no zeppelin.

He pulled himself to a more upright position, straining on the rope, pulling with his fingers and palms as he had not pulled since high school gym class. It was no easier now than it had been then. He dropped back to the end of the rope, dangling once more, and took from a leather strap looped around his belt a pouch filled with the scientific instruments he had chosen to take with him to the bottom of the Chicago River, chosen as eternal companions—as pharaohs were entombed with *their* most precious possessions. Careful of gravity's selfish pull, he removed a tiny telescope from the pouch. He shook his head to keep the blood from clouding his vision and held the extended telescope to his eye.

The distant, flying object was no zeppelin!

The tiny white sphere rose almost straight up with a lift that Loren Woodville had never before witnessed in the flight of a conventional aircraft. It rose higher. Once more, he gripped the rope with one hand—believing that this might suddenly have become an inopportune time to have fallen off a bridge.

"Yes!" he shouted.

The white sphere ascended from a position somewhere between the bridge under which he dangled and Lake Michigan. He could distinguish small identifying marks that ran around the tiny space-craft to form an insignia of some kind. Or perhaps they were landing lights. In any case, the identifying marks were red—the color he recognized as the universal signal for danger, or SOS. Just such an emergency would explain why an alien spacecraft was so close to a metropolitan area. The Martians had no choice. Loren closed his eyes and rubbed them to ensure that what he saw was more than a product of a desperate imagination or tired eyesight. He opened his eyes.

The tiny white sphere was real.

A single tear slid over Loren's eyebrow, trailing down his forehead to his hairline, where it paused—gathering itself like an uncertain suicide—before dripping into the Chicago River.

Loren replaced the telescope in the leather pouch and removed a protractor and compass. He had perceived a gradual arc in the flight of the sphere. The geometric consistency thereof suggested that the tiny craft conformed to the most basic law of physics, gravity—that it presently moved under the accumulated momentum of some awesome initial thrust which had launched it into the air. Or perhaps the craft was coasting to conserve fuel. In any case, through observation and simple mathematical computation, its course was *predictable.* Loren smiled as he fumbled with his instruments. "Let's find out where you're going to land, friends."

Loren balanced the protractor on the taut rope from which he hung, sighting up the straight line into the sky. He closed one eye—moving nearer, then away, lifting himself up, falling back, like a pool player studying a difficult shot. He gauged the angle. His lips formed silent numbers. From his trousers pocket he removed an inscribed pocket watch: *They are free who do not fear to go to the end of their thought.* He counted aloud the seconds as they passed around the face of the watch. He shook his head, smiling, and let the watch fall into the river below. It seemed to Loren that he may indeed have come to the end of his thought just seconds before having come to his end altogether.

He removed a slide rule from the leather pouch. The instrument was sufficiently worn by constant use that its markings had long since been rubbed away. But he didn't need any markings. He played the slide rule as Paganini played the violin. Fretless.

"Fifteen," he said, counting once more. Backward this time. "Fourteen, thirteen, twelve, eleven . . ." His fists were clenched. Beads of sweat had formed on his forehead, dripping—like the tear—from his dangling hairline down to the river. The sphere raced higher. "Three, two, one!"

His calculations were correct.

A crashing *boom!* descended upon the city of Chicago. Like thunder ripping through stormy air, the burst of aural violence (from out of the clear sky) shook even the city's most formidable structures to their foundations—to the strained limits of their nuts and bolts. The awesome rumble sent sound waves over the Windy City that knocked to the ground the saplings freshly planted in Horner Park, broke windows in the office of Mayor Bill Thompson (who dived behind his desk in fear that his silent partner Al Capone had betrayed him), tore the hands from the clock atop the Wrigley Building, and pried loose bricks from the outfield wall at Wrigley Field. The "sunny thunderclap," as the *Tribune* would call it the next day, shook the nerves of Chicagoans to the point at which they stood, like the stock market not long before, on the brink of collapse.

Meanwhile, Loren Woodville swung joyfully beneath the bridge in a forty-foot arc.

"This is magnificent," he whispered. "The speed of sound! Splitting the atmosphere, breaking the sky itself like, like . . ."—in his moment of triumph he recalled his years of defeat—"like the empty sky can break your heart."

Loren turned once more to the slide rule. Using a formula similar to that by which he had predicted the precise moment when the sphere's acceleration would carry it past the speed of sound, he mumbled numbers that corresponded to longitudinal and latitudinal points on a pocket map of America which he carried in his leather pouch. He unfolded the map, fighting the swirling air beneath the bridge as he swung pendulumlike over the river. He glanced across the western half of the map. "Where will you land, friends?" he asked.

According to Loren's calculations, the Martians would glide to the very edge of the American continent.

"California," he said. "Three days."

He dropped the slide rule into the river. He would need it no more. He cupped his hands to his mouth. If he was ever to reach the Pacific coast in time to meet his Martians, he would surely have to find a way back *onto* the bridge. He shouted into the air, "Lift me up!" Shouted as if the words had been forming somewhere deep within his heart for some time, "Lift me up!" Shouted as much to the heavens themselves as to any passerby who might give a pull to the rope from which Loren Woodville dangled.

"Lift me up, lift me up, lift me up!"

The ball game was over. The Yankees had won 5–4 on Babe Ruth's fifth-inning home run. In the visitors' clubhouse Ruth sat before his locker in only a towel and a baseball cap. He was surrounded by reporters who held tiny notebooks in their hands and wore press passes in the hatbands of their fedoras.

"How'd you do it, Babe?"

"What kinda pitch did he throw you?"

"You ever called your shot before?"

The Bambino took a long swig from a Coca-Cola bottle that smelled to the reporters suspiciously like rum. He smiled. His white belly hung over the edge of the towel and his face was flushed from the afternoon's activity.

"Can you do it again tomorrow?"

"Yanks gonna sweep 'em?"

"How'd you *do* it, Babe?"

The Bambino removed his cap. Wet cabbage leaves fell to the clubhouse floor. On warm days he wore them in his cap to cool his head. With his bare foot he kicked the leaves into his open locker. He tossed the cap in after them.

"How'd it feel, Babe?"

"How'd 'ya know Root was gonna throw a strike?"

"You got any more surprises saved up?"

A clubhouse boy broke through the circle of reporters. In his arms he carried a cardboard box filled with notes, letters, and correspondence of all kinds. He set the box down beside the Babe's stool. The boy spit a brown wad of chaw into a spittoon near the Bambino's duffel bag. "Today's fan mail, Babe," he said. "Chicago-type fan mail."

"More threats?" Ruth asked the boy.

"I imagine."

The Bambino reached into the box. He removed a single postcard. He looked at the picture. The towering Wrigley Building. On the back was scribbled, *Shove it up your ass, Ruth.*

"Boys," the Bambino said to the reporters, holding the postcard in the air. "Sometimes it ain't easy."

He tossed the card back into the box.

"Did the crowd anger you, Babe?"

"You got anything to say to Root?"

"You got anything to say to Chicago?"

The Babe shook his head. He kicked the box back to the clubhouse boy. A sealed white envelope sat atop the pile of correspondence. "Put 'em on the bus," he said.

The boy picked up the box and was gone.

"I burn 'em for fuel in the winter," Ruth explained to the reporters. "The letters, I mean, not the fans. The Chicago fans themselves I burn during the World Series. Like that, boys? Can you use it?"

"Sure thing, Babe," the reporters said.

Ruth took a swig of the Coca-Cola. "Boys?" he said. The reporters held their pencils poised upon their papers. Ruth scratched the top of his head, mussing his thin hair. "Did any of you happen to see that ball I hit come *down*?"

The reporters looked at one another. They shook their heads.

Ruth smiled. "I didn't see it neither," he said. "But it sure as hell felt like I got all of it."

"You did, Babe!"

"I've never seen nothing like it, Babe!"

"Where do *you* think it might have come down, Babe?"

Ruth took another swig of the Coca-Cola. "Hell," he said. "I think it's still up there!"

The reporters laughed, scribbling the comment on their notepads, and afterward patted the Bambino—victorious and half drunk—on his wide back.

"Good one, Babe," they said.

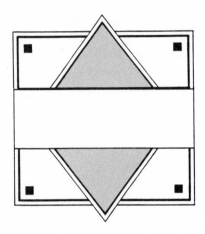

There was a great crowd inside the La Salle Street railroad station. Some lingered near the loading platforms with luggage at their feet and pocket train schedules held like Bibles to their breasts; others lined up with military precision before the noisy ticket windows; others bought newspapers from the same boys who had earlier today hawked game programs at Wrigley Field; others ate pieces of pie in the station cafeteria where the clanking of silverware was so great that the rumble of a train itself was but a whisper by comparison; others made notes on the backs of envelopes. Ladies blotted their lipstick in the station's spotless powder room while gentlemen were shoe-shined by gravelly-voiced black men who handled their soft cloths as Toscanini handled a baton. Porters pushed carts piled high with luggage past children who sat on polished hardwood benches reading comic books or slapping at one another. Young couples held tight to each other's hands, tethered like boats in a storm, to keep from being separated in the jostling of the great crowd. Men in business suits looked at their wristwatches, then to the six-foot-wide clock on one wall, then back to their wristwatches. Seven o'clock in the evening.

Inside the La Salle Street station, one hour looked very much like any other. There were no clear divisions to the day. No crisp morning, no warm afternoon, no balmy evening. No bedtime even for children (except that moment when they simply fell asleep in their parents' arms). Rather, there was *always* a crowd, always those in a hurry, always those waiting, always the same yellow light from the chandeliers, always hunger, always food, always noise, always arrivals, always departures. And always, in this timeless place, a pressing need to know the time.

"Last call for the Madison Zephyr," announced a calm voice over the loudspeaker. "Leaving in five minutes from track forty-seven for Racine, Madison, Dubuque, Des Moines, and points west."

"What was that?" Buddy Easter shouted from within the great crowd at the La Salle Street station. "Points west?"

He pushed through a crowd of men dressed in pin-striped suits and dodged a group of nuns who ran past murmuring Latin phrases, their habits flying, their eyes darting up to the clock on the wall like quarterbacks in the last minute of a big game. He stepped past a family sitting on a worn trunk set in the middle of the room. The family shared a single apple. It was probably their dinner.

Above the ticket booths was a large board upon which the arrivals and departures were spelled out by mechanical letters. Every few minutes, the destinations and times on the board changed with a great clanking and shuffling. The letters were obscured in a frantic flipping of alphabet upon alphabet until, almost magically, the shuffling stopped and upon the board were words. New destinations, new times. It was a marvel.

"Points west," Buddy said to himself.

He had run all afternoon beneath the arching baseball. As unrelenting as the earthbound shadow of a kite—needing only light to continue—he had run west down Addison Street, past Lane Technical High School, over the bridge that crossed the Chicago

River, and past Kilbourne Park before he realized that when the baseball at last came down it would be in a place far more distant than any boy had ever run before. Even a boy with as much to gain as Buddy Easter. He stopped running. He watched the baseball rise higher. It continued west like a distant relative of the sun, trailing behind it a flaming tail composed of sandlot dust. After a moment's deliberation, Buddy turned back toward the ballpark, retraced his steps along Addison, turned right at Clark, and raced downtown—toward the La Salle Street train station. Sure, the Bambino might have got all of it, he thought. But I've got applied science on my side. I've got the Union Pacific Railroad.

What Buddy didn't have, however, was a train ticket. He didn't have any money either. So he climbed a hardwood bench at the center of the bustling station, rising above the sea of Chicagoans, took from his back pockets his best baseball cards (which he carried always with him), and cleared his throat. He shuffled through the cards, nodding farewells to the ballplayers—to Cobb and Johnson, to Pepper Martin, Grove, and Gehrig. Then he shouted to the crowded train station, "May I have your attention!"

No one heard the boy's request over the clamor.

Buddy tried again. "May I *please* have your attention!"

The La Salle Street station grew suddenly quiet. Most present would agree that the hush coincided with Buddy's second request merely by chance. The conversing thousands gathered in the great waiting room merely chose the same moment to gather their thoughts. The announcements over the loudspeakers stopped simply because there was a lull in rail traffic. The slamming of suitcases and the dropping of trunks upon the marble floor ceased only because the suitcases and trunks had already been dropped. The group of anxious nuns, however, stopped praying when they heard Buddy's polite request. They believed the subsequent silence was a miracle intended to demonstrate the power of simple courtesy. To this day, the good sisters relate the story to unruly students.

"I am auctioning today the finest baseball trading cards in all of Illinois!" Buddy announced boldly. He was not afraid to speak before the great crowd. He pretended that Abner stood at his side whispering encouragement. Whispering, "Do what you must do, Buddy."

As suddenly as the crowd had become quiet, however, it became noisy once more. Travelers turned to one another to comment on train schedules or the weather in Wisconsin. Bags crashed once more to the marble floor, bells rang, silverware clanked, and over the loudspeaker came "Now boarding for the Twentieth Century Limited at track twenty-nine. . . ."

"Didn't you hear what I said?" Buddy shouted, fanning out the handful of trading cards like a dealer at a poker table. "Look at these guys! And I'm willing to take a lot less than they're worth. All right, everybody, who'll start the bidding for a Lou Gehrig in mint condition?"

One man answered. "I'll give you a nickel, kid."

The other travelers merely continued with their private conversations, limiting their thoughts to those of places that can be reached by train. Missing out on the places that can only be reached by knowing, like one's own name, the expression on Lou Gehrig's face, or the statistics printed on the back of Walter Johnson's tobacco card.

"I have a bid of one nickel!" Buddy shouted, turning toward the man who had called out. He was bald and nearly as wide around as he was tall. On his lapel was pinned a daisy so fresh that Buddy could smell it above even the tobacco and fruit pies, leather, sweat, and grease of the train station. His nose was flat and his eyes small within folds of pink flesh. "Do I hear a dime?"

"A dime," the fat man said.

Buddy shook his head. "You don't have to bid against yourself, sir," he said.

"A quarter," the man said.

"What?"

"A dollar," the fat man continued. He stepped toward the hardwood bench upon which Buddy stood. When the man smiled his teeth flashed gold. He reached into his pocket and withdrew a shiny silver dollar.

"I have a bid of one dollar," Buddy called, gazing over the fat man's head into the disinterested throng. "Going once, twice, sold!"

The fat man held the silver dollar up to Buddy, who snatched the coin from the man's hand. He slipped it into his own pocket and held out the Lou Gehrig card. "Here you go, sir."

The fat man shook his head. "Keep your card," he said. "I want something else."

"Who?" Buddy asked. "I've got a Grover Cleveland Alexander and a Ty Cobb in excellent condition."

"Keep all your cards."

"So what do you want?" Buddy asked.

The fat man smiled. He sat down on the bench, brushing his shoulder against the side of Buddy's leg, and gestured with one fat finger for Buddy to sit beside him.

"What do you want?" Buddy asked again, not moving.

The fat man continued gesturing with his index finger.

Buddy sat down. "What's the deal, sir?"

"What did she say to you?" the fat man asked.

"Who?"

"Miss de Minuette," the fat man answered, slipping his arm around Buddy's shoulders in a manner that suggested paternal warmth. The man's touch, however, was not warm. It was strong. Buddy suspected that the grip could grow even stronger. This is why, though the smell of the daisy suddenly nauseated Buddy, he did not try to escape.

"Who?" Buddy asked.

"We saw you talking to her, kid," the fat man said. Even his breath smelled of daisies. Buddy wondered if he *ate* them. "Back near Wrigley Field. A few hours ago."

Buddy shook his head.

The fat man tightened his grip. "Talk to me."

"There's policemen in here, you know," Buddy said, shooting the fat man the formidable glance that Abner had taught him some time before. However, Buddy had never quite seemed to get it right.

"Cops," the fat man answered. "They're on the boss's payroll.

Now, why don't you tell me what you know. Otherwise I'm gonna have to take you up to see the boss."

Over the loudspeaker: "Now boarding for the Peoria and Western Bullet on track sixteen. . . ."

"That's my train," Buddy said. He tried to stand.

The fat man pulled him back onto the bench. "Make it easy on yourself, kid. We've cracked tougher nuts than you, so don't be no hero."

"You can have your dollar back, sir."

The fat man squeezed tighter.

"I don't know nobody," Buddy said, hoping the double negative might lend credence to his lie.

"She *belongs* to us, kid," the fat man said. "Like a mouse belongs to a cat. You understand? So don't mess around with nature."

"I don't know who you're talking about," Buddy said. But of course he did know. How could he have forgotten? How might he have considered even for a moment that the fat man was interested in any woman but the one who had saved Buddy's life outside the Parkview. How could *anyone* be interested in another woman? "I don't know nobody," Buddy repeated.

"Talk to me, kid," the fat man said, tightening his grip on Buddy's shoulder. "Or I'll squeze the words outta ya like pus out of a pimple."

Buddy shook his head. He liked the blond woman. He did not like the fat man. He did not trust the fat man. It seemed to him very simple. "No," he said.

The fat man unbuttoned his suit coat. The coat popped open at the insistence of his great gut. Inside was a black gun in a shoulder strap. The fat man touched the gun with his fingertips. "This is my friend," he said. "I call her 'Daisy.' "

"I don't care," Buddy said. He would not betray the woman who had saved his life, who had suggested by her actions that his life was *worth* saving.

"You want to meet Daisy?" the fat man asked.

"Doesn't matter," Buddy said. A woman who makes a boy want to live is a woman for whom a boy might be willing to die.

"Are you working with her?" the fat man demanded.

"I don't know what you're talking about."

Amid the great, distracted mass of humanity, the fat man's tightening grasp on the boy was as obscured as a misstroke on a Picasso canvas.

"I'm losing my patience, kid."

"Me too," Buddy answered. Never before had he met so many difficult people in one day. First Frankie Pilaretti, now this. He shook his head. He had had enough.

"Help!" he screamed.

The travelers who milled about the hardwood bench turned toward Buddy. They looked confused, then annoyed, as if the noise and bother within the train station was distraction enough without having to endure a boy's call for help. Buddy tried to pull free of the fat man. He yanked and flailed. The fat man merely tightened his grip.

"Come now, son," the fat man said, loud enough for all around to hear. "Your grandmother's cooking's not *that* bad."

"Help!"

The travelers turned away, shaking their heads at the boy's impertinence. "He should be grateful he even *has* a grandmother," they muttered to one another.

"Don't try nothing else funny, kid," the fat man whispered.

"Abner," Buddy implored, pulling fruitlessly against the fat man's grip. "Help me."

"Let's go, kid," the fat man said, standing up.

"What goes on here!" demanded a woman's voice from out of the crowd.

Buddy turned.

The Mother Superior.

With black robes flying behind them, the good sisters—who earlier had been so impressed by Buddy's courtesy—appeared from out of the disinterested throng like sweet avenging angels. Their rosaries flew up about their shoulders. Their stern faces were racked with concern.

"What goes on here?" the Mother Superior repeated.

The fat man's eyes grew wide at the approach of the nuns. He swallowed hard; his Adam's apple (the size of a golf ball) moved up and down in his throat. "What's that, Sisters?" he asked. His grip on Buddy's wrist loosened.

Buddy didn't hesitate. He jumped away from the fat man, brushing against the starched, noisy garments of the youngest nun, and leaped over the hardwood bench. The fat man lurched forward, reaching past the nuns, and grabbed a handful of Buddy's shirt. The fabric ripped in the fat man's hand.

"Come back, you little sonofabitch!"

"You're not his father!" the Mother Superior said, stamping her foot on the marble floor. "You're a profane man. Leave that child alone! Do you hear me?"

The fat man pushed past the nuns. With elbows swinging, he crashed through the meandering crowd like a great ship pushing through floes of ice, leaving the sisters behind like Byrd's cutter leaving behind outraged penguins.

"Come back, kid!" he shouted.

Buddy ran on, dodging the piles of luggage and groups of travelers gathered in circles on the marble floor. He could hear his own heart pounding. Nothing else. Just his heartbeat. And Abner's voice reminding him, "Do what you have to do."

"Stop, kid," the fat man called.

Buddy continued past the lines at the ticket windows, past the great clock on one wall, past the souvenir shop, past the newsstand, past the shoeshine stand, past the cafeteria, the lost and found, and the baggage area. Buddy was grateful for every fattening morsel of food his assailant had ever eaten—frightened to consider how fast the man might be without the extra weight to slow him down.

"Give it up, kid," the fat man called.

Buddy turned down a long, empty corridor marked Track 42. The walls, ceiling, and floor were made of tile. Buddy's footsteps echoed. The corridor smelled of tobacco and was lit by bulbs placed every fifteen feet along the ceiling. Buddy glanced back.

The fat man had stopped at the entrance to the corridor. He held his gun propped on one arm. He aimed at Buddy.

"Freeze, kid!"

Buddy kept running. There was nowhere to go but forward. No doorways into which he might slip. No baggage carts behind which he might duck. Only the promise of darkness at the far end of the corridor. He pushed himself harder, imagining that he was Ty Cobb stretching a single into a triple. The fat man pulled the trigger.

A light bulb popped above Buddy and a wrenching explosion burst within the corridor. The gunshot echoed until the single squeeze of the trigger came to sound like a barrage. Shards of glass fell about the boy. He kept running. There was no stopping now. Further delay in Chicago would mean he might never catch up to the soaring baseball, never catch up to his own destiny. If such was to be, he resolved, he would rather the fat man shoot him dead now.

"Stop!" the man called.

Buddy kept running.

The fat man squeezed the trigger once more. Another bulb popped over Buddy's head and another explosion burst within the tile corridor. Buddy covered his ears. He kept running. The end of the corridor was near. He felt the cool night air grow closer with each step. He felt the rumble of the trains reverberate through the tile walls. Trains going to great places. To great things. . . .

"Freeze, boy, or I'll plug you!" the fat man called.

Buddy kept running. The last bulb burst above his head. He raced from the corridor and onto the loading platform. Outside! The open air smelled of grease, steam, smoke. He glanced into the sky. His baseball appeared as a faint star, moving just perceptibly against the steady background. He turned again toward the tile corridor.

The fat man's approaching footsteps echoed.

Buddy leaped onto the tracks and started across the railroad yard.

Loren Woodville crouched silently in the corner of a dark, stationary boxcar. Through the open door he saw the shadowed outlines of other railroad cars on other tracks; he saw the lights of the yard glimmer green or red; he smelled the grease and coal and heard the violent clanging of railroad cars being joined to one another. Occasionally, he heard men pass. He saw the lanterns they carried swing at their sides. He listened to their voices, holding his breath, wary that they might be railroad security guards, who were known to beat freeloaders senseless.

Now was not the time for senselessness.

Hours before, Loren Woodville had wanted nothing less than oblivion itself. He had yearned for it. A swift blow to the skull administered by a vicious railroad bull would have seemed perfect. He'd have *paid* for it. It seemed to him a far more efficient demise than drowning in the Chicago River. But with the sighting of the Martian sphere everything changed—not just for Loren, he believed, but for the whole of humanity as well. It seemed to him now that no man was *ever* more in need of his faculties—every bright, burning brain cell—than was Loren Woodville, first ambassador to Mars. He crouched deeper into the shadows, relieved each time the burly railroad men passed by. He waited. Unsure.

"Sh-h-h," he whispered to himself.

Loren Woodville had never hidden in a boxcar before. He had never plotted a course across the country by penciling on a pocket map the routes of a half-dozen freight lines which, before tonight, he didn't even know existed. He had never sought to follow *any* plotted lines but those noted on the star chart that hung from his apartment ceiling. These things were new to Loren Woodville. For he had never before coupled a compelling need to reach the Pacific coast with an altogether empty pocketbook. He had never before given away his last dime (assuming that money would do him no good at the bottom of the Chicago River). He had never before been a pauper with a place to go.

"Sh-h-h," he whispered once more to himself.

The afternoon had been like this: After being pulled up from beneath the Addison Street Bridge by a passing Boy Scout who graciously asked no questions, Loren Woodville started for the La Salle Street station. There was no place else for him to go. No friends, not anymore. No family. Only the white sphere that glistened above him in the sunlight. After a long walk, he slipped through the crowd in the station waiting room—taking special note of the departure board—and for more than an hour crept among the steam engines and wooden cars in the railroad yard. Afternoon turned to evening as he nodded confidently to kerchiefed engineers and brakemen who passed in the cinder beds. He dared not ask them where he might find the Denver Behemoth—a freight train with a name like a pugilist. Rather, he withdrew a notepad and pencil in hopes of being mistaken for a journalist or, better yet, a railroad inspector who would never *dream* of jumping a train—of stowing away like a common bum or hobo or Ph.D. in physics, mathematics, and astronomy.

It was dark when Loren at last came upon the Denver Behemoth. The name was painted in delicate script on the side of the massive engine. Heat glowed orange inside. Steam spewed from around the huge metal wheels like dragon's breath. The machine rumbled even as it stood still, hissed even when Loren whispered kind things to it.

"You're going to be famous, Denver Behemoth."

He slipped past the engine and moved cautiously past each car, lingering about the doors, glancing inside, whistling a popular tune, making notes as if checking an inventory. There were crates of tomatoes and Raggedy Ann dolls, of books and maps and Paul Whiteman 78s, of Christmas handcrafts made by convicts from Joliet and quilts made by women from the South Side. In one boxcar were crates filled with lettuce. The myriad green heads brought to Loren's mind guillotined victims of a French Revolution on Mars. Of course, *real* Martians' heads were far smaller than heads of lettuce. And Martians were not violent by nature. Still, the sight made Loren shudder. He would not ride in that boxcar.

Loren moved on to a car half filled with piled crates of shoes. There was room in this car for a stowaway to stretch comfortably on a long ride. Loren glanced back toward the engine. Large men moved in the orange light, but none paid him any attention. He looked toward the distant caboose. There was no movement there at all. Night. He considered going farther back—putting greater distance between his hiding place aboard the train and the men in the engine. He looked into the sky for guidance. Among the stars was a new, glowing sphere that arched higher and higher. It was no star, though it was indeed of star stuff. A guest in the night sky. Loren pulled himself into the boxcar, a guest in the shoe shipment to Boulder.

The car was dark inside. It smelled of leather. Loren ran his hand along a row of crates until he came to a break in the stacked line. Slipping his fingers down a side edge of the crate, he knelt on the wooden floor. Slowly, quietly, he slipped his folded legs from beneath him, turned around, and sat with his back to the crates, his eyes on the door. He could see very little within the boxcar. On the crates nearest the door he read Red Ball Shoes. Rays of moonlight slipped through tiny cracks between the wooden slatted sides of the car. Outside was light and movement. He watched for security men—the violent sort who would be unimpressed by his ambitious plans. With each gust of wind, each short call of a train whistle, each passing of a brakeman or engineer, Loren shuddered in his shadows. Had he been religious, he'd have prayed. Loren was a scientist. He calculated.

"When the train starts out of the yard," he whispered, "Alpha Centauri will coincidentally be aligned with both the Serpens nebula and the Trifid nebula."

Loren Woodville thought this was a sign.

He didn't know precisely *what* it signified. Long before, however, he had learned not to dismiss the medium merely because he could not understand the message.

"A sign," he whispered, vaguely relieved.

The Denver Behemoth was watered and stoked and prepared for its journey through the great flat middle of America. Loren heard the massive engine fire, rumbling like a hungry god, and at last allowed himself a deep breath. He let his muscles relax. He stretched his legs. Then he gasped.

In a single silent movement, a small man carrying a large shadowy object leaped into the boxcar. Loren jerked backward, bumping his head against a wooden crate. The man froze in the doorway. Loren tried to stand but his legs gave way beneath him. He slipped once more to the hard wooden floor.

The man stepped into the boxcar.

Loren scrambled to his feet.

The shadowed man nodded. "Evenin'," he said.

Loren stepped forward. "Haven't you ever wanted something so bad," he asked, his voice barely controlled, his hands shaking, his heart pounding, "that you're willing to break the law to get it? To trespass? To freeload? Don't you think there are ideas in the universe that are worth doing such things for? Well, that's all I'm doing. For mankind's sake I *have* to be here! Do you understand?"

"Beats walkin'," the small man said. "Hittin' the long old lonesome go?"

"You see," Loren continued, "I'm going to change the world."

"Me too," the small man answered. He struck a match.

In the flare of light, Loren was able to see the man. He was short and wiry with a full head of curly black hair. He wore a red-checked shirt and worn blue jeans and carried a guitar. His thin face was tanned and weathered, but his eyes were soft. He held out his hand. "My name's Woody," he said.

"You're not a security man?"

Woody laughed. His palm was dry, his handshake firm. "I'm 'bout as far from bein' a security man as a rabbit is from bein' a hound."

Loren took a deep breath. "My name's Woodville," he said. "I'm a scientist."

"Yeah?" Woody asked.

Loren nodded.

"Lotsa folks trampin' these days," Woody said. "You meet 'em all over the place. Lotsa troubled, tangled, messed-up men. Travelin' the hard way. Dressed the hard way. Hittin' the long old lonesome go. Nothin' to be ashamed of. But a scientist? I believe you're the first scientist I've traveled with. Least since the last time I hoboed with ol' Albert Einstein."

"Albert Einstein?"

Woody nodded. He brushed past Loren and sat cross-legged on the hard floor. He set his guitar beside him. He took a cigarette from behind his ear and struck another match. Loren might have cautioned his companion about the railroad security men had not Woody seemed so at ease, so natural in this setting. Strange shadows danced in the dark boxcar with the flickering of the match.

"You understand ol' Albert's Theory of Relativity?" Woody asked.

Loren nodded. "It's ripe with genius."

"Well," Woody said, drawing on the cigarette, "ol' Albert and me wrote a song about it once when we were trampin' from Redlands to Escondido. You wanna hear it?"

"You and Albert Einstein wrote a song?" Loren asked, sitting down beside Woody. "You expect me to believe that?"

"You expect me to believe you're a scientist, don'tcha?" Woody answered.

"But I *am* a scientist," Loren said. "I know that now."

"You want to hear the song or don't you?" Woody asked.

"Do you think it's a good idea?"

"Relativity?" Woody asked. "Yeah, it's a good idea. But I guess it all depends on where you're standin'."

"No, I mean do you think it's a good idea to play music just now?" Loren continued. "Considering all the danger out there."

Woody picked up his guitar. "Considerin' all the danger out there, I think about all we *can* do is play music." When Woody held the guitar against his body, the curves of the wooden instrument fused with the bony curves of his torso until the two became as one—like a mother suckling her child. He strummed a chord. Loren cringed. He thought of the security men. But Woody seemed to know what he was doing. He seemed an experienced railroad freeloader. He strummed another chord, twanging the strings until the instrument rambled into tune. "Bother you for this guitar neck to stick up in your face?" he asked.

Loren shook his head no.

"You want a cigarette?" Woody asked.

"No, thanks."

"The Special Theory of Relativity Song," Woody said. He strummed a light, steady rhythm. His voice was sturdy when he sang:

> "If I cain't go east nor west,
> If I cain't go north nor south,
> I can still go in and out,
> I can still go round and around!
> I can still go round and around!"

Woody strummed the final chord with a flourish and patted his guitar as if it were alive. His foot continued tapping long after the last note had been struck.

"Very nice," Loren said.

"Me and ol' Albert got a million of 'em."

Loren nodded.

"Pretty true, ain't it?" Woody asked. "I mean scientifically speaking?"

"Well—" Loren began.

"Yeah, ol' Albert's a real kidder!" Woody interrupted. He leaned his guitar against a crate. "Ol' Albert's got a sister. I don't know if you ever heard about her. Name's Rosalee. Rosalee Einstein. Hotter'n a depot stove! But she'll break your heart, believe me. I've seen men tear each other's eyes out and throw each other out of boxcars that are clipping along at sixty miles an hour. Seen guys knock hide and hair off each other's heads. Seen blood fly. Seen splinters dug into the hands and faces of men tromped on the floor. But I never seen no man hurt another man as bad as a woman can. I know what a woman can do. Specially one like Rosalee Einstein. Tear your heart out like you was a plucked chicken on a Sunday afternoon. But sweet when she wanted to be sweet. I still dream about her. I mean, a man's gotta dream about somethin'. Can't dream about freight trains, now, can you?"

"No," Loren answered. "You can't."

It was nearly time for the train to depart. If Loren could get out of this dark railroad yard, he thought, it would be a sweet dream indeed. If he could feel a cool breeze slip into the car, watch the moon through the open boxcar door rise higher into the night sky—the same moon by which the Martians navigated and upon which, Loren imagined, they had constructed subtle rock gardens far surpassing in beauty and subtlety those of the Japanese. If he could pursue with his body that which he had pursued for so long with his heart and mind, *then* could he truly consider the sweetness of dreams.

"What do you dream about?" Woody asked.

"I was just thinking about that," Loren answered. "I dream about Martians."

"Martians?" Woody asked. "Like from Mars?"

"They're real, you know. I've written a dissertation on them. I have evidence. I'm on my way to meet them now."

Woody nodded. "Yeah?" He leaned back slowly, hands knit behind his head, until he lay flat on the boxcar floor. "You ever dream about women? You know, like Rosalee Einstein?"

Loren shrugged his shoulders. "A man has to remain focused. He has to resist the distractions that spring up everywhere he looks. Otherwise his vision is altered. Singularity of thought is defeated, and with it any hope for a higher understanding, for real insight, for transcendence."

"Sure, but do you dream about 'em anyways?"

Loren nodded. "Yes, I do," he said.

The boxcar jerked violently forward. Loren and Woody were thrown against the back wall of the car. Woody's guitar slipped across the floor; it twanged an open chord when it crashed against a wooden crate. The train was moving. Moving west! On the far side of the car a crate tumbled from its stack. There was a crash. From out of the darkness came a high-pitched voice: "Ouch!"

"What was that?" Loren asked, sitting up once more, his eyes wide. He stood up slowly, careful to keep his balance in the moving car. He glanced out the door. The yard passed at three miles an hour. The steam engine strained and pulled, very slowly at first, gradually gaining speed, as a strong man in a circus pulls a wagonload of elephants. The metal wheels clanked beneath the car. "Did you hear it?" he asked Woody.

"Hear what?" Woody said, sitting up.

"Somebody said 'Ouch.' "

"I thought that was you."

Loren shook his head.

Woody stood and walked toward the dark crates on the other side of the car. He moved with a steady ease—like an old sailor on a Sunday cruise—as the floor rocked and pitched beneath him. He struck a match and held it to the crates of shoes.

"Come on, friend," he said. "There's no need to hide back there among those mean, splintery boxes. You're gonna be pickin' wood outta your behind for weeks if you don't come here and set yourself down with us where there's room to stretch out. You hear? Why, you're gonna be all twisted up tighter than the E-string on my guitar if you stay back there the whole trip."

No response.

Woody turned back toward Loren. He winked. When his match burned out he lit another and held it up again to the crates. "You the high-strung type?" he asked.

From behind the crates came a woman's voice, "I'm quite all right, thank you."

Woody blew out the match. He stepped back. He turned to Loren and shook his head, smiling. "Is that a soft, beautiful, female-type voice I hear?"

"Yes," came the reply from behind the crates. "And I'm quite comfortable back here. I have a gun."

"I didn't mean no offense," Woody answered. "I didn't know you was a woman. Still, I hate to think of you all cramped up behind these boxes. How far you goin'?"

"As far as it takes," she answered.

The train jammed on its air brakes.

The guests of the Red Ball Shoe shipment were thrown to the hard floor of the boxcar. Loren and Woody crashed into the piled crates, which tumbled back toward the hidden woman like giant dominoes. Loren reached out to grab a crate but managed only to grab a handful of splinters. The wooden boxes fell with a crash nearly as loud as the screeching of the train as it came to a complete stop.

"You all right?" Loren asked, climbing from the heap on the floor. "You been hurt, miss?"

Woody scrambled to his feet.

Sitting amid a pile of broken wooden crates, a dozen pairs of shoes in her lap, was a woman in a sky-blue silk dress that was torn along the hem and caked with railroad dust. Her face was streaked with dirt, but her hair shone golden and her skin was soft and white.

Woody stood speechless, his mouth wide open, as she brushed down the wrinkles in her dress.

"Are you all right?" Loren repeated.

"Well," Alice answered, "I've been better."

The train jerked forward.

Once more, the guests of the Red Ball Shoe shipment threw their arms wildly about them and twisted their hips like beginning ice skaters to keep their balance.

"West!" Loren announced.

The Denver Behemoth steamed through the railroad yard, accelerating gradually past dimly lit switching houses and steady green lights. All around was a complex network of track and movement, of whistles and bells and shouted voices from out of the darkness. Nearly a quarter mile distant, the station was lit by ten thousand light bulbs. Beyond that was the skyline of Chicago, and beyond that a mystery and grandeur that only the clanking of these steel wheels could deliver.

Woody stepped toward Alice and extended his hand. "I'm Woody Guthrie," he announced. "The singin'est soldier of misfortune you'll ever meet."

"My name's Alice," she answered, touching his hand for only a moment. "Who do you work for?"

Woody stepped back. He scratched his head. "Well, that's a most unusual question," he said. "I've ridden these rails with men trained as doctors and lawyers, executives, stockbrokers, lotsa ex-millionaires, and even a former President of these forty-eight states who asked me not to mention his name. And one thing they all had in common was that when they was ridin' these rails *that's* what they did for a living. Ridin' the rails. Nothin' else. But I've always been a little different. See, I make my living with that racket box." He pointed to the guitar. "Singin' for tips and friends. Why, I don't mean to brag but I can get a hot meal just 'bout any ol' time I please simply by throwin' down my hat and playin' any one of about ten thousand songs. Can get a meal for my lady friends too, I might add."

She nodded and turned to Loren. "What about you?" she asked, her voice firm.

"My name's Loren," he said.

"Who do you work for?" she asked. Her gaze remained at once beautiful and forbidding. "You don't look like the sort of man I expected to meet in a boxcar, if you don't mind my saying so. Do you work for Al?"

"You don't exactly look like the sort I anticipated meeting in a boxcar either," Loren answered.

"Did you follow me here?"

"I'm a scientist," Loren said.

"Like ol' Albert Einstein," Woody added.

"A scientist?" she asked. She narrowed her blue eyes just enough to communicate disbelief.

Loren nodded. "Ever hear of the Woodville Theory?"

"You don't work for Al?" she asked.

"Al who?"

She smiled and sat down on a crate. "You two are just *traveling* in here? That's all?"

"Why else would we be in a boxcar?" Woody asked. "To meet girls?"

"No," she said, shaking her head, "I don't suppose a fellow would have much luck if he had anything like that in mind. Especially since I really do have a gun." She patted her beaded purse.

"Too bad," Woody said. "But we'd of been gentlemen anyways. Right, Professor Woodville?"

Loren turned to the open door. He strained his eyes as though gazing through Hubble's hundred-inch telescope. "Of course," he answered.

The Denver Behemoth rounded a wide bend, passing first a water tower half the size of Soldier Field and then the ramshackle dormitories of the station employees who worked sixteen-hour shifts, as it headed toward the long straight stretch of track that would lead west out of town. Other trains steamed past on parallel tracks, all moving like corpuscles in the perfect organization of a transcontinental bloodstream. The lights of the station twinkled more distant.

"Where you headin', miss?" Woody asked.

Before she could answer, however, a burst of gunfire sounded from outside the boxcar. Alice's face grew pale. "Capone!" she said.

Loren clenched his fists and wiped with the backside of his wrist a sudden cold sweat from his brow. "Get away from there!" he called to Woody, who had run to the open door, hooked one arm around the handle, and leaned out of the car to gain a look at the skirmish. "Don't let the security guards see you!"

The train moved faster now and Woody's curly hair waved in the breeze. "What goes on out here?" he yelled, his voice swallowed up by the chugging of the train. More gunshots. He jerked his head back inside. "I'll be damned!" he said.

Buddy Easter had run across the railroad yard, slipping between the coupled boxcars and passenger coaches of half a dozen different trains—weaving in and out, over and under, as if racing through a complex maze. Still the fat man managed to keep close behind, firing warning shots and shouting threats that would freeze the blood of any boy less determined than Buddy Easter. Beneath the coal car of the Twentieth Century Limited as it rolled past the loading platform, over the caboose of the Zephyr Rocket, which rested on a track near the great water towers, through the dining car of the Santa Fe Empire Builder, and beside the steaming engine of the Peoria and Western Blueblood, Buddy and the fat man ran.

"Stop, or I swear I'll plug you!" the fat man called into the night.

Bullets glanced off the gravel around Buddy's feet.

It was the flickering of a candle or match that first attracted Buddy to a boxcar some distance from the station. The train was a freight and, unlike the luxurious passenger trains, was not surrounded by station employees who might stop to question a running boy just long enough to put him in mortal danger. The train was moving.

"Stop!" the fat man called.

Buddy changed direction, leaping over the heavy steel tracks, and started at such an angle through the yard that he might meet the train just before it steamed past the stationmaster's house. The fat man followed.

"Freeze, kid!"

The fat man pulled Daisy's trigger once more. Gravel bounced up around Buddy's feet. The boy turned. Somewhere in the railroad yard the fat man had shed his coat. He ran now in shirt sleeves, his shoulder holster flapping under one arm.

"Stop, goddammit!"

By the time Buddy intercepted the train it had gained such speed that he was able to keep up with the engine only for a moment. Painted in script on the black iron: Denver Behemoth. As the engine pulled away, Buddy was left to run in a hot cloud of steam.

"Stop, kid!"

The coal car thundered past Buddy Easter. The train gained speed. Buddy reached for the handrail that ran around the water tank but missed as the car sped past. He nearly lost his balance. Only the windmilling of his arms enabled him to continue running. The fat man shot again. Two boxcars roared past Buddy. The train was moving faster now than any boy could run. Another boxcar. Buddy reached up to the open door. The car thundered past. Then another car and another. Buddy could see the lights of the station-master's house growing nearer. Beyond that lay only straight track—no more obstacles around which he might dodge, no more railroad cars beneath which he might squeeze in his effort to lose the fat man. He reached up for another boxcar, grabbing hold of the doorway. Pulled by the train's momentum, he ran faster than he had ever run in his life, completely out of control as if running down a steep grade. The gravel was unsteady beneath his feet. But he could not let go. There was no stopping. There was only the next long step to be taken—stretching from one railroad tie to the next. He glanced over his shoulder. The fat man fell behind. Buddy held on.

A hand reached from out of the dark boxcar. Buddy felt the calloused skin on his own. The hand tightened around his wrist. Buddy's ankle gave way beneath him just as the man in the boxcar lifted him into the air. For a terrible moment, Buddy sailed—almost horizontal—beside the open doorway. His feet were off the ground. He flapped like a banner in the wind. Then the man in the dark boxcar pulled him up and inside.

Buddy Easter landed on the wooden floor in a heap with the man. He scrambled to his feet, pulling free, and raced back to the doorway through which he had been pulled. He leaned out. The speeding night air slapped at the back of his head as he surveyed the yard. In the distance, he saw the fat man collapse to his knees beside the tracks, his puffy hands held to his chest. Then the fat man fell in a heap to the cinders.

The train raced past the stationmaster's house.

"What the *hell* was that all about, kid?"

Buddy turned.

The small curly-headed man who had pulled Buddy into the car sat up on the wooden floor. "You a criminal or something?" he continued. "You a thief?"

Buddy shook his head no.

"Well, it don't matter as long as you don't steal nothin' here," the man said.

Buddy nodded. "Yes, sir."

Another man, tall and thin, stood shadowed in one corner. He said nothing—only wrung his hands together and swallowed so hard that Buddy could hear the gulp across the boxcar.

"You all right, kid?" the small man asked.

"I got some good baseball cards," Buddy answered. "I'd like both of you to have one. Good ones. Maybe a Gehrig. Or a Dickey. Or a Lazzeri. I'm grateful to you."

"You got any *money* on you, kid?" the small man asked, sitting straighter on the wooden floor. He ran his hands through his curly hair and spat skillfully out of the boxcar.

"I have money," Buddy said, taking from his pants pocket the shiny silver dollar that the fat man had given him a few minutes before. He held it up to the moonlight that slipped into the car. "See?"

The small man smiled. "So you do," he said, standing.

"I'm no urchin," Buddy continued.

" 'Course not," the small man answered. "My name's Woody. You like music, son? What do you think a good song's worth? 'Bout a buck? I got a million of 'em."

"Well," Buddy said, "I don't have a million bucks."

"I don't have to play 'em all," Woody answered.

"Leave the boy his money," said the man in the shadows. He was a head taller than Woody but moved with a diffidence that undermined his physical advantage. He stepped forward. "You don't need it, right?"

Woody turned. "That's right, I don't need it. I wasn't gonna *take* it, Professor." Woody shook his head. "I was just askin'. For curiosity's sake. Didn't you know that? You think I'd take money from a kid? You think I'm that kinda guy? Jeez, you don't know me very well yet."

Buddy held the silver dollar out to Woody. "I don't care," he said. "Take it. I don't want it. Go ahead."

Woody shook his head no.

"I don't want it," Buddy repeated. "I don't want anything to do with it. It's the fat man's money. I don't need it. He didn't take his baseball card anyway. It'd be like stealing."

"I don't need it neither," Woody answered.

"Just keep it," Loren Woodville said to the boy.

Buddy shook his head no. He wound up like a baseball pitcher and delivered the silver dollar through the open doorway, out of the speeding boxcar and into the dark Illinois night.

"What'd you do *that* for!" Woody asked.

"Nobody wanted it," Buddy answered.

"Well, I'd of *taken* it," Woody said, shaking his head. "If it would of made you feel better. You didn't have to go and strain your arm."

Alice de Minuette stepped from behind a pile of broken crates. The dark boxcar was illuminated by a warm yellow light, barely perceptible—but undeniable—that emanated from her golden hair. In her hand she held a tiny pistol. "Buddy?"

The silver dollar was quickly forgotten.

"Alice?" Buddy said.

"Did you follow me here?" she asked.

"Alice!" Buddy continued. He swallowed hard. He took one step toward her. "Did you see Frankie Pilaretti take off running when you fired that gun?" he asked. "Nobody's ever done a thing like that for me. At least nobody made of flesh and blood. Nobody that you'd actually be able to *see*."

"Did Al send you, Buddy?" Alice asked. "Have you been following me?"

Woody removed his hat. "You two know each other?"

"Nobody sent me," Buddy said. "Unless you count the Babe."

"Ruth?" she asked. "Babe Ruth?"

Buddy nodded. "The Bambino himself."

Alice moved nearer the boy. "What did he say?" she asked. "What did he tell you?"

"Well, I didn't *talk* to him," Buddy answered. "He just hit the baseball, remember? That's how he sent me."

"What baseball?" Loren asked.

"Did Al give you that silver dollar?" Alice asked.

Buddy shook his head. "He was fat," he said. "And he smelled like daisies. You know him?"

Alice shook her head. "Was it Al Capone?"

"You know *Capone*?" Woody asked. "Jeez!"

"We don't want to hurt you, miss," Loren said, stepping farther out of the shadows. "We're just here for business. We just have to get from one place to another."

"Are you in on this too?" she asked.

"In on what, miss?"

Alice merely shook her head. She was tired. Confused. Outside, the wheels of the boxcar clacked over each joint in the track. Steamy Chicago jazz played for fleeting seconds each time the Denver Behemoth steamed past one of the ramshackle trackside juke joints spread across the South Side. Alice wished for calm. Quiet. She wished she could think straight.

"I didn't tell him a thing," Buddy said. "I pretended not to know you."

"Capone?" she asked.

"Al Capone is *chasing* you?" Woody asked. "Jesus Christ!"

"It wasn't Al Capone," Buddy said. "I've seen pictures of Capone. This guy was fatter."

"It was one of his men," Alice said.

"Why the hell is Al Capone chasing you, miss?" Woody asked. "I mean, if we're gonna ride in the same boxcar I believe I got a right to know."

"It isn't important," Alice answered.

"Must be important to somebody," Woody said.

She shook her head.

"If he's gonna start shootin' it'll be damn important to *me*," Woody said.

"Why did you follow me, Buddy?" Alice asked.

"I didn't," he answered. "I been following the baseball. Remember, like I showed you this afternoon? The Babe hit it. He got all of it. Remember?"

She nodded.

"What do you mean, a baseball?" Loren asked the boy.

"A baseball," Buddy answered. "Regulation, big league, signed by Judge Landis with one hundred and sixty-two stitches."

"The boy was bein' chased by a fella 'bout half the size of Illinois, miss," Woody said. "That's why I pulled him up. If somebody's out to hurt you, it ain't him. Maybe Capone, maybe the fat man doin' the shootin'. But they're both behind us now. So why don't you put that squirrel shooter back in your purse and rest easy?"

Loren stepped toward the boy. "What do you mean a *baseball* was flying through the air?" he asked.

"Babe Ruth hit it," Buddy explained.

Woody stepped toward Alice. "S'pose I ask *you* a question, miss." His voice was soft, calm. "I mean, you sure been askin' us a bundle. Who the hell are you? And why are you ridin' in a boxcar while wearin' a dress that's worth more money than my guitar and my soul put together? And why the hell is Al Capone tryin' to catch up to you?"

"My name's Alice," she answered. "That's all you have to know."

"How far did this so-called baseball fly?" Loren asked the boy.

"It's still up there," Buddy answered, turning to Loren. "I'd say it'll be up there for a long time. But when it comes down, I'll be there to catch it."

"Once I heard a story," Woody said. "Lotsa folks believe it's true. But I'm not sure. They say there's a hobo that comes upon men at twilight. Sometimes in a hobo jungle. Sometimes in a boxcar. But usually only to boys in groups of two or three, like me and the Professor and Buddy, here. But this particular hobo ain't exactly human. It's a ghost. And it comes to the poor doomed men in the form of a beautiful woman."

"I know the name of the fat man's gun," Buddy said, turning back to Alice. "I don't know if it's any help to you."

"You're telling me that a baseball was hit so hard that it's still in the air hours after the impact?" Loren asked.

"Its name is Daisy," Buddy said.

"The gun or the baseball?" Loren asked.

"The gun, of course," Buddy answered.

Alice shrugged her shoulders. "I don't know any gun named Daisy," she said.

"And this beautiful woman takes the souls of the poor boys in the boxcars and swallows 'em up like a wino downin' a bottle of cheap port," Woody continued. "Nothin's left. Just the empty bodies of the poor boys. And this beautiful ghost moves on to the next hobo jungle. Or the next boxcar."

"Alice is no ghost," Buddy said. "She's real. I know about ghosts."

Loren shook his head. "Don't you know what's really in the sky tonight?" he asked the boy. "I mean, it's very exciting to think about a home run, but you're missing what's really there. And it's far more exciting than baseball."

"Nothing's more exciting than baseball," Buddy said.

Woody took another step toward Alice. "I can think of one thing," he said.

"It's Martians up there!" Loren continued, moving across the boxcar to the open door. A cool wind pressed against his face. The train passed over a steel bridge that spanned the Chicago River. The deep, dark Chicago River. Loren Woodville held tight to the boxcar door.

"Did you say Martians?" Buddy asked.

Loren turned back into the boxcar. "Come and see for yourself."

"What did the fat man want to know, Buddy?" Alice asked. "What did he say?"

"Why don't you put that gun away, miss?" Woody suggested. She shook her head no.

"He wanted to know what you said to me outside the Parkview," Buddy answered.

"What did you tell him?" she asked.

"I told him I didn't know what he was talking about," Buddy said to Alice. "I told him I'd never met you. I lied."

"According to my calculations," Loren announced, turning

back toward the heavens, "the Martians will land in Long Beach, California, three nights from tonight. You're all a part of history— whether you believe it or not—merely by being on this train. All of you. Actually, we're part of history merely by being on this planet."

"Then why was the fat man chasing after you?" Alice asked.

"If you think those're Martians up there, you're crazy!" Buddy said, turning to Loren. "Crazy!"

"Why?" Alice repeated.

"Because it's a *baseball*, that's why," Buddy answered.

"No, why was he chasing after you?" she asked.

"Galileo was called crazy," Loren said.

"Because he didn't believe me," Buddy said to Alice. "He thought we were working together or something."

"Working on what?" she asked.

Buddy shrugged his shoulders. "He didn't say."

"Oh."

Buddy turned to Alice. "*Are* we working together, Alice?" he asked. "I mean, it kinda feels like we are. Only I don't know what we're working *on*. I don't even know who you are, really. But we *are* in this together, aren't we?"

She nodded.

"I don't just mean this boxcar," Buddy continued. "I mean you and me, this thing. Like with me and Abner. Doesn't matter what we're doing. We don't even have to be together to be together. It's like there's an invisible string between us. Even when Abner's far away I feel tugs on the string. I've thought about it a lot. About Abner and me. But I never knew I was tied to somebody else. Not till now. I've felt you tugging all day. I can't explain. Do you feel it? Do you understand?"

"I felt it too, Buddy," she said. "But I don't understand."

"You know, I've seen guns go off by accident," Woody said. "If you'd just put that ol' piece of trouble away, we could all rest easier."

Alice looked at the gun. "I don't want to shoot anybody," she said.

" 'Course you don't," Woody answered. "Besides, we're the good guys."

"I don't want to shoot anybody," Alice repeated. She tossed the gun out of the speeding train.

"Jeez, lady!" Woody said. "You didn't have to do *that*. The gun might of come in handy. You're as bad as the boy. Tossin' money off a train. Jeez! You two might as well be related."

"You shouldn't be scared, Alice," Buddy said. "Not anymore. You're with me. I won't let anything bad happen. I got too much to do, too many great things, to be stopped, even by Al Capone. You'll be all right."

Woody stepped toward her. Before he could sit beside her on the wooden crate, however, she motioned him away with a movement of her hand.

"I think I need to be alone right now," she said.

Woody stepped back.

"Lots of people have looked into the night skies over the millennia," Loren began. "And they imagined *they* were alone. But that's the most beautiful part of it. They never were. There was always somebody up there. Watching. Waiting for the right moment. And in all of history, they chose us!"

Woody walked to the far side of the boxcar. He sat down, cross-legged, beside his guitar on the wooden floor. He lifted the instrument, placing it gently in his lap. He strummed an open chord. He hummed a lullaby.

Buddy moved to the doorway.

"See it?" Loren asked. "It's beautiful."

"Of course I see it," Buddy answered. "I've been watching it all day. I saw Ruth *hit* it, for pete's sake!"

"It's a Martian scouting craft," Loren said. He did not hear Buddy Easter. His thoughts were as distant as his gaze. "They're very tiny creatures. But their hearts are very big," he continued. "Big enough to hold the whole sky."

Alice moved beside Buddy in the doorway. She sat on the wooden floor with her legs hanging outside the car. Chicago sped past. The tallest buildings and brightest lights had already been left behind. A whole life. But the western suburbs burned with a life of their own. Wood-frame houses from which glowed a warm light. Quiet schools. Neon cafés.

"Do you see it?" Buddy asked, sitting beside her. He pointed into the sky.

"I see a million stars," she said.

Loren sat beside them. In a single line, they rocked and bobbed with the movement of the train, each gazing into the Illinois sky.

"It's the point of light at the foot of Ursa Major," Loren explained.

"Is Ursa Major one of those shapes people are supposed to see by drawing lines from star to star?" Alice asked.

"It's called a constellation," Loren said.

She nodded. "I've never been able to see the shapes up there. Crabs and horses and a man wearing nothing but a belt. I think somebody made the whole thing up. Those stars might just as easily be South Side seamstresses or waitresses or dance hall girls. At least as far as I can see."

"They're frozen pieces of a baseball made of ice that was busted by a single swing of the bat," Buddy explained. He looked at Alice. She would surely be the most beautiful woman in the ice grandstands on the day of the Winter Game. He inched beside her until his leg brushed against hers. She was solid—flesh and blood—but the charge that sparked between them was as electric as the spark that had bound Buddy to Abner. Buddy moved away. He needn't touch her. To be in her field was enough—almost too much.

"Constellations have always been man's way of explaining the mysteries of the world," Loren said. "What's in the sky is what's in a man's heart. That's all."

"You don't sound much like a scientist," Alice said.

"So I've been told," Loren answered.

Woody strummed a slow chord progression. He leaned back against the wooden crates. He watched his traveling companions silhouetted in the doorway.

"See the baseball?" Buddy asked Alice, leaning toward her so that when he pointed into the sky her eye might be more nearly aligned with his arm.

"Baseball?" Loren asked, smiling. "That's a Martian craft. I've made all the calculations. It conforms to the laws of gravity while, at the same time, demonstrating a degree of vertical lift impossible for a manmade object. Don't be disappointed, kid. This is far better. And after I'm famous I'll buy you a baseball. All the baseballs you want. All right? How could it be a baseball? How could it be anything but what it is?"

"Babe Ruth hit it," Buddy answered.

"Yeah," Alice said. "Babe Ruth hit it." She smiled at Buddy Easter. Her face was warm, believing, faithful. "He could do it too. I know. I really do."

"Hey!" Buddy said, jumping to his feet. "Is this train going west? I have to stay under that baseball! I didn't even think to ask where we were going."

Woody's voice was strong and steady when, in answer, he sang:

> "This train don't carry no gamblers,
> Liars, thieves, and big-shot ramblers;
> This train is bound for glory,
> This train!"

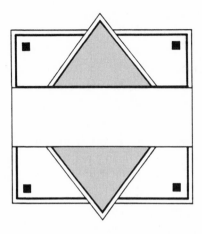

The Denver Behemoth rambled through the great woods that lie two hours west of the La Salle Street station, spewing from its surging engine a plume of white steam that captured and held in each vaporous drop the first light of the moon. Outside passed fields of pale grasses and thick stands of birches and shadowed elms whose twisted limbs pointed in every direction like crazy signposts. Far above, in the silent night sky, soared the arching evening star of Ruth—lighting the way for the Denver Behemoth like a firefly guiding a beast through the night.

"Well," said Loren Woodville, settling back like his companions on the wooden floor of the boxcar, gazing up at the ceiling as the countryside raced past, "I'll go first. But it isn't exactly a story. I mean, it's true. Every word of it."

Woody slept. Buddy and Alice listened. Beneath them, the clanking of the train's wheels upon the metal joints of the track established a single time—like a metronome—for the disparate melodies that played in each of our heroes' hearts.

I was once alone in these woods. I was a boy. Maybe fourteen. How old are you, Buddy? Yes, about your age. Camping. It was summer. The night was beautiful. Very clear. Do you know such nights? The sky is frightfully near on these nights. Near enough almost to touch and smell. And the quiet—though there must have been a multitude of sounds. Night birds and the wind in the trees. But I remember only silence and the nearness of the sky.

This was new to me. I was from the city. Never before had I felt airborne while lying on the ground; never before had I sensed the silence of the void, of space itself; never before had I *known* the sky. I was not afraid. I had my father's rifle. And a campfire. I'd read of courageous boys fending off wild animals with clubs alight, torches, waved like the batons of crazy maestros. What had I to fear? I had fire. I had courage.

Then the bear. . . .

When it appeared from out of the trees I thought neither of the gun nor of the fire. It was a brown bear. Very large. Yet I thought nothing of "the wild." Nothing of danger. Rather, I thought of Ursa Major. The constellation. The Great Bear. It seems senseless now, but I had *seen* them, Alice. The shapes in the sky, in the stars—even without the dotted lines. The bear stepped through the brush. I felt the animal's hot breath and smelled the musk and filth of its coat. But I was not afraid. I did not move. I watched the animal, but I thought of the constellation. Ursa Major. I felt it. Not some vicious beast come to play with me as a cat plays with a mouse. I thought of stars.

Of course, I wasn't looking into the sky any longer. After all, the bear . . . I paid him at least as much respect as to keep him in my sight. I have sometimes been oddly inspired, but I've never been altogether *mad*, not even as a boy. No matter what you might have heard.

I don't know how long the bear sat at the edge of the clearing. I watched him watch me. It might have been quite a while. It's easy to lose a sense of time in such instances. Time and place. The temporal. Meaningless, really. Woody's friend Albert Einstein speaks of this. Though I'm not altogether sure how it explains the bear. I'm not altogether sure how anything explains the bear.

It moved forward. I didn't think about the gun. I didn't think about the fire. I watched the bear. I was never afraid. The bear was too big to fear. Like the sky. If it chose to swallow me up I would be as consumed by *it* as the day is consumed by the darkness. But the day doesn't fear. Light doesn't fear dark, any more than Orion fears Scorpio's stinger or Cancer's claws. They are together, but they are apart.

The bear sat beside me at the fire.

This was no dream. It might have been, but I don't dream. At least not while I sleep. And waking dreams are hardly dreams at all. Waking dreams are almost as real as the fleas that leaped off the bear's coat into the fire like tiny lemmings. I remember this. I saw it. I had flea bites afterward to prove it. The bear and I watched the fire. Watched the crazy shadows cast among the trees. The bear's muzzle was twice the size of my fist.

The bear gazed deeply into the flames.

I looked away. I had grown comfortable sitting beside the beast, occasionally brushing elbows with it as one brushes against strangers on a shared armrest in the theater. The bear and I were that close. Yet after a time I felt secure enough to look away from the animal. Of course, what I saw in the sky changed my life.

Before that night I had not actually committed myself to real astronomical study. Still, I was acquainted with star charts. The heavens were a serious interest if not yet a true vocation. I *knew* the sky. I knew what it looked like. I had watched Venus rise and set over the course of a season. I knew the moon's phases as if they were my own. I saw the constellations even without the dotted lines. I needed to see something I could understand. The heavens. Which never change.

So I looked up.

But something was wrong. The sky was out of balance. Then I understood. Ursa Major was gone! The constellation. The stars. They were not in their proper place. They were nowhere in the sky. Just darkness in their corner of the heavens where a moment before I had *seen* the constellation. Ursa Major had simply *disappeared*. Well, not disappeared. I knew where Ursa Major had gone. I knew where the Great Bear was. It was sitting beside me at the fire, breathing hot breath and stinking of mildew and filth. I turned back to the fire, to the bear.

The bear was gone. I'd not heard it leave.

I looked once more into the sky.

Ursa Major had returned to its position among the stars. The grandest constellation. Silent, in mid-stride, across the night, its starry muzzle twice the size of my fist. The sky was in balance once more. I was alone again at the campfire.

But I had *touched* the stars. . . .

On the coast I will again touch the heavens. I will once again know the sky.

■ BUDDY'S STORY ■

I camped in these woods once too. At night. But I wasn't alone. A whole dormitory of boys was with me. The loud ones shouted and laughed until needles started raining down off the pines, while the quiet ones huddled together talking about the safety we had left behind—talking about bears who don't just sit beside boys at the campfire but who roast them and eat them like marshmallows. The camp counselors tried to calm both groups. Some counselors shouted warnings to the loud boys that too much noise might attract murderous animals, while other counselors whispered to the scared boys that there *were* no wild animals within a hundred miles. Of course they were all lying. But they had good reason. The loud boys *were* too loud, and the frightened ones were too darned frightened. Nothing's worse than boys who are too darned frightened.

I wasn't actually with the loud boys *or* the scared boys. I was with Abner. He's my best friend. He's older. A lot older, really. But he's not *too* old. He understands what it is to be— well, what it is to be me. Sometimes he understands a lot better than I do. That's why he's my best friend. That's why I'm here now, sort of.

So on this night in the woods we pitched our tents—the loud boys quieting down, the quiet boys livening up—and we settled around the campfire for a story. More than one story, actually. But I've forgotten all but one. The other stories were too much alike to remember. Ghost stories that were unrealistic. See, I know about ghosts. Real ghosts. As a matter of fact, Abner's a ghost. But *these* ghost stories were ridiculous. Ghosts chopping people's heads off and cutting children into tiny pieces and making off with newlyweds in the dead of the night. Crazy.

The story I remember wasn't about ghosts at all. It was much more realistic. It was about the Mothman.

It's *supposed* to be true. But I wouldn't take any bets on it. You can never tell about this kind of stuff. After all, the ghost stories were supposed to be true and I didn't believe them for a minute. But at least this story *might* be true. And that's about all you can say for anything. Or anybody. Might be true.

The Mothman lives in the woods, like around here, and also in the farmlands to the west and the swamps down south. He's never been photographed, but he's been seen by plenty of respectable people who wouldn't have a reason in the world to lie. He's about seven feet tall, trim build, and he's got wings that glow in the dark when he opens them.

They come out from just behind his shoulders and open to a span of twenty feet or more. They look to people who've seen them to be very powerful, but when they move they don't make a sound and they're as graceful as a butterfly's wings. They just flap once or twice and this Mothman, who has huge red eyes and a shiny silver body, takes off into the air and flies as gracefully as any bird.

He's usually seen only at night, though there are a few stories of people who've seen him in the day. He flies over dark roads where few people pass because he's naturally shy. And he likes to glide over railroad tracks, hovering like a hawk circling a rabbit. Nobody knows exactly what he eats, though, because he's never been seen eating. But this much *is* known: whenever the Mothman is sighted, you can bet that soon a fat banker will turn up missing and never be heard from again. That's why almost everyone agrees that the Mothman eats fat bankers.

In fact, if you're a fat banker, the Mothman's a *terrible* monster. Lurking in the tops of trees waiting for a banker to walk down a deserted country road at night . . . terrible! Once, a bank held a picnic for its employees. The president was the last to leave the picnic. That is, he and his two assistants. The bank president was very fat. The assistants were trimmer. Together, they all walked down a country road. It was dark, but they thought they were safe—why wouldn't they?—when suddenly they heard a *whoosh* in the sky above them and, looking up, managed to catch a glimpse of the Mothman landing in a field nearby. His wings glowed, and he was easy to see. He landed real soft. When he turned his head to look at them, his red eyes glowing, it struck so much fear into their hearts that they turned and ran down the road at full speed. All three of them—the president and his two assistants. Well, naturally, the president was too fat to keep up with the others, maybe as fat as that man chasing me in the railroad yard tonight. Pretty soon, he was alone in the road. The assistants were gone. He ran and ran, his arms pumping at his sides, chugging like this train, when he saw a huge shadow block the moonlight above him. Then he felt strong hands or claws or something tug at his arms and he was lifted into the air, his feet swinging from under him. The Mothman had him. The banker flew over the trees and looked down to see his assistants running ahead along the road. Well, when they saw *him* they realized their terror had made them forget all about their boss. This thought put so much guilt into their hearts that they died right on the spot because they couldn't stand themselves anymore, not even enough to keep on living. They were found the next day looking dead and real sad. The fat banker was never heard from again.

Meantime, the Mothman flapped his wings a few times and was gone forever. Or until the next banker walks down a dark country road.

That's the story I remember from around the campfire: the Mothman. Naturally, we were quite impressed. We were glad not to be bankers. But I had a question. As terrifying as the Mothman must be, I asked the boys seated around me, just imagine how awful he must have been *before* he became the Mothman. When, if my biology books are right, he must have been the Worm-man. Isn't it a terrible thought? Doesn't it make you grateful for metamorphosis?

But I didn't really want to tell you about the Mothman. I mean, that's not my story. I really want to tell you about Bobby Crabtree, who was there that night around the campfire. In these woods. He had been one of the quiet, frightened boys. He probably should never have heard a story like the Mothman. It was too much. He was the nervous sort.

A week or so after the camping trip, on an ordinary school day, we looked up from the playground and spotted someone standing atop the main school building. Four stories high. He was dressed in a silver outfit with a red mask over his eyes and giant cardboard wings strapped to his back. We didn't know then that it was Bobby Crabtree. But we knew from the start that it wasn't the real Mothman. Everyone laughed.

Then Bobby jumped. He didn't fly at all. Not even for a moment. He just dropped. The wings flapped off his back, and the mask tore off of his face. All this in about two seconds. Then he hit the pavement.

So much, so fast. You wouldn't believe it.

Abner wouldn't let me go near the body, though the other boys ran for it as if there was something they could do. There was nothing. Nobody even knew what Bobby was trying to do. Fly? Just get a laugh? *Be* the Mothman? I wanted to go to him too. But Abner kept tugging on my arm. I didn't know what to do. I didn't know what to think. I thought I was going to pass out. You can't imagine what this is really like. But then Abner asked me a question, calm in the middle of all this terrible panic.

"After the Worm-man has become the Mothman," he whispered to me, "what do you suppose he becomes next?"

It was a good question. The sort of question that either drives you crazy or keeps you from going crazy, one or the other. For me, it worked. I don't think I'm crazy. "What do you suppose he becomes next?" Abner asked. But he didn't expect an answer. You don't have to *know* the answer. You only have to know the question. And let the answer work itself out for you one way or another.

That's the story I wanted to tell you.

■   ALICE'S STORY   ■

You're probably wondering why Al Capone is chasing me. It's a reasonable question. And I suppose the answer makes for a kind of a story. Not a very nice one, though. Nothing so soothing as a fairy tale. "Rapunzel, Rapunzel, let down your hair." I wish it was that simple. To be locked in a tower seems nothing by comparison. Especially when all a girl has to do to escape is to wait until her hair grows long enough for a handsome prince to climb up. Is that so tough? But maybe it's not waiting for the hair to grow that's difficult. Maybe it's waiting for a prince to show up. I don't know. I'm not waiting for anything. And this is no fairy tale.

Last night I had a date with Al Capone. I didn't *know* I was going to be with Capone. I'd never even met him before. It was a blind date. I never go on blind dates. But this seemed different. He had been so persistent. And mysterious. Roses every night at my apartment. Unsigned poems. Corny, but after six months it's hard to ignore. Do you mind if I tell you what happened? I've never camped in these woods. I don't know many other stories. In truth, I don't really even know *this* story. I mean I don't understand it. I don't know why what happened, happened. But it did. It's real. Maybe if I tell it to you it'll become clearer to me. Do you mind?

Good. But it's not very nice.

I was picked up outside my building by a long black limousine. It was a beautiful car. The driver was handsome and very polite. His hands were graceful as he opened the door for me. His teeth were white when he smiled. I slid into the back seat. Alone. No one was there. Only a single rose. I still hadn't had a glimpse of my date. But it was very nice. Champagne. A new copy of *Vanity Fair* magazine. Nice.

As the limousine pulled away from the curb it felt like the whole state of Illinois had been lifted a foot off the ground and was being carried aloft by a smooth breeze. *Whoosh*, we moved through the city. Traffic parted for us. I didn't know where we were going. But the flowers had been so frequent, the poetry so sincere (even if it *had* actually been written by Elizabeth Barrett Browning), and the car was so gorgeous, I thought the mysterious secret admirer must be the most romantic man in Chicago. Al Capone was the farthest thing from my mind.

I'm not sure what I was expecting—*who* I was expecting. It's been a long time since I've really known a man. Can I say that? Is it offensive? It's been a long time since I've spoken to a man. Really *talked*. Even like this. I've danced with plenty of them. I've exchanged compliments over watered-down drinks at the dance hall. I know details about men's wives. But I don't know the men themselves. Sometimes I think I'd like to know a man again.

It was eight thirty when we pulled up in front of the hotel. The limousine driver told me nothing as we drove. I asked him about the secret admirer, but he was as silent as the deaf-mute who had delivered flowers to my apartment every night for six months. I flirted and joked with him. Nothing. Just a clue? Nothing. But now, of course, I understand. If he had answered a single question, Capone would have broken him into tiny pieces to smoke in his cigar.

Two men in pin-striped suits and loud ties showed me upstairs to the penthouse. I still didn't suspect that a monster lay in wait for me. Well, perhaps I suspected *something*. The evening had been too well planned. Too perfect. Except that I hadn't yet been allowed to lay eyes on my devoted and patient admirer. I suppose I suspected something. But by then it was too late. What could I do?

Capone greeted me in the foyer of his apartment wearing only a powder-blue satin robe that stopped at mid-thigh. I knew I was in trouble. Of course I recognized him. But he's uglier in person than he is in the papers. His face is bloated and pale. He wears powder to cover his scars. It doesn't work. His eyes are the most frightening. They're light. More than that, they're *lighted* in a way that doesn't come across in black-and-white pictures. His face looks stupid, except for those eyes. They are intelligent. They are terrifying.

He took my coat. He is much impressed with himself. He pushed himself up against me, smiling, nodding his big head. More men in loud ties stood smiling at each other on all sides. It was pretty bad. I knew I was in trouble. But what could I do? Run? Fight?

I kissed him hard on the lips.

It worked. He told the smiling goons to wait quietly and then pushed me into a bedroom that overlooked the street. We were alone, though I could hear his men laughing on the other side of the door. I looked around. There was a fire escape outside the window, but I knew I'd never outrun him. Besides, he probably had goons on every floor. Still, I wasn't going to let him touch me. I didn't know how I would stop him, but I wasn't going to give in to him. He took my purse the moment we walked into the room. He set it on top of a stack of papers on his desk. I knew I'd never manage to dig through the purse for my gun. Besides, I wasn't too confident about firing the thing anyway. Real life is like that sometimes, you know? There might be a gun in the room, but you know you'll never fire it.

He told me he had watched me every night for the past six months. That he had snuck into Marnie's to watch me dance. He said he loved me. I wanted to kill him. At least I *thought* I wanted to kill him. I would think so right up to the moment I had the chance. Then it's not so easy to kill somebody. Even if he deserves it.

He pushed me back onto the bed. He was still wearing the blue robe, though it wasn't doing much to preserve his modesty anymore, and he took from one of the satin pockets an envelope which he set on the bedstand. He was grinning, going on about love and devotion, as he opened the envelope. I thought there'd be money inside, which would have been bad enough. But it was worse. Much worse. A half-dozen shiny razor blades rattled out of the envelope. I don't know what he had in mind. I've heard the girls tell stories. I don't like to think about it.

But I know what *I* had in mind: a way out. Suicide.

He trusted me. I had been friendly to him. I had listened to his stupid words. I pretended to believe he was a poet. I pretended to like what I saw of him. But the moment he moved near me on the bed I acted. I reached for the razor blades. What a mistake to have trusted me.

I grabbed a blade. I planned to cut my throat. A single slash across the artery and all this would be over. The razor blade felt good in my hand. The steel felt good against my skin. All this in less than a second. And then I thought, if I'm going to commit suicide, I might as well take Capone with me.

You should have seen his face when I turned on him with the blade. He was deathly white and stammered something I couldn't understand. Everything happened in slow motion, like a traffic accident. Everything was over in two seconds but it felt like years. I had him. He was dead. But I couldn't do it. It's not easy to slice somebody's throat. He was coming toward me. I had to do *something*. Anything. But I couldn't kill him. I just couldn't. You think very fast in such moments. It occurred to me that if I slashed his leg I might escape through the window without actually *killing* him. I wanted to cut his leg. Deeply. Some place that would hurt and slow him down but wouldn't ruin his life. His face was scarred enough. I swear, I was aiming for his leg. All this in about one second. There's plenty of time to think, but not much time to take aim. I tried to slash his leg. I really did. But he was moving. . . .

I missed his leg. Not by much.

Still, I got him. He went down in a heap. I was horrified. Blood was everywhere. He was all curled up on the floor. But he wasn't going to die. I mean, I might have slashed his throat and he would be dead. That would be worse, wouldn't it? Don't you think? Besides, I was just trying to slow him down. It would have been worse to kill him, right? I mean, he's *already* fathered a child. I read about it in the papers. It's not like he hasn't had a full family life. Besides, I was aiming for his leg. I didn't mean to—well, cut him *there*. But I don't think he'd see it that way.

Capone kept moaning, "Help me, help me." But nobody came.

His men were outside the room. They must have misunderstood.

Then I remembered my purse. I ran over to the desk. I wasn't thinking. I was just acting. Capone kept moaning and bleeding. I was afraid he might grab for my ankle. I didn't even look at the purse. I reached—and wound up grabbing the purse *and* an envelope Capone had set it on top of. I grabbed it all. Grabbed and ran. I wasn't trying to steal anything. I didn't care about his private papers. I just wanted my purse. I just wanted out!

So I slipped down the fire escape. I made it. But of course I had no place to go. Capone knows where I work. He knows where I live. He knows everything about me. I had to make a plan. I hid in an alley for an hour or so and thought things through.

Finally, I remembered an old friend who might help me. An out-of-towner visiting Chicago for a few days. A very strong man, in his way. You'd know his name. He's acquainted with folks who are almost as powerful as Capone. Like the President of the United States. So I started across town to find him. I knew he'd be busy, but I thought he'd take time for me. I wrote him a note on the back of the envelope I had taken from Capone. I didn't have anything else to write on. I don't know what was inside. I didn't want to know.

So I sent the envelope into the ballpark. But after a minute I started thinking again. Listening and thinking. I had second thoughts about asking for George's help, anybody's help. Bringing somebody else into this mess didn't seem such a friendly thing to do. It seemed dangerous. Selfish. I had to get out of town *on my own*. I left the ballpark before George could come out to meet me.

I needed another plan. *This* plan: being in a boxcar bound for anywhere. That's why I'm here.

■ ■ ■

On the morning of October 2 (one day after Babe Ruth's monumental home run) Alice de Minuette opened her eyes and sat up in bed. Her brow was damp with cold sweat and the palms of her hands were sore where she had dug into them with her clenched fingernails. She was not completely awake but rather lingered in the gray place between dream and waking, participating in neither, vaguely aware of both. She could see the morning light. She could feel the fresh breeze that slipped through an open window and filled white cotton curtains the way wind on Lake Michigan fills the sails of sleek racing boats. The bed was soft beneath her. In this world of half-light, she could also sense the details of the terrible scene left behind—replayed like a Bijou matinee in the screening room of her mind.

She enjoyed for a moment the comforting notion that the two gunmen on the train platform that morning had been part of a dream. A nightmare as insubstantial as the monsters played by Lon Chaney that simply disappeared when the movie house turned on its lights. She rubbed her eyes. Then she slipped from the gray into the white. Into full wakefulness. She gasped. It had been no dream.

"Where am I?"

She jumped off the bed. The room was tidy and altogether unfamiliar. On the walls hung framed paintings of planets and constellations. A small desk was piled with schoolbooks. Above the desk was a felt pennant that read Smallville High School. Outside the window were rolling fields of wheat and endless blue skies. In the distance, a man bounced along a rutted dirt road atop a red tractor.

Alice had never before seen the room.

It was fitful memory that had stirred her from dark sleep. Awake, she remembered everything: the ordeal with Capone, the flight through the city, the train ride through Illinois, Iowa, and into Kansas, Loren's story, Buddy's story, the quiet in the boxcar as her companions finally slept, the first light of morning, the tiny Kansas train station, the platform, the vicious faces of the gunmen, the black muzzles of their guns, the bursts of fire in the clear air, the darkness. It was no dream. It was real. She remembered everything. Yet she understood nothing. Least of all how she could still be alive. Had the gunmen missed? And where was she now?

She swallowed hard. "Can't be," she said.

If it is impossible to survive a machine-gun assault by two of Capone's gunmen, Alice de Minuette reasoned; then—no matter the appearances afterward—one *has not* survived. Simple enough. Therefore, she continued, since the gunmen's bullets surely found their mark, she must now be dead and this must be no ordinary bedroom. Simple logic. Yet she felt very alive. And the room *seemed* ordinary, except for the texture of its newly painted walls: as smooth as Marnie's best line on a slow night. And the bedspread: as soft as the downy hair of an angel. And outside the window the light was clear and white and the flatness of the land was of biblical proportion.

After a moment, however, she shook her head. "I'm not dead," she said aloud. "This place isn't heaven. It isn't hell. It's Kansas, for God's sake. And I'm alive. Somehow. Alive, alive, alive."

She walked to the small desk. She smelled bacon cooking downstairs in the kitchen. Whose kitchen? She picked up a newspaper set atop the schoolbooks. She needed to know more. She needed to know *something* before leaving the quiet bedroom to confront whoever had brought her here. Wherever this was. The bacon smelled heavenly. It reminded her how long it had been since she had eaten bacon and eggs. Or a hamburger. Or a hot dog. Or anything. It reminded her how long it had been since she had arranged her fine china on the kitchen table in her apartment (setting for one). How long it had been since she had rubbed her finger along the rim of her crystal water glass to make the beautiful ghostly music that was heard by no one. How long it had been since she had secretly smoked a Havana cigar after dinner while listening to Fanny Brice on the radio. The smell of the bacon reminded her how endlessly long even the day before yesterday can seem to a woman who no longer knows where she is or how it is she is still alive.

She looked at the *Smallville Trumpeter*, a daily newspaper beneath whose banner was written Truth, Justice, and the American

Way. She scanned the front page. There was an article about a local beauty contest to be held that night, which offered as a prize a trip to Denver, Colorado. There was another article about the erection of lights at the local ballpark. There were other stories about President Hoover's speech to the Congress, Amelia Earhart's solo flight, and the latest rage to sweep the nation (if one considers the Depression something other than a rage): miniature golf. In the bottom corner of the front page, however, was an article that caught Alice's attention.

NEW STAR SIGHTED IN KANSAS SKIES

SMALLVILLE—A new star has been sighted in the Kansas skies by Mrs. Thelma Percy of Rockwell Avenue. Mrs. Percy, a teacher at Smallville High School and amateur astronomer, called the *Trumpeter* offices shortly after 8 P.M. to report the unusual sighting.

"I was shocked to look up from my porch and see a new light in our beautiful autumn skies," Mrs. Percy told the *Trumpeter*. "The star is located at the foot of Ursa Major. All my students know where Ursa Major can be found."

Scientists explain that new stars are formed when many different gases come together until they form a ball of gas so dense that it collapses under its own weight and explodes into a burning ball of fire.

Rev. John Stanley of the First Street Evangelical Church, however, disagrees with the scientific explanation for the birth of stars. "God makes stars," Reverend Stanley told the *Trumpeter* when contacted at his home. "And the Lord makes them for a reason. In this case, it seems that he has sent a star from out of the east to lead us to our salvation."

Reverend Stanley will address the appearance of the new star in next Sunday's sermon.

Mrs. Percy has asked that the new celestial body be called "Percy's Star" until formal confirmation from government authorities gives to it an official identity.

"That's Buddy's baseball," Alice said.

"What's that, miss?"

Alice turned. The broad-shouldered young man who had leaped between Alice and the bullets as Capone's gunmen fired their first volleys at the train station stood now in the doorway. He carried a tray on which was arranged a plate of bacon and eggs, a tiny glass of orange juice, a cup of steaming coffee, and a pitcher of milk. The young man moved with a natural grace which, in Alice's hopeful mind, made it less likely that he might prove one of Capone's thick-fingered stooges. He wore slacks, a white dress shirt, and a tie upon which was the tiny monogram C.K.

When he smiled Alice felt short of breath.

"What happened this morning?" she asked. His face was young, but in his eyes was a knowing that Alice thought far beyond his years. He was very handsome.

"I thought you might be hungry," he answered, setting the tray on the desk.

Alice felt a chill when she looked into his eyes. She shuddered, at once attracted and afraid. She had never felt such a rippling shudder before. She had *seen* it—in the bodies of men who were moved by *her* beauty. She had imagined their helplessness. She had used it. But her imaginings proved short of the reality. As he stepped near, she thought her heart would stop.

"Are you all right?" he asked.

"No," she managed.

In his eyes she saw the rarest combination of strength and compassion. His beauty was almost otherworldly, his intelligent face almost godlike. His body rippled with muscles. Alice was ashamed. She was stirred. How was a woman to deal firmly with a young man of such grace?

"Are you hungry?"

"Very," she said.

He smiled. "That's a good sign."

"Who are you?" she asked.

"My name's Clark," he answered.

"Nothing like this has ever happened to me before," she said.

"I should hope not," he answered.

"Forgive me if I seem awkward."

"You're fine."

"My name is Alice."

"That's a very nice name," he said.

Alice was attracted to Clark not only because of his beauty and strength and the strange sense of the unknown that surrounded him, but also because of a single stubborn lock of jet black hair that had fallen to his forehead in a noble curl—a few unrestrained strands that were perfect in their imperfection. As a single drop of black is added at the factory to a vat of white paint in order to intensify the whiteness, so the curl resting on Clark's forehead served to highlight his perfection. Alice knew she was in trouble again.

"You're not hurt, are you?" he asked.

She shook her head no. "Where are we?"

"This is my bedroom," he said.

"Oh, I see."

He turned away to set the silverware on the desk. His hands worked carefully: fork on the left, knife on the right. However, as she watched him from behind—the nape of his neck, the set of his hips and shoulders—the terrible moment on the train platform returned. The confusing implications of all that had happened remained even in the sublime peace of Clark's bedroom. Alice had to *know*.

"Here's your coffee," he said.

"What's going on, Clark?"

"Breakfast," he answered.

She looked away from him. She set her jaw. "You were there. You know what happened. Tell me."

Clark nodded. "I was there," he said as he sat on the bed. His body was large, yet there was hardly a wrinkle in the bedspread where he sat. "Everything's all right now."

Alice shook her head. "It's not all right," she said. "I saw you jump in front of me as they were shooting. I remember thinking what a foolish thing you did. That maybe they wouldn't have killed *you*. I remember. You jumped in front of me. Like you were made of steel. It's the last thing I remember."

Clark looked away. "It was just a reaction," he said. "I didn't stop to think about it. There wasn't time. Bullets are pretty darn fast."

"So what happened? Why are we still alive? They couldn't have missed. They never miss. Tell me what happened. Are you in on this? You don't work for Al, do you? Where am I? What in the hell happened?"

"You're in Smallville, Kansas," he answered. He spoke slowly as if weighing the consequences of each word. "You're in my parents' house. You say you don't remember anything about what happened after they aimed their guns at you?"

"Just that you jumped in front of me. What do *you* remember?" Alice's eyes were wide with frustration. If it weren't for Clark's bright baby blues she might have thrown something at him: the plate of eggs or the cup of coffee. But the bright baby blues. . . . It was all she could do, even while angry, to keep from throwing *herself* at him. She knew this weakened her. It didn't help to know it. "What's going on, Clark?"

"I went to the station to catch my train," he answered, gazing out the window. "I was leaving on the six fifty-five. I have a job interview tomorrow with a newspaper editor. I'm going to be a big city reporter. I just completed a correspondence course in news writing. The career fits nicely with my other plans—"

"Please," Alice said, sitting beside him on the bed. "We can talk about that later. Just tell me what happened at the station. How I got here. And why we're still alive."

"All right." Clark stopped.

"Well?"

"Right," Clark said. He shifted his weight on the bed. He cleared his throat. "Why we're still alive? All right. I'll tell you. I was standing on the platform waiting for my train when your freight pulled in. I saw you slip out of a boxcar. I was surprised to see someone so—" He stopped. He looked away.

"So what?" Alice asked.

He blushed. "Pretty," he said.

Alice smiled. "Thank you," she said. "I usually don't ride boxcars but yesterday was—well, you just wouldn't believe what kind of a day it was."

Clark nodded.

"So then what happened?" Alice asked. "When the men with the guns came out."

Clark shrugged. "It was all very fast. They burst out of the waiting room with those paper sacks. I should have looked more closely at the sacks, but who could have guessed what was going to happen? It had been such a quiet, *peaceful* morning. Then, suddenly, they were aiming machine guns. I moved without thinking. Sometimes it's like that, you know?"

"I remember all that," Alice said. "What happened next? And don't tell me they missed."

Clark turned away.

"Don't tell me they missed," she repeated.

"They missed," Clark said.

"No!" Alice answered. "I don't believe you. They were ten feet away. They had tommy guns. They never miss. *I* could have hit somebody from that close. What's going on here?"

"I'm not a child," Clark said.

"I know that," Alice answered. "Believe me, I've noticed."

"Then don't talk to me as if I were a child."

"All right," Alice said.

Clark said nothing.

"So what happened?" Alice asked.

Clark looked away. He tapped his fingers on his knee. He cleared his throat once more. "Well, the truth is this," he said at last. "They were shooting blanks. They just wanted to scare you. I don't know why. When you passed out they left. So, see, I didn't really accomplish anything by jumping in front of you."

"Blanks?" Alice asked.

"But don't get me wrong," Clark said, turning once more to face her. "I don't think badly of you for having passed out. They were very convincing."

"They just wanted to scare me?"

Clark nodded.

"After what I did to Capone?" Alice asked. "He just wanted to *scare* me?" She smiled. "That's nothing."

Clark cleared his throat. "Well, don't be so sure," he said. He stood, slipping his hands into his pockets and pacing the room. "I wouldn't be too sure that next time they won't have real bullets in their guns. I mean, I wouldn't let my guard down."

"What do you mean next time?"

"I don't know."

"I mean, if they wanted to kill me, why didn't they do it today?" Alice asked.

"Like the old saying," Clark answered. "Blanks today, bullets tomorrow. Everybody says it."

"Who says that?"

"Lots of people who know about things."

"Oh," Alice said, stepping toward Clark.

"I mean, you can't be too careful."

"I know," she said, standing before him. She looked up into his eyes. "Thank you for your courage."

Alice had been lonely for too long.

"It's nothing," he said.

"Not true," she answered.

Alice de Minuette placed her arms around the strong young man. She pulled herself close to him, resting her head against his chest, where she heard the beating of his heart and the gentle rhythm of his breathing. The muscles in his arms were hard and pressed against the soft linen of his shirt. She moved her fingers just enough to feel more precisely the skin beneath the cloth. She hated herself for wanting him so; she suspected that her desire was a product not only of his beauty and her solitude but also of the terrible anxiety of the past day. How could she have lived through so much and *not* yearn for the touch of another human being? Still, she was ashamed. She stepped away.

"I'm sorry," she said. Being sorry, however, didn't change the way she felt. "You know, if those bullets *had* been real they'd have bounced off that steel chest of yours."

Clark stepped back. "No," he said, his voice cracking. He tightened and turned away from her. "I'm no stronger than a normal human," he continued. "I don't know where you got that idea. It's unsound thinking."

"Oh," Alice answered. "Unsound thinking, huh?"

He nodded, turning back to her. As if to prove that he was less strong than he looked, he removed from his shirt pocket a pair of black horn-rimmed glasses that he placed awkwardly on his nose as if wearing them for the first time. "See?" he asked.

Alice nodded. "I just want you to know that I appreciate what you did for me. It was brave. That's all."

"Oh, I see."

"I didn't mean to make you uncomfortable," she said.

He removed the horn-rims, returning them to his pocket, and nodded. "I knew you were just kidding about that man-of-steel business," he said. "Now it's time you ate breakfast. Otherwise your eggs'll get cold."

But Alice didn't move. She had been struck by a sudden inexplicable sense of embarrassment. Also excitement. She didn't understand. She could only blush. It was not altogether unpleasant. It was as though she were suddenly standing naked before this beautiful man. It made no sense. But the feeling was undeniable. Almost overwhelming. As though he had secretly come to know every mole and curve of her body and yet was somehow able to restrain in his prying blue eyes the betrayal of such knowledge. It was as if he had chosen to look right *through* her clothes. She felt a shiver. "Oh, Clark," she said. "I've just had the most awful chill."

"Let me close the window," he answered. As he turned away from her the feeling passed.

"Better," she said.

Clark's wide shoulders blocked much of the light that came through the window. He stood tall and straight. "My mother and father will want to meet you after your breakfast," he said. "I told them I found you passed out in the station waiting room. They don't know about the gunfire. I didn't think it was necessary to tell them. They'd only worry."

"Good," she said.

"Why did the gangsters want to hurt you?" Clark asked.

Alice took a deep breath. She said nothing. Clark was too young and beautiful—too reckless also, she feared—to know the truth. A man impulsive enough to step into a line of machine-gun fire *might* be foolish enough to try and fight organized crime if he learned Alice's story. Clark seemed just that sincere and naïve. Alice shrugged her shoulders. "I don't know why they wanted to hurt me," she answered.

"You're still in danger," Clark said.

"I wish you weren't leaving," Alice answered.

"The next train's not until four thirty this afternoon."

"I can spare the time," Alice said.

Clark moved to the door. "Eat your breakfast."

"I'm not hungry anymore," she said.

Clark stopped. He turned. His eyes soaked up the light in the room until everything was dark and Alice could see only his bright baby blues. She heard his soft breathing. He swallowed, gathering himself.

"My mother and father are going into town this morning," he explained. "We have a guest room in the attic. They'll be gone all day. Will you meet me up there after they leave? It's something I don't want them to know about. Will you?"

He was young. Very beautiful. Strong. As Alice herself was beautiful and strong. She took a deep breath. But he was *too* young. Besides, Alice had been too long alone to allow herself such passionate company so quickly. It seemed unhealthy. After all, one takes only tiny portions of food, increased gradually, after enduring a fast. Otherwise, illness. Alice suspected that friendship rather than passion was her best diet against such hungry loneliness. Friendship as she had felt the night before with Buddy Easter. Special friendship. Purity. Clark was too young. Alice had been lonely for too long. She knew these things.

But what she knew didn't matter.

It seemed to Alice that she might have been spared from death for this very moment. Nothing else mattered. She looked at Clark. She nodded yes.

Clark turned and walked out of the bedroom. The light, equally distributed once more, became as white as the Kansas sunlight. Alice sat on the bed. She fell back into the folds of a soft pillow. She looked at the ceiling. Everything happens so fast, she thought, when it happens at all. There is no moderation. Excess or emptiness. It didn't seem right, but it was real life. And being alive, Alice thought, was a good thing that she didn't want changed for her by any damned hired gunman. She would never return to Chicago. The world is too big for a woman to grieve the loss of a single city. Alice was happy. She resolved to live her life with courage.

Alice de Minuette was in love.

Buddy Easter awoke. His first thought was of the baseball soaring far overhead. He imagined the view of the country to be gained if only the baseball had eyes. The great wheat fields. The jagged, snow-capped Rockies to the west. Beyond that, the glistening blue of the Pacific Ocean. The farmers tending their fields, the cowboys branding their herds on the open range, the wives hanging clothes on the line, the children walking to school—all seen from far above, where a perspective might be gained that would give to each movement a meaning imperceptible from the ground. Buddy had once seen a painting at the Chicago Institute of Art that was nothing more than jumbled dots of color when viewed closely, but a beautiful landscape when seen from a distance. The baseball enjoyed such a view, such a vision of the Truth. To catch the baseball seemed to Buddy Easter the next best thing to *being* the baseball.

His second thought was of Alice.

"Hey," he said, sitting up on the wooden floor. He looked around the boxcar. "Where *is* she?"

Woody and Loren sat beside each other in the open doorway of the speeding car. Outside passed sunny fields of corn. Woody's curly black hair pointed in all directions. He held his guitar on his lap, absently strumming chords. Loren was pale in the sunlight. He penciled nervous calculations on a paper package emptied of its cigarettes. The steel wheels clanked beneath the boxcar.

"Where's Alice?" Buddy repeated.

"Morning, Buddy," Woody said, looking up from his guitar. "Sleep good?"

"Fine," Buddy said. "Where's Alice?"

"She left," Woody answered.

"She what?" Buddy asked.

"Early this morning," Woody said. He strummed a minor chord on his guitar. He frowned. He slapped the instrument as if scolding a pet. Then he strummed a cheery major chord progression. "Better," he said.

"Why did she leave?" Buddy asked.

"She asked me to tell you so long," Woody said. "And she wanted me to give you this." He removed a folded sheet of paper from within the body of his guitar and flipped it across the car to Buddy without missing a beat.

"Why didn't she wake me?" Buddy asked. He stood, stretching his arms and legs.

"Don't worry about it, kid," Woody said.

Buddy rubbed his blurry eyes. It had been a long night. He moved to the back of the boxcar, nestling among the same broken Red Ball Shoe crates among which Alice de Minuette had secretly nestled. He unfolded the paper. His lips moved silently as he read:

Dear Buddy,

I should probably just say goodbye to you. But it seems to me important that I say more than that. It seems important that I explain. I want you to know something about me, Buddy.

Nobody knows this. But after you've read it that won't be true anymore. You will know. Then anything can happen to me, but nothing can happen to *this*. You will keep it. Forever. And this will be so: somewhere, sometime, the truth was known by someone.

When I was a girl, barely older than you are now, I fell in love with a man who was very charming. He was kind to me and took me to restaurants and clubs that I'd only dreamed of visiting. He was a ballplayer, Buddy. You'd recognize his name. And I knew him better than I had ever known anyone. But knowing him made me know certain things about him, whether I wanted to or not. The worst was this: I knew that he loved his freedom more than he could ever love me. Or anyone. I knew that it was this freedom that made him able to do the wonderful things he did on the baseball diamond. Nothing else. Not speed or strength or smarts. He was older than me, but I knew more about some things than he did. For example, he never understood why he could do these wonderful things. But the answer was simple. In his heart he was *free* to do them. To do anything, everything. That's all. I wouldn't have put it in such words when I was sixteen, but I knew. It was what made me love him.

Then something happened. Something terrible and wonderful. Such things happen, sometimes, to young foolish people who love each other. It just happens. We made a baby. And I had to make a choice. At least that's how it seemed to me at the time. I thought the choice was this: either take from him his boyish, magical sense of freedom, or disappear and lose him as my special friend altogether. That's how it seemed to me then. If only I had known more—or less. . . .

Oh Buddy, that children have to make such decisions!

I never saw him again. I never said goodbye, I just disappeared. Isn't that foolish? I think he was sad. But finally, I think he'd have been sadder if I had chosen differently. In fact, I know this because I've watched him go on doing wondrous things. I'm sorry if this is confusing. Can you understand?

Now Al Capone wants to kill me. He'll kill anybody he finds with me, I'm sure. That's why I have to leave you. I will miss you. And this time I want to leave no questions unanswered. I want to say goodbye.

Goodbye, Buddy.

I will be very still sometimes waiting to feel a tug of the strings that hold us together, Buddy, even when we are apart. So go ahead and tug. Anytime.

Catch your baseball! And take care of the crazy pair in the boxcar with you.

Alice

"What'd she say?" Woody asked when Buddy Easter at last emerged from behind the wooden crates.

Buddy shook his head.

"Is she all right?" Loren asked.

Buddy folded the letter in half. Then in half again.

"She's all right as far as I'm concerned," Woody said. "Can I read her letter, kid? Did she say anything about me?"

Buddy shook his head no.

"She said something about me?" Woody asked.

Buddy slipped the letter into his pants pocket.

"Something unkind?" Woody continued.

"No," Buddy answered.

"Well?"

"She said you play that racket box all right," Buddy said. "That's all. Nothing else."

"Yeah?" Woody asked. "Let me see."

Buddy stepped back. He shook his head.

"What'd she say about me?" Loren asked. "For history's sake."

Buddy smiled. He stepped forward. "You, Loren?" he asked. "What she said about you? Heck, she said you were as 'crazy as a loon.' She said that what you *think* is a Martian spaceship can only truly be one thing: a baseball hit by Babe Ruth for a home run. That's what she said!"

"A baseball, huh?" Loren said, shaking his head.

The Denver Behemoth blew its whistle. The shrill call split the quiet morning. What sounds blue and lonely by the glow of the moon sounds like the very voice of adventure in the white light of day. Buddy stretched his arms and legs. The baseball remained for the catching. There were still great things to accomplish, great friends with whom to be reunited. Abner Doubleday, for one. Alice de Minuette for another. Buddy swore to return for Alice as soon as he caught the baseball. Abner would like her. They would understand one another. They were both made of electricity. Buddy *would* find her. He was as sure of this as he was sure of his own name. He moved to the doorway. Outside, the baseball was a tiny, gleaming point in the morning sky, invisible to all but the most directed observer. All was not lost—

Then the train jammed on its air brakes.

Buddy Easter hurtled to the floor, crashing into a pile of wooden crates that tumbled around him. Woody and Loren, entangled, as they had grabbed each other to keep from being thrown out of the car and onto the tracks, slid struggling across the wooden floor. The train lurched, shivered, and screamed. Sparks from the distant brakes raced past the open doorway of the boxcar in which our heroes rode. The Denver Behemoth screeched to a stop.

Red Ball Shoes were everywhere.

"Damn!" Woody said, untangling himself from Loren where they lay on the hard wooden floor. "This is the goddamn jerkiest flat wheeler I've ever had the mispleasure of ridin'!"

Loren crawled toward the doorway.

"You all right, Buddy?" Woody asked.

Buddy nodded from among the slivers.

"We've got company," Loren announced.

Woody turned to the doorway. "Martians?" he asked.

Buddy moved beside the men. It was not Martians.

Outside the train was parked a long line of black Cadillacs from whose smoked windows protruded the snouts of countless automatic weapons. Parked across the railroad track was a school bus filled with screaming, frightened children. Outside the school bus stood men in pin-striped suits. They held Thompson submachine guns. The Denver Behemoth was going nowhere. The train engineer and brakeman jumped down and were pushed onto the track with their hands atop their heads. White steam gushed from beneath the engine.

"They're not looking for Red Ball Shoes," Loren said.

The Cadillacs fanned out, raising clouds of dust as they cruised about the track on which the Behemoth set.

"No sense runnin'," Woody observed. A cornfield lay thirty feet away. "We'd never make it."

"Maybe we could hide in here," Buddy said.

"Where?" Woody asked.

The wooden crates had been broken into splintered boards.

"Just stay where you are," Loren said. He took a long breath. "We can't hide and we can't run, so we might as well let them know where we are. After all, we can't *appear* guilty. We have nothing to hide, right? Alice is gone. We don't know where she is. We have nothing to say. We're all right."

"Yeah," Woody said. "Ramblin' men hittin' some hard travelin'. Hittin' the long old lonesome go. Nothing more. Simple workin' folk. How can they hate us?"

"They won't hurt innocent people," Loren said.

"You sure?" Buddy asked.

"Even criminals have a certain code of ethics," Loren explained. "It's based on honor. I've read about it."

The longest, blackest Cadillac raced toward their boxcar. A cloud of dust rose from beneath its wheels as it slid to a stop on the gravel beside the tracks. Buddy, Loren, and Woody remained in the doorway.

"Be very calm," Loren said.

"We're just ramblin' men hittin' the long old lonesome go," Woody answered.

The Cadillac's doors opened slowly. Other black cars gathered nearby. Dust clouds rose in tiny twisters. With doors flapped open like wings, the descending fleet seemed to Buddy more like a flock of vultures than the most impressive automotive collection this lonely stretch of Kansas highway had ever seen.

"Just hittin' some hard travelin'," Woody whispered.

Out of the longest Cadillac stepped the fat man from the La Salle Street train station, smelling of daisies and red in the face. The snouts of two dozen machine guns covered him as he straightened and stretched on the gravel. At last, with frightening arrogance, he stepped forward. When he smiled up at Buddy (who remained motionless in the boxcar doorway), his eyes disappeared within folds of pink flesh. "Well, kid," he said. "We meet again."

Buddy swallowed hard.

The fat man patted the bulge in his breast pocket. "Daisy's been bored since you left town," he said.

Next out of the long Cadillac stepped Al Capone.

Buddy, Loren, and Woody moved back, as if choreographed, when the light of the morning fell upon the stout face of the famous gangster. He removed his hat. On his thick lips was a small smile. His face was pale, powdered white, and a long scar ran from just below his left ear almost down to his jaw. In his thick fingers he held a cigar.

"Meet the boss," the fat man said.

Capone wore a powder-blue suit, meticulously tailored, and pearl-gray spats. On his middle finger was a huge diamond that sparkled in the morning light like the baseball soaring far above. His eyes were gray. He carried a shiny new walking stick and moved with a slight limp. Buddy and Loren knew why he limped. Capone grinned, but he did not seem a joyful man.

A driver placed a stepladder at the entrance to the boxcar. Capone climbed up. The fat man followed. Buddy, Loren, and Woody backed to the far wall of the car.

"Morning, boys," Capone said, taking a puff on his cigar. His voice was high-pitched for a man so large. "I hear we have a mutual friend. Small world, isn't it?"

"Who's that?" Loren asked.

"We're just ramblin' men hittin' the long old lonesome go, sir," Woody explained. "We meet lots of folks. But we don't never know nothin' about none of 'em. We never ask a body to explain nothin'. That's the way of the road."

Capone nodded. "The way of the road?" he asked. "You mean some kind of traveling ethic, huh? I suppose your sort has a code of honor and all that. Am I right? Unwritten rules of manhood to live by?"

Woody nodded.

"Exactly," Loren said.

Capone puffed his cigar. "Code of honor? Ethics? Bullshit."

Loren Woodville swallowed hard.

"Where's Alice de Minuette?" Capone asked.

"Bastard," Buddy whispered.

"What'd you say?" Capone demanded, stepping toward the boy.

"Sonofabitch," Buddy said. His voice remained steady as he looked into the gangster's gray eyes. His hands were clenched in fists at his sides. "Goddamn sonofabitch."

"Oh, you funny little boy," Capone said.

Buddy Easter flew at Al Capone.

It was very quick. The gangster slapped the boy to the floor of the boxcar with a single swipe of his walking stick. His powder-blue suit was not even ruffled.

"We don't know where she went, sir," Woody said. "She got off the train some time ago."

"Where?"

Woody shrugged his shoulders. "You all right, Buddy?"

Buddy nodded, face down.

"Where!" Capone demanded. "She took something very valuable that belongs to me."

"Damn right she did," Loren whispered.

"I don't know," Woody answered. "It was still dark when she left. Probably someplace back in Illinois."

Buddy sat up. A trickle of blood ran from his scalp.

"More, kid?" Capone asked.

Woody stepped between Buddy and Capone. "Don't pay no mind to him, sir," he said. He nodded furiously as he spoke, as if his nonverbal affirmation might prove more convincing than his words. "He's a little light upstairs."

Loren cleared his throat and stepped beside Woody. He gestured toward Buddy, brushing at the air with his hands as if to brush aside the boy's remarks. As if swatting away flighty thoughts unworthy of Capone's profound attention. "I could help you," he said. "If I knew how long ago this woman deboarded, and the average speed of this train since then, I could calculate the approximate place where you might find her. But I'm afraid I don't have that information, Mr. Capone." His voice hardened. He stepped toward Capone. "So I can be no goddamn help to you."

Capone shook his head. He touched Loren's shoulder as if touching a friend. "I got a question that you *can* figure out," he said. "Here goes. If you make one more stupid remark, do you know where your family is going to have to go to find *you*?"

Loren said nothing.

"It don't take no slide rule to figure," Capone continued.

Loren nodded.

"Do you like music, sir?" Woody asked, taking his guitar off the boxcar floor. He tuned. "I got a million songs."

Capone stepped forward. He took the guitar from Woody's hands. He admired the polished wood. Then he smashed it against the hard boxcar floor. The racket box twanged in agony. Woody's face bent as he watched his meal ticket shattered and tossed out the boxcar door.

"I love music," Capone said.

Woody said nothing. Loren looked away. Buddy muttered.

"What is it?" Capone asked. "Money?" He reached into his suit coat. He withdrew his billfold. He took three hundred-dollar bills from a wad of green thicker than the shipment of lettuce in the next car. He held it in the air, shook it, then offered it to the passengers of the Red Ball Shoe shipment. "Take it. It's yours. A gift from me to you. Enjoy."

"We don't want no charity," Woody said, slapping the money away. "And we sure as hell don't got nothin' to trade for it. No goods, no music—"

"No information," Loren added.

"Nothing," Buddy said.

Capone nodded. He took a blackjack from his suit-coat pocket.

"Nothing," Buddy repeated.

"Boss!" someone called from outside the boxcar.

Capone stopped.

A young man in a green suit jumped into the boxcar. He carried a machine gun in one hand. He closed his eyes when he spoke as if concentrating to find just the right words. "We got news of her," he said. "But you ain't gonna like it, Boss."

"Where?"

"Scalise and Anselmi caught up to her getting off this train about thirty minutes ago. At a little station in a place called Smallville."

"Well?" Capone asked.

The man in the green suit shook his head.

"What?" Capone asked. "Is she dead or what?"

The young man stepped back. "She got away," he said. "We'll get her, though."

Capone said nothing.

"The way the boys tell it is this," the young man continued. "They were no more than ten feet away from her when they let her have it—tommy guns blazing, right?—when this kid who happened to be standing on the same platform jumps in front of her like he's going to take the bullets. Real bodyguard material. So the boys go ahead and shoot. But what happens? I swear this is exactly what they told me. The bullets bounce off the sonofabitch. He's standing there just blocking the bullets with his chest like he was made of steel. Must of been some kind of special bulletproof vest or something. I don't know. It's just what they told me. The girl's passed out by this time so they aim for her, trying to shoot *around* this guy, but he reaches out and knocks the bullets down with his hands. Crazy, huh? I swear this is what they told me. Maybe they been on the sauce, or working too many late nights. I'd be real firm with them if I was you, Boss. 'Cause they turned and ran when this guy started catching their bullets, and when they finally worked up the courage to go back, he and Miss de Minuette was gone. That's what they told me. That's exactly what they told me."

"Is this a joke?" Capone asked.

"That's what they told me, Boss."

"Then this is bad news," Capone said. He remained composed,

calm, unmoved but for the twitching of the little finger on his left hand. "You understand that, don't you?"

The young man nodded. He wiped his palms on the lapel of his green suit. He stepped away from Capone. His Adam's apple moved up and down like a rat in the gullet of a python.

"It's bad news because it means two very bad things," Capone continued. His voice was patient, almost kind. "First, it means that two of my best men have betrayed me and have offered this story as a personal insult. Christ, they were probably in on this whole thing from the beginning. They probably tipped the broad off about the envelope. That's bad enough. But second, it means that *you*, my green friend, are too stupid to know what kind of message you carry. Too stupid to know that you're looking me in the eye and delivering an insult that'd break my mother's heart."

"No, it don't mean that," the young man said.

"Then you're insulting me on purpose?" Capone asked.

"No, it's just what they told me."

"I have to do something about these things," Capone announced. "It's my job. Do you understand? My responsibility. If I don't do it, it won't get done. This is the burden of greatness. It is *my* burden. It is *your* ass."

"I'm sorry, Boss."

Capone nodded as if he understood. He moved forward and took the machine gun from the young man's hands. He stepped back. He aimed the weapon at the messenger's heart. "I'll show you how bad this news grieves me," he whispered.

"Please don't," the young man said.

"All right, kid." Capone lowered the aim of the gun, pointing it at the young man's feet. He smiled. "I'm gonna help you," he said. "After all, if you can't walk, you can't deliver no more insulting messages. I'm gonna turn your whole life around. You'll thank me. Really."

Capone pulled the trigger.

The boxcar was rocked by the gunfire. Buddy, Loren, and Woody crouched in a corner, covering their ears with shaking hands. For all of Capone's bravado, they had not believed he would do such a thing. The bullets tore holes in the boxcar floor. Wood and flesh danced in the air like insects in a fire. The young man lay screaming near the doorway, his green suit soaked red, his feet reduced to gushing pulp. Two seconds. The terrible moment had seemed to last forever.

"Goddammit!" Capone screamed, throwing the tommy gun through the doorway and onto the gravel below. He motioned for two of his men to remove the bleeding mesenger (who had mercifully passed out) and to attend to his terrible wounds. He wiped his face where it had been splashed with the young man's blood. He took a deep breath. He turned to the rear of the boxcar.

Woody was passed out.

"I won't be bothering you anymore," Capone said to Buddy and Loren. He turned and stepped out of the boxcar. A half dozen of his men climbed into the car in his place. Buddy and Loren watched the gangster through the open doorway as the pale goons encircled them. Capone motioned for the engineer to fire up the massive steam engine. He shook his head, brushing down the wrinkles in his pleated, bloody slacks. At last, he called up to the fat man who had remained in the boxcar.

"You and the boys tear the car apart. I mean everything!"

The fat man moved beside Buddy Easter. He grinned.

Another man in a pin-striped suit approached Capone with a new powder-blue suit coat to replace the bloodstained garment. Capone changed coats as he spoke. "If you don't find nothing, you can toss these freeloaders onto the tracks after the train reaches sufficient speed. The Union Pacific Railroad would want it that way. Nobody rides for free. Got it?"

The fat man nodded.

A half-dozen machine guns turned toward Buddy and Loren.

"What exactly do you mean by 'sufficient'?" Loren asked.

Capone said nothing.

Three miles down the track, Buddy Easter, Loren Woodville, and Woody Guthrie (roused from his lightheaded reverie) found out.

■ ■ ■

Alice touched the door of the guest room. The wood was smooth, hard. She held a hand to her breast. Her heart had begun pounding the moment she heard the family's pickup truck pull out of the front yard. Mom and Dad gone to town. Kind, good people. They had asked Alice no difficult questions. They had insisted she drink with them a cup of tea and honey. They had left the house as if on cue. Alice felt a girl again. Good people. And their son was the most beautiful man she had ever seen. She knocked on the door.

Clark stood in the doorway. He had opened the door so quickly that it seemed to Alice she was looking at him even before she had removed her knuckle from the wood. She might have commented on his quickness had she not felt again the distracting thrill of an irrational—but undeniable—sense that he was looking *through* the material of her dress. Her breath caught in her throat as his eyes moved down past her waist.

"Come in," he said, his voice strong and firm. He stepped backward into the room. Alice followed, closing the door behind her with delicate care.

"Hello, Clark," she said.

The room was painted white. The curtains that billowed toward the center of the room, flapping like twin trains of a bride's gown, were white as well. The bedspread upon which Clark sat down was white. When Clark smiled at Alice, she was struck by the whiteness of his teeth.

"Did you like my parents?" he asked.

"They're very nice."

Clark motioned for Alice to sit on the bed beside him. "They're actually foster parents," he said. "I was orphaned at an early age."

"I'm sorry," Alice said, sitting beside him.

Clark shook his head. "Don't be sad for me. I never knew my parents. It hardly feels a loss. These are good people. I've been very happy."

Alice looked at Clark. He was somehow unlike any man she had ever known. He was handsome. His body was so near perfect that the pressing of each rippling muscle against the linen of his shirt made Alice shiver. But it was not his appearance alone that set him apart. She had known beautiful men before. It was something else. His manner was one of awkward charm; farmboy innocence that had remained genuine despite his intelligence and knowing. Alice had met other men who possessed a charm composed of diverse elements. It was something else about Clark. Something almost—she hesitated even to think the word, reflecting on her incredulity the night before when Loren Woodville pointed out a spaceship in the night sky—something different. Something almost *otherworldly*.

"I like you," she said, touching Clark's chin and guiding his head toward hers so she could look into his eyes. "You're not like anyone I've ever known. You're different, aren't you?"

Clark stood up off the bed. He slipped his hands into his pockets. He paced to the door and back, stopping once to grasp the doorknob as if about to walk out. "I'd rather you not talk about how I'm different," he said, turning back to her. "I don't want things spreading around."

"Don't worry, Clark," Alice reassured. "Nothing that happens in this room will ever get spread around."

"I can trust you with this?" he asked. He ran his hand through his hair. When it fell back into place, the perfect curl on his forehead was different. It was tighter than before; the circle was smaller. But it was still perfect.

"Of course," Alice said.

"You're not here because you feel indebted, are you?" he asked. "I don't want you to feel indebted. What I did this morning was really nothing. You have to believe that."

"I'm here because I like you," she said, standing up.

"No!" He pointed once more to the bed. "Please stay there. This is difficult for me."

Alice nodded. "Is this the first time you've ever done something like this?" She sat down once more.

He nodded.

Alice smiled. "Don't be nervous."

"I'm not nervous," he snapped. But his strong hands were shaking.

"I like you, Clark," she reminded him. "I think you like me, too."

"I do," he answered, turning once more toward her. His blue eyes began to suck the light from the room. Alice took a deep breath. They sucked the air from her lungs as well. She thought she might die. It was wonderful.

"Good," she said.

"You do sew, don't you?" he asked, turning away once more.

"What?"

"Do you sew?" He pronounced the words as if they were a secret incantation.

"I don't understand."

"Do you sew?"

Alice leaned forward on the bed. "A little," she said, confused by his question but enticed by the unpredictability of his thinking. Perhaps there were things to be done with a needle and thread undreamed of in heaven or hell. This would be new even to the girls back at Marnie's. "You mean like sewing clothes?" she asked.

Clark nodded.

She was grateful he had not asked about razor blades.

"*I'm* very bad with a needle and thread," Clark explained.

"Oh, I see," she said, though she didn't.

Clark looked down at the rug. "This has to remain a secret. I'd explain more except that I can't burden you with such responsibilities. You don't want to get involved with the wrong kind of people."

She stood up. "I'm getting a little tired of this secrecy business," she said. "What do you think I'm going to do, go around advertising our afternoon here? Maybe we should just forget the whole thing."

"No, of course not," Clark said. He stepped toward her. He shook his head. "I'm sorry. It's just that this is so important to me. I've been waiting so long. And I can't wait any longer."

She nodded. "It's important to me too, Clark."

"Have you sewn for long?"

"What?"

"Did you make that dress?"

"No."

"Too bad. It's very nice."

"Clark?"

"Yes?"

"I hate to seem naïve," she said, "but what are you talking about?"

Clark looked away. He wiped his damp forehead with the back of his hand. He cleared his throat. Alice had never seen a man so self-tortured in this circumstance. She was afraid he might pass out.

"Clark?"

"Alice, I'm different," he said. "I'm not like everybody else."

"I know that," she said. She wanted to hold him close enough to feel his great heart beating inside. She wanted their heartbeats to find a single rhythm. One heartbeat. She wanted their blood to course at the same speed, to ebb and flow like the tides at the command of a single heavenly body. She had always wanted this. "That's why I'm here, Clark," she explained. "Because I've sensed all along that you are different."

Clark's eyes were damp.

"Come here," she said.

He held up his palm. "I can't sew," he said. "But you—" He turned to a wooden chest of drawers that stood beside the window. He knelt and opened the bottom drawer. He rummaged through a pile of thick wool socks, tossing them over his shoulder as he dug deeper into the drawer. When he stood, turning to face Alice, he held in his hands a bright pile of red and blue fabrics.

"Red silk?" she asked. "What is this?"

He smiled and sat beside her on the bed. He rubbed the silk between his fingers. "It's going to be my cape." Holding up the blue fabric, he said, "And this is going to be my tights. I can see the whole thing in my head. All I need is somebody to sew it for me. Somebody I can trust. You can sew, right?"

Alice stood up off the bed. "I don't understand."

"You do sew, don't you?"

"This is why you asked me up here?" she asked. "All the secrecy. To sew you some kind of outfit?"

He looked up at her. He nodded.

She stepped away, her eyes wide in angry surprise. She held one hand to her forehead. She shook her head. "What kind of girl do you think I am? A seamstress?"

"It's very important to me," Clark answered.

She looked at the bright red silk on top of the pile. A cape and tights? She clenched her fists in frustration. "You're *not* like other men, are you?" she asked. "No real man would ever wear something like that!"

"I told you I was different."

"You're not a real man!"

"Well, I wouldn't go that far."

"Red silk cape and blue tights? It's disgusting. No wonder you don't want your parents to know. Such nice people. No wonder you were willing to throw your life away at the train station. I've heard of men like you! In fact, one of the bouncers at Marnie's turned out to be that way."

"He did?" Clark asked, unable to disguise the shock on his face. "I thought I was the only one."

"God, no," Alice said. She turned away. Her vision was clouded by tears less welcome at this moment than even one of Capone's bullets might have been. She shook her head as she touched the hard, cold doorknob. She could not hate Clark. She could only grieve his loss. And feel a terrible fool.

She was alone again after all.

"But the colors are America's colors!" Clark pleaded. "That's why I chose them. It's for the good of the whole nation. Heck, the whole free world!"

"Oh, that's just *great*," Alice said as she opened the door and stepped forever from the room.

She ran down the stairs. The farmhouse was quiet. As she got to the front door, Clark called from upstairs. His voice was frightened. "Alice! You don't understand!"

"Right," she whispered to herself as she stepped out the front door and into the yard. Alice believed she understood everything too clearly. She yearned for misunderstanding. She ran for the road as if she knew where she was going. As if she had someplace to go. One foot in front of the other. . . . A single tear followed a course down the curve of her cheek with the same compliance to the conventional laws of physics with which a baseball soared through the Kansas skies above her. The tear fell in the barnyard of Clark's parents' farm. Years later, a tree would spring from it upon which grew apples in the shape of shiny red hearts.

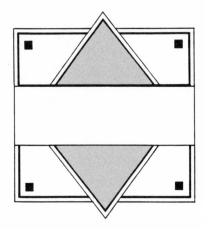

It was nearly night when Buddy Easter and Loren Woodville caught sight of a town in the distance. Their walk through the vast wheat fields had been long and difficult, as each had been battered and bruised when tossed from the speeding Denver Behemoth hours before. Only the thickness of the wheat and the tilled civility of the black soil had allowed them to survive the fall. Flipping headlong—arms flapping like the limbs of rag dolls—Buddy, Loren, and Woody had left three long skid marks in the fertile Kansas soil. Unconscious, they had lain sprawled, like forgotten human baggage, among the stalks of wheat until nearly midday.

Woody Guthrie chose to remain beside the railroad tracks, resolved to await the passing of another train, to avoid the least possibility that he might once more encounter the violent pinstriped boys from Chicago. It didn't matter to him which direction the next train might be running. He had been cut and bruised and wanted only to escape the suffocating wheat fields and the gangsters' wrath. "A crazy boxcar on a wild track headed sixty miles an hour in a big cloud of dust due straight to nowhere. That's where I'm goin'," he said. "And I'll wait as long as it takes for my ride."

Buddy and Loren, however, could not be so carefree in their decisions. After all, they were travelers with a clear destination: the Pacific coast. Destiny. Merely to wait beside the railroad tracks as the soaring white sphere raced farther west over their heads, to watch the sun set, to shiver in the cold night, to watch the next day's sunrise—all the time uncertain that *any* train might pass their lonely spot in the wheat field—seemed to Buddy and Loren a torture too great to endure.

"Goodbye, Woody," Buddy said. The sun glared above the three like a naked light bulb in a cold-water flat.

"Adios, amigos," Woody said.

"Sorry about your guitar," Loren added.

Woody took from his shirt pocket a shiny harmonica. He winked at the anxious pair, then blew slow blues chords as Buddy Easter and Loren Woodville set off through the wheat field in search of civilization and a way west.

It was a long walk.

"Damn woman," Loren murmured, tromping through the wheat.

"It's not her fault," Buddy said.

"Damn woman."

Three hours passed before the pair came upon a stretch of two-lane blacktop that ran through the great wheat field like a tiny vein through the massive bicep of Charles Atlas. Still distracted by a ringing ache in their heads, Buddy and Loren limped along the road, hoping to catch a lift into any town where transport west might be gained. Buddy cradled his left hand, swollen, throbbing, sprained or broken in the fall, pointing in two directions at once. Loren held a handkerchief, hard with dried blood, to his own swollen forehead. His eyes were blackened and his back ached with each step. One foot in front of the other. There was nothing else to do. The road stretched forever.

Only hours—no cars, no trucks—passed.

Loren stopped. He knelt in the middle of the road. Buddy sat on the gravel shoulder. Loren took a thin stalk of wheat and held it up to the sky. He closed one eye, aligning the stalk with the tiny white dot that soared far above. Loren's lips moved—forming numbers that fit into mathematical equations, reworking complex calculations—though no sound came form his mouth. Buddy watched. He noticed that Loren was missing one of his front teeth. Buddy was too weary to laugh.

"Oh, my God," Loren whispered. He turned toward the sun, extending his thumb and closing one eye like a painter to better assess its position. He moved his thumb to the soaring sphere. After a moment, he announced, "It's getting away."

The dark asphalt stretched hopelessly in both directions, silent and empty, before finally fading into tiny dark points on each horizon. The world was framed by wheat (which seemed capable just now of *consuming* rather than being consumed), and the sky was of a clarity and depth of color unlike any Buddy had ever seen in Chicago. Buddy wondered if Abner knew such clarity. The baseball, like the sun, seemed near enough to reach out and touch, though it moved farther away with each moment. Did Abner know such clear vision? Buddy wondered if he would ever have the opportunity to ask his electric friend.

"Everything's getting away," Loren concluded.

The afternoon waned. With each silent step across the great plain, the possibility that the soaring baseball might escape Buddy Easter—might slip through his anxious grasp like a passed ball in the bottom of the ninth—became more real. With each step, as the shadows grew long and Buddy's breath became increasingly short, he grew more frightened of failure. Of losing the baseball. Of losing Abner. Of losing the strength ever to come back for Alice.

"Everything's getting away," Buddy said.

"Are you all right?" Loren asked as they marched on.

"I'm all right," Buddy answered.

But neither was all right. It was not the physical beating they had endured that threatened to debilitate them. Rather, it was worry itself. Worry that the long journey from Chicago had been undertaken for nothing. Worry that they might soon be reduced to the same obscure despair that had proved for each almost overwhelming before Babe Ruth's monumental swing of the bat. Most painful of all: worry that they had looked at the face of greatness, looked deeply into its eyes, only to have it turn away at the last moment. They were once again only two tiny human beings walking through an enormously vast wheat field in an enormously vast country that would never know their names.

"But you want to know something?" Loren asked as they rested once more, downed like broken kites on the rich Kansas soil. "It's not for me that I feel sorry. It's for the people who look into the sky and see nothing but distant, cold, dead things. For the people who think they're alone. The people who will never understand that the faces of their best friends were painted in the sky all along."

Buddy nodded and stood. "Let's go on," he said.

When at last Buddy and Loren came within sight of a small town nestled among the wheat like a flea within a dog's coat, they were struck by its quiet. For a moment, it seemed the stillness was an illusion, a trick of the setting sun, a hallucination. Buddy ran his hand to the top of his head, where he found among the silky strands a swollen lump nearly the size of a regulation major-league baseball. He touched it with his fingertips. Thin lines of dried blood crossed the surface of the lump like the hard laces around a baseball.

"We're there," Loren said.

"Do you hear anything?" Buddy asked. "Or is it just me?"

Loren shook his head. "Nothing," he said. "Not a sound."

Buddy looked at his companion. In the twilight, Loren's face resembled a much-used artist's pallet on which was stained an unnatural collage of color: reds and blacks and blues. "Is it just us?" Buddy asked.

"It's just quiet," Loren answered.

As the sun set behind it, the silent town looked to Buddy Easter like a two-dimensional façade—like buildings constructed in Hollywood studios that give the illusion of depth while actually consisting only of height and width. But there were no actors here.

No lights in the windows. No movement. The town reminded Buddy also of a graveyard on a hill near the School for Boys. The graveyard had a skyline, rounded headstones, and marble crosses. The stillness was the same. But this was no graveyard. It was no movie set. It was a farming town in the middle of America.

"Why is it so dark?" Buddy asked.

"Power failure?" Loren answered, starting toward the town.

"I don't think so," Buddy said, following.

The last rays of the sun slipped beneath the great, rolling sea of wheat to the west. Still, the sky yielded enough purple-orange glow to illuminate for Buddy and Loren the broadest details of the darkened town.

Main Street was altogether deserted. Nothing stirred but a single sheet of newspaper that blew out of a dark, silent alley and continued down the street, puffed and curved against the wind like the sail of a boat. The newspaper wrapped itself, flapping, around a darkened street lamp at the base of a large granite building on which was carved CITY HALL. An American flag flew over the entrance to the granite building, which, like every other, was dark inside. Red, white, and blue bunting hung from the eaves of the silent buildings as if the town were celebrating the Fourth of July. But all was silent and deserted.

"Where is everybody?" Buddy asked.

The Bijou Theatre, which advertised a Douglas Fairbanks movie as its current hit, was locked up and dark inside. In the barred window of the box office was a hand-printed sign that read CLOSED. No Douglas Fairbanks. No electricity.

"This is a little spooky," Buddy said.

"Sh-h-h," Loren answered.

Across the street was a small park. There were wooden benches and flowers and in the center a granite statue of a civic hero from some time in the romantic past of central Kansas. The hero stood nearly twelve feet tall, and in the dim light his stony face cast upon the park an expression either of unwavering courage or merciless cruelty. The difference in perception lay only in the way the shadows fell.

"You think this is a trap?" Buddy asked.

"Maybe," Loren said.

It was nearly pitch dark now.

"Star light, star bright, first star I see tonight, I wish I may, I wish I might—" Buddy stopped.

What *would* he wish for? To ask only that the town might come back to life, that Buddy Easter might feel safe once more, was to wish only for the same despair he had felt before entering this dark place. He had felt safe, but failed. This was not good enough. However, to wish for the things he *really* needed (the baseball, Abner, Alice) seemed to Buddy too much to ask. He looked at the stars. Among them moved one of exquisite beauty.

He wished for nothing.

Then, light!

From out of the west a brilliant white glow sent sharp beams over the darkened rooftops, down the alleys, and across Main Street to where Buddy and Loren stood. The light trickled like water through the smallest spaces and cracks, pouring in every direction from a single brilliant source perhaps a mile distant. The light illuminated the empty downtown. Illuminated the wonder on Loren Woodville's bruised face. Illuminated the pictures on the sides of the orange crates piled in the alley beside which our heroes stood— pictures of sun-drenched maidens in California.

"Dawn," Buddy said.

Loren shook his head. This was no natural light. No fiery death of a distant star. No reflection of the light of the silvery moon. This light cast harsh, clear, straight-edged shadows. It was artificial light, indoor light, somehow made powerful enough to light the outdoors. The whole outdoors. As if it were day. Loren had never seen anything like it. In the pitch blackness of the Kansas plain, its brightness seemed more intense than all the bulbs ever to have lit the Windy City put together.

"Where's it coming from?" Buddy asked.

A roar of distant voices echoed in the otherwise silent streets. The voices were ghostly—like cries of the ancients responding to a dramatic ritual. Not fear, but great wonder.

"That way," Buddy said, pointing west.

Loren looked into the dark sky above. He closed his eyes. Then he slapped his hands together and turned to Buddy Easter. His bruised face was pale. He swallowed hard and took a deep breath before speaking. "They've landed *here!*" he announced.

"Who?" Buddy asked.

"Them," Loren answered. "The Martians!"

"Martians?" Buddy turned to the sky. The brilliant light had made the stars invisible. The baseball was invisible too. Gone. Buddy felt a sudden panic. "Can't be," he said.

"Martians," Loren answered, grinning. "Right here!"

"Can't be," Buddy repeated. But there *was* something unusual about this empty town, this night, this light. Something *almost* unearthly. "Can't be. . . ."

"Come on!" Loren said, turning toward the west.

The light grew brighter as Buddy and Loren weaved through the deserted streets. It drew them like moths to a flame, past locked shops and cafés, soup kitchens and relief offices, and quiet lawns standing before quiet wooden houses.

Some moments before the unearthly illumination gave light to the dark town and to Loren Woodville's most fervent ambitions, a round man in an emerald-green waistcoat stepped up to a microphone on a makeshift stage in center field at the Smallville Municipal Ballpark. The man was called Professor Marvel. He was mayor of the dark town. Dim floodlights run by a portable generator lit the stage a dingy shade of yellow. Beyond the yellow lights, all was darkness.

On the field and in the grandstands waited the citizens of Smallville. Only young Clark Kent (who had left town that afternoon) and a Miss Maybelle Lewis (who had locked herself in her house, convinced that there were gangsters about the peaceful town) were absent. Otherwise, an entire citizenry moved about the field in half darkness, able to see one another only by the light of the stars or the matches they held lit near their faces. The night air smelled of wheat and sulfur.

The mayor held index cards. His voice boomed over the loudspeakers with a practiced clarity that inspired confidence among even the most reticent. "This, friends and neighbors, is the greatest night in the history of Smallville, Kansas!" He paused as the audience cheered. "For we have gathered here tonight to usher in a new era, a new triumph, a new world. Night baseball!"

Applause echoed in the old ballpark's wooden rafters, though the townspeople had not come to hear the mayor speak. They had come for the lights, which stood darkened on standards high over the outfield wall. Anticipation rumbled through the crowd like hunger—though to make their impatience known, they feared, might seem disrespectful to the man who had made the miracle possible, Professor Marvel. So they applauded at appropriate moments and waited patiently.

"The construction of these great lights stands as a tribute to you, the people of Smallville," Marvel continued. "These are the worst of times for many, yet together we rise tonight above Depression to give America its first night baseball park!"

Applause.

"Our achievement tonight stands tall in answer to all attacks. What difference does it make if Smallville doesn't actually have a baseball team to play under these new lights? I ask you, what could serve as greater enticement for a professional organization to place a minor league team here than the possibility of playing its games under our lights? Nothing!"

Applause.

The ballpark was not new. The wooden bleachers dated back to before the turn of the century, when the Smallville Municipal Ballpark served as a rodeo ring for Wild West shows that passed through town. Buffalo Bill Cody had stood in this ballpark. Annie Oakley. Until the mayoral election two years earlier, no one dreamed that the old structure might enjoy a future even more illustrious than its past. Then Professor Marvel arrived—the very day of Smallville's mayoral election. The construction of outdoor lights was a critical political issue in the election. Professor Marvel's campaign slogan was, Let There Be Light.

The election was a landslide.

Before becoming mayor, Professor Marvel had made his living as a carnival soothsayer, hot-air balloonist, and part-time wizard. "After tonight," he promised, "when the people of America think of Smallville they will think, 'Smallville: City of Light, City of Dreams!'"

The townspeople applauded once more, though their anticipation had grown nearly unbearable. Those who stood on the hard dirt infield or in the outfield near the wooden stage bounced nervously from one foot to the other. Those who sat in the grandstands tapped their feet on the wood beneath them. The huge lights remained dark. Yet with the single flick of a switch—

"It is small sacrifice indeed," the mayor continued, "for the town itself to remain in darkness on nights when this ballpark is lit. When the switching station in Peabody becomes more powerful we may be able to light the ballpark *and* the town at the same time! Won't that be something?"

Applause.

"Allow me to introduce the folks who share the stage with me now," he continued. There was a gentle moan throughout the ballpark. Professor Marvel pointed to a row of dignified farmers who sat, in Sunday best, to one side of the podium. "Our esteemed city council," he said.

Applause.

Marvel turned toward a row of young women on the other side of the stage who sat with legs daintily crossed. "Selected just this afternoon," he announced, "I'd like to introduce the finalists in the Miss Smallville contest."

Four of the five finalists were farmer's daughters who had grown up in the town. The fifth, older than the rest, was from Illinois. She had been selected for her beauty—her pale skin, her blue eyes, her incomparable blond hair. Though she was new to the town, her appeal was undeniable. But her manner was short. She had nearly been eliminated from competition during the "congeniality evaluation" when she claimed to have entered the contest only because she needed the prize: an all-expense-paid trip to Denver, Colorado. Still, those lips, those eyes—

"Let's hear it for our lovely ladies!" Professor Marvel concluded.

Applause.

Professor Marvel smiled. "And now the moment of truth," he announced. "Let there be light!"

Riotous cheering.

He pulled the switch.

Nothing. The townspeople of Smallville, all of whom were on their feet by now, stared in disbelief at the tall light standards. No light! Only a low humming sound as electricity raced through the wires. The foot-wide bulbs remained dark. The townsfolk turned to one another, lighting matches to read the disappointment on their neighbors' faces. Then a faint glow in the thick filaments. Barely enough light to cast shadows on the field. Then more light! The filaments glowed more strongly. Excitement renewed the heart of each citizen as electricity built within the lights. Then, as if answering some inaudible Edisonian cue, the lights flared brilliantly to full power. They radiated a powerful glow that lit the field below in an unearthly white and cast straight shadows on the faces of the townspeople. The faces were smiling.

It was like nothing they had ever dreamed.

Electricity hummed in the ballpark like a billion bees in a hive. The night was as bright as the day. The straight lines of the old ballpark were clear and the wooden scoreboard in center field as legible as ever it had been on a sunny afternoon. The townspeople lifted their hands to the sky and cried in full voices to express their awe. The roar was deafening, as if a local boy had hit a home run in the World Series. The bleachers rattled. Green paint chipped off the outfield wall.

"It's a miracle!" Professor Marvel cried into the microphone.

The crowd cheered louder. "Hurray for Marvel!" yelled a farmer, cupping his calloused hands around his mouth. "Night baseball!" called a fat woman in a print dress. "City of light!" another woman yelled as she swiped at a glowing moth that flew about her head. "We did it!" cried an unemployed city engineer who had donated his time to the project. "God bless us!" implored an old man who stood near home plate, his fists thrust into the air. It was real. Mayor Marvel wiped away a tiny tear that slipped from the corner of his eye. The little ballpark shone on the otherwise dark Kansas plain like a cut diamond.

"Yes, let there be light," Professor Marvel said.

Yet there remained a darkness in the ballpark.

Al Capone stood unnoticed near the stage. All around him was joy and uplifted expressions. However, Capone was neither joyful nor uplifted. He stared not at the lights but at Alice de Minuette, who seemed as oblivious and awestruck as the other Miss Smallville contestants. When a tiny moth flew about the gangster's head he caught the creature and crushed it between his fingers.

"Bring on the beauties," he whispered.

"Being Miss Smallville is very important to me."

Alice's voice echoed in the night air.

"More important than you can imagine," she continued. "Unless you too have once been in need of a new name. A new start." Her hands clasped the microphone stand in the same passionate manner with which good band vocalists hold on during romantic ballads. Her hair shone as golden as the sun under the brilliant artificial lights. The movements of her body were unmistakable, even from three hundred feet away: the dip of one shoulder as she pronounced a long word, the turning of her hip just so, the minute smile that crossed her lips when she paused between sentences. "If I am chosen Miss Smallville," she concluded, "I will go to the courthouse tomorrow morning to legally change my name to Alice Smallville as a token of my pride. Of my new identity. Miss Smallville. *That* is how important it is—"

Alice stopped.

She saw Capone beneath her.

She took a short breath. She felt her heart pound in her chest. Her blood pulsed cold through every part of her body. "How important it is—" she said again into the microphone before her voice cracked and disappeared altogether. Capone was not far away. He swiped at a flying insect that hovered about his head. He smiled at her. She reminded herself that he didn't really want to kill her. That the gunmen on the train platform had merely shot blanks. That everything was all right. "Everything's all right," she said aloud.

"Is something wrong, miss?" Professor Marvel asked, swatting at a moth that flew between them. The night sky was becoming crowded with flying insects. "Have you finished your speech?"

"No!" Alice said. "Nothing's wrong. I'm not finished."

"Would you like me to help you back to your seat?" Marvel asked. He put his hand on her shoulder. She jumped and slipped from beneath him.

"No," she said. "Don't touch me."

"You've gone pale."

"I'm all right," she answered. "Let me finish."

"Thank you very much, miss," the mayor said, tugging gently on her arm.

"Don't touch me!"

"Please, miss."

"I have to go on," she said. "I haven't told you why I need a new start. Don't you want to know? I have to go on."

"No you don't!" Capone called to her, his voice audible even over the murmuring of the crowd. "You're *through!*"

"The gentleman's right," the mayor said, shielding the microphone with his hand. "The other girls deserve a chance to deliver their speeches too."

"But I can't stop," Alice said, her voice booming over the loudspeaker. "I won't!"

Her determination pushed past proper beauty contest etiquette. Not only was her chance for Miss Congeniality lost, but because she failed to show proper respect for a town official of Marvel's stature, the final judging of the Miss Smallville contest might have gone against her as well had it not been for the latest wave of flying insects attracted to the powerful lights. The bugs descended upon the ballpark in such number that the townspeople were too occupied slapping and cursing the winged creatures even to notice Alice's indiscretion.

This glowing jewel of a ballpark—the one light for thirty miles in all directions—the most powerful surge of electricity that central Kansas had ever known, had attracted every moth and flying insect then living on the great midwestern plain. The air became thick with creatures. The buzz of electricity as it coursed through the thick wires was overpowered by the incessant beating of the insects' wings. Women in the grandstands and on the field waved their hands madly in the air while their men crushed the insects in their palms. The townspeople had left behind the euphoria of the light. With each moment, they moved nearer something very like panic.

Near the huge bulbs themselves, the insects grew so thick that the light descending onto the ballpark became no longer white but rather took on the subtle reds and blues of the insects' translucent wings. Moths that flew too near the powerful lights burned and sizzled like frying bacon. The air above moved as though it were a single living organism.

Professor Marvel took the microphone from Alice de Minuette. "Please," he shouted. "Don't panic, brave citizens of Smallville! They're just moths. They won't hurt you. Perhaps if you don't swing at them they'll go away. Leave them alone!" But even as he spoke, Marvel himself took swipes at the insects. "Please, leave the bugs alone!" He clapped a moth between his hands. "Don't panic!"

But it was too late. More insects arrived. Weary but happy travelers, they had come from all over central Kansas. The brilliant light of the ballpark was too much to resist.

"Don't panic, friends," Professor Marvel shouted. But the beating of wings in women's hair and the prickly sharp insect feet on bare arms and faces were too much. The night of Smallville's greatest triumph turned rapidly to disaster. And the worst was yet to come.

Capone removed a long black revolver from beneath his suit-coat and climbed onto the stage. Alice didn't see him. The moths were so thick—a fog bank—that visibility had become a problem.

The beating of millions of tiny wings created a stiff breeze that blew Alice's hair up around her head. Capone moved unseen toward her, pushed the mayor away from the microphone, and reached for Alice with thick hands. "It's all over," he said, a mere instant before being hit and tackled hard from behind.

Al Capone and Buddy Easter landed in an angry tangle and wrestled for a moment before one of the Chicago gunmen pulled Buddy off the most powerful private citizen in the world. The henchman lifted Buddy into the air as though lifting a puppy by the scruff of its neck. Buddy's dangling feet kicked. Capone brushed himself off. He turned back to Alice.

"Leave him alone!" she yelled. Though Alice stood only a few feet away from Capone, her voice was barely audible over the cries of the crowd. She swatted viciously about her. "It's me you want!"

"That's right." Capone cocked his black revolver.

"Don't panic!" Marvel yelled.

At that moment, however, there appeared from out of the thick cloud of moths and other flying insects a shape so horrifying that even Professor Marvel issued a scream that shook the rafters of the old ballpark as it echoed through the amplification system. It was the Mothman.

Capone turned to the sky.

The Mothman wheeled in the busy night air, turning cartwheels over the frantic townspeople, who ran into one another like confused ants. The creature glided over the ballpark with a grace that defied entomological definition. Nearly seven feet long, the Mothman's body was more like that of a silver-coated human being than that of an insect. Its translucent wings spanned twenty feet. Long antennae on the creature's head twisted and turned as if it was through *them*, and not the brilliant red eyes, that the Mothman watched all that went on below.

Buddy Easter shook himself loose from the startled grasp of Capone's henchman. "Bobby Crabtree," he said. The boy from the top of the main school building. The boy with cardboard wings. "Bobby!" he called. It seemed to Buddy Easter that some ghosts appear in forms altogether different from that to which he had grown accustomed during his friendship with Abner Doubleday. He moved toward Alice, his eyes still on the sky.

The Mothman swooped toward the townsfolk, pulling up at the last minute like a crop duster, to send the people of Smallville to their knees. The Mothman wheeled once more into the crowded night sky, flapping its wings and sending a cool rush of air over the crouched citizens. It made a gentle loop, gliding on air currents like a great bird, barrel-rolling like the barnstormers who annually passed through Smallville, and cast a dark shadow over the frightened, upturned faces of a whole town.

"Somebody shut off the lights!" cried a sensible voice from among the wailing throng. In the confusion, however, the switch had been broken. When Professor Marvel flipped it to OFF, nothing happened. The lights continued burning. The Mothman descended once more over the townsfolk, gliding with a loud *whoosh* that blew ladies' dresses up over their knees.

Capone grabbed Alice by the arm, looking away from the Mothman for the first time since the creature's appearance. He pushed Alice to the wooden stage floor. Buddy moved toward him but was knocked from the stage by the back of Capone's hand. The gangster grabbed a tommy gun from one of his henchmen. "Stand back," he said. "Enough of this nonsense."

"Alice!" Buddy called from below.

Capone closed one eye and sighted in on his target. The machine gun moved in slow circles, pointed at a 45-degree angle into the air to follow the path of the Mothman. Capone's hands were as steady as his income.

"Kill the thing!" the city councilmen cried, noticing for the first time the gun-toting stranger. Alice tried to stand but was pushed back to the stage floor by one of the henchmen. "Kill it!" the local Miss Smallville finalists cried. "Kill the damn bug!" Professor Marvel screamed.

"No!" Buddy called.

The discharge of the machine gun ripped through the already thunderously loud night. The tommy gun spat at sixty rounds a second. The frantic citizens of Smallville, who lay flat on the baseball diamond to avoid the Mothman's swooping dives, watched and prayed that Capone's aim might prove true. *Rata-tat-tat-tat-tat.* First, there was only the slightest hesitation in the Mothman's movements. As though a thought had crossed the creature's mind. Next an arrhythmic flapping of its wings and then a burst of brilliant red along the entire side of its body. The townsfolk were rained upon by the warm blood of the Mothman.

The creature cried out in a voice almost human, flapping one wing frantically, as Capone released a second volley that ripped through the other side of its body. The sound of the bullets entering the strange form was like the sound of fabric being torn. The Mothman's cries silenced the shouting of the townsfolk below. It turned in the air, one long antenna dangling uselessly at the side of its head, and wheeled upward once more with a final thrust of its bloodied wings. The monster turned sideways, perfectly white now instead of silver, and crashed at full speed into the top of a buzzing light standard, bursting into the foot-wide bulbs and opening its wings against the impact. There was a flash of light where the Mothman had hit, followed by a loud crackling sound as the electricity of all the lights was directed into the creature's body. The Mothman sizzled high above the townsfolk. Then, with a pop and a final burst of white light, the circuit shorted and the ballpark was thrust into darkness.

"Alice!" Buddy called from the playing field. He groped toward the stage, feeling the wet, frightened faces of the townsfolk all around him. He listened: a dull thud in right field where the Mothman's body crashed. "Alice!" he called again. He put his hand on the stage. He strained his eyes. After the brilliant illumination of the electric lights, however, the scant glow of the stars was worthless. He tried to smell Alice's perfume but could distinguish only the scent of grass, the disquieting odor of three thousand panicked citizens, and the drifting stench of the Mothman's charred remains. He listened for Alice's voice but could hear only Al Capone's announcement over the loudspeaker.

"Don't anybody move or I'll plug the whole damn bunch of you!"

Buddy continued forward. He hoisted one foot onto the stage and pulled himself up when, from out of the darkness, he was kicked square in the forehead. He reeled backward off the stage and crashed once more onto the thick grass. When he touched his forehead his hand became wet with blood.

"Don't nobody else try to climb up here or I'll kill you!" Capone yelled. "Now turn on the damn lights!"

The citizens of Smallville continued toward the exits. In the darkness they held on to one another. There was much shouting and crying and calling of names—"Daddy! Daddy!"—and angry, profane suggestions directed to the once popular mayor of the town (who—like everyone else—had disappeared in the darkness). But added to the cacophony was an intrusive sound that drifted over the townsfolk from a position not far from the stage, a sound incongruous among the despairing cries for its jaunty *melody*. A sweet harmonica in the black air. Then Woody's clear voice as he sang unaccompanied:

> *"The mysterious Mothman,*
> *color of a tin can,*
> *soared in the Kansas night*
> *till a man struck him down*
> *with a tommy gun round*
> *and put out the Mothman's light."*

Capone fired his machine gun straight into the air, discharging a stream of bullets that traveled nearly as high into the night sky as had the soaring baseball, which was just then passing unnoticed over distant Springfield, Colorado. The citizens of Smallville cried out at the sound of the gun—a general gasp, then a wail. "Nobody leaves here till we get these damn lights back on," Capone announced. "We will have order!"

The townsfolk continued toward the exits.

Woody began another song:

> *"So long, it's been good to know yuh,*
> *So long, it's been good to know yuh,*

So long, it's been good to know yuh . . .
And I've gotta be driftin' along."

When at last the small generator that powered the dingy yellow lights was restarted, making visible again the small area in center field, it became clear that no man (not even Al Capone) might have maintained order during the frantic moments of darkness. Shadowed by the dim, flickering light, Capone stood expressionless with tommy gun at his side; Professor Marvel hunched behind the podium, head in hands; the local Miss Smallville contestants, wrapped like children in one another's arms, their tearstreaked faces made all shades of color by the running of their makeup, straightened their long wrinkled dresses and patted into place their coiffures; the city councilmen shook their heads in ardent denial and disapproval of their disgraced mayor; and the henchmen from Chicago turned in confused circles, looking for Alice de Minuette.

But Alice was gone.

A half mile outside Smallville, a million stalks of wheat blew in the moonlight as if choreographed—like kelp beneath the sea responding to the current's cue, or the pennants atop Wrigley Field dancing in graceful, uniform movements. All in rhythm to a music of silence. Near silence. The cries and shouts of the townspeople in the distant ballpark were audible only as echoes among the tall stalks. The wind itself sang more boldly.

This was another world altogether.

Loren Woodville sat behind the thick curtain of golden wheat and waited. Waited for something, though he no longer pretended to know what might come next. He no longer allowed himself the indulgent fantasy that he was in *control* of his own life. He had seen different. Cruel fate. The years had borne this out. However, with the renewal of his great celestial dream, he had momentarily felt the fire of self-determination relight in his heart. A spark of control. The past hours, however, had proven too volatile for the tender flame. The pilot light of self-determination was consumed by a chaotic explosion that finally shut out light altogether. Gangsters, Mothmen, electricity, delay. Now, the spherical spaceship was out of sight, drifted west, spotted an insurmountable lead, forever lost. Simply gone. Loren's hopes might better have remained unlit, he feared. He would have been spared the ashes and smoke.

Alice de Minuette sat beside him on the soft dirt.

"Are you all right?" she asked.

Loren nodded. They were alone in the wheat field.

"Goodness," she said, patting her chest with the palm of her hand in rhythm with the rapid beating of her heart, "I've run farther in the last two days than I ever even *walked* in all the years of my life. Did you know that, Loren?"

He nodded.

"Are you all right, Loren?"

"It's good for the cardiopulmonary system," he answered. He regretted his words the moment he spoke them. They were boring words. Textbook words. Expressive of nothing. He sat up straighter. He was weary. But not so weary that he didn't recognize and respect the weighty obligation of speaking sense to a beautiful woman on a moonlit night.

"Cardiovascular," she said. "Your heart and lungs?"

Weary, but not dead. She *was* beautiful.

"Right?" she asked.

He nodded. "Running keeps a person alive longer," he explained.

"So I've learned," Alice answered.

Loren turned to the clear sky. Great spaces of darkness broken by pinpoints of light. The conventional heavenly objects. Whole worlds light-years away, from which spring small creatures who visit the earth in spherical ships. Who glide over great distances in perfect mathematical arcs. Who bring hope as the sun brings light. Whose presence will never be proved.

"You were wonderful at the ballpark," Alice said.

Loren turned from the stars and looked at Alice. She had wrapped her arms around her knees, bringing her legs close to her body, and sat on the soft dirt wrapped in a graceful ball. Her skin was white, her fingers long and thin where they entwined, and the ends of her golden hair fluttered just perceptibly when a cool breeze passed over her. There was a strange light about her head. Loren looked more closely.

"Alice, did you know that your hair shines?"

In the dim starlight Alice's hair radiated a glow of its own, as if within each strand burned a tiny golden fire. Not a reflection of light, but a source. Loren had seen a similar independent glow in the eyes of winos, which he attributed to their massive consumption of port wine. But since it was not alcohol that lit Alice's blond hair, what fuel was it that burned within her warm body? Loren wondered.

She shifted on the soil to face him. She brought her hands together. "Loren?" She stopped. Then she rubbed her hands to ward off the gathering chill. "How did you lead us through the ballpark? It was so dark. Too dark."

"The stars," he answered. Her eyes were the color of cornflowers. "Mariners use the stars to cross oceans. If you understand the heavens, a dark little ballpark is nothing."

"I see," Alice said.

"Conventional heavenly objects," Loren added. "At least they're good for something."

"You can wish on them too," Alice added.

"You can what?"

She shook her head. "Nothing."

"What do you wish for, Alice?" he asked.

She looked into the sky.

"Safety?" he asked.

She shook her head. "I was safe two days ago," she said. "Safe from Capone, at least. But it wasn't enough: safety. Because it's not real. It can't be. Ever. Because you're never safe from *yourself*. From the things that happen inside you. Things that happened years ago. Things that you think today and things that you *will* think tomorrow. Safety is a dream not worth having."

"Peace?" Loren asked.

"How can you be peaceful in a world so unsafe?" Alice answered.

"So what do you wish for?"

She looked at Loren. "Right now," she said, "I wish I had a big juicy hamburger, potatoes on the side, and a tall glass of Coca-Cola. That's a wish worth making."

"That's all the stars are good for?" Loren asked.

"No." She looked away. "You can also wish not to be alone. You can wish that one until your heart breaks. The stars are good for that too."

"Exactly!" Loren said, jumping up from the dirt. "You understand! That's why they're there. The stars. That's why anybody with a lick of sense knows I shouldn't really have to *prove* the Woodville Theory. The proof is in the sky every night of the year. We are not alone."

Alice shrugged her shoulders. "I don't know about all the science."

"You don't have to know," Loren answered. "Just look."

"Is that your wish?" she asked. "That people look?"

"It would be nice," Loren said.

"I'm sorry if I've slowed you down."

Loren shrugged. "Nothing you could do about it."

"Well, I'm sorry Capone threw you off the train."

"Forget it."

"Oh, Loren, we're lost," Alice said. "Aren't we?"

Loren glanced into the sky. He shook his head. "I know exactly where we're at."

"No," she said. "I mean *lost*."

"Oh," Loren answered. "Well. Maybe not."

"Maybe not," she repeated. "It's a darn big wheat field."

Loren nodded.

"Will Buddy find us here?" she asked.

"We stopped here to rest this afternoon," Loren answered. He slipped his hands into his pockets. "Buddy knows where it is. He may find us."

"I appreciate your help," Alice said. "I wouldn't be here

without you, Loren. But tomorrow I'm leaving on my own. I have to. Just like before. It's too dangerous for you to be around me. And Buddy shouldn't be getting tossed off trains. He's just a kid. I've slowed you down enough. Besides, I have a plan."

"A plan for what?"

"A plan to get out of town," she answered. "To walk away right under Capone's nose. I've seen it done lots of times. I saw it first in an Alice Faye movie. Then in a play called *As You Like It*. Shakespeare. I liked it. It's clever. Nobody figures it out. You know why?"

"Why?"

"Because when Buddy gets here I'm going to borrow his jacket and trousers, and maybe you'll lend me your hat, and I'll dress like a boy." She beamed.

Forgetting his manners, Loren Woodville allowed his eyes to slip south from her face. Down her long white neck. Down past her round breasts and the tiny nipples that pushed in the cool air from behind the soft linen of her dress. Down past her firm stomach and the gentle curve of her hips, the shapely outline of her thighs where they pressed against her dress, and finally past her knees to the place where her smooth legs became visible in the Kansas moonlight.

At last he said, "It won't work."

"Rosalind," Alice answered. "That was the woman's name in the play. It worked for *her*."

Loren shook his head. "That was a comedy," he said. "This is not."

"Sure it is," Alice answered. She pointed into the sky. "Tomorrow you'll catch up to your spaceship. To your friends, the Martians. To your dream. That's a happy ending, right?"

Loren said nothing.

"Right?" she asked.

Loren turned away. "That's right," he said, though he knew differently. He knew this: the space sphere was by now too far west *ever* to catch up to it. Loren would not be in California to meet his Martians. They would land unattended, unrecognized. There had been too much delay. Unless, Loren thought, he sprouted wings like the Mothman and *flew* to the coast. But metamorphosis is slow. And airline passage was out of the question. "Yes," he said. "A happy ending."

"See?" Alice asked. "Comedy."

"Do you have an airplane in your purse?" he asked.

"Do I what?"

"Nothing," he said. "I was being comic." He looked once more into the night sky. After so many years, the heavens had become as familiar to Loren Woodville as his own reflection in a mirror. As many stars in this single galaxy as there are grains of sand on Earth. But among all this light and energy, Loren had seen only one space sphere and now, like a star radiating itself into nothingness, it was gone. *Poof!* "It's gone," he said to Alice, unable to conceal his disappointment any longer. "What will I do?"

Alice said nothing.

When Loren turned he discovered why. She slept.

"What will we do?" Loren repeated.

Alice lay on her side on the soft black soil. Her hands were clasped beneath her head, like a pillow, like the hands of a child. Her eyes were closed but her golden hair still glowed in the dim starlight. Loren watched her breathe, slow and even. He stepped quietly to her, sat beside her, and spread his coat across her shoulders to keep her warm. "Good night," he whispered.

He watched her sleep. Watched the twitching of her cheek as she dreamed. Watched the way his coat—Loren Woodville's own tweed—moved up and down with her breaths. He watched her so closely that at last it seemed to him he could almost hear her heartbeat from where he sat. Hear it or feel it. It seemed to beat in the same rhythm as his own. He lay beside her on the black earth. He slipped his arm around her shoulders to keep her warm. She opened her eyes. Loren smelled the soil and her perfume. She was awake. He felt her soft hair against his face. She turned to him. Silent. He listened. Their heartbeats *did* keep perfect time with the wind in the wheat.

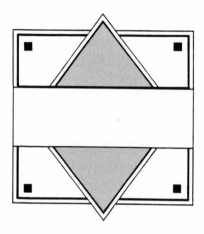

"What's the matter, Babe?"

In the half-light of his hotel room, Babe Ruth turned to the woman beside him in the rumpled bed. Her long black hair fell about her shoulders in a disheveled manner which, for a moment, mirrored the wisp of cigarette smoke that drifted, black and tangled, to the carved ceiling above her. Her bare shoulders were white, her teeth yellow. Ruth had already forgotten her name.

"Nothing's wrong, doll," he said. "I was just thinking."

"About us, Babe?"

He took a deep breath.

"About our future?" she asked.

He had met the woman an hour before at the hotel bar. She had entered with a tall man in a bowler. The tall man spotted Ruth drinking alone in the corner. He moved toward the Babe, pulling his reluctant, raven-haired date behind him. Ruth obliged the man's request for an autograph, invited the two to join him for a drink, listened politely to the man's story about sugarcane fields in Haiti, bought another round of drinks, listened to the woman's story about mosquitoes in Alabama, gave the man tickets for game five of the World Series*, and then politely informed him that he (Ruth) and the raven-haired woman would be going upstairs now to spend a not-so-quiet evening together.

The man in the bowler hat was confused. He shook his head, his jaw slack. "When did this happen?" he asked, as his date rose smiling from the booth to take the Bambino's hand.

But it was not a question of *when*. It was a question of *where*.

And the answer was: under the table.

"No, I'm not thinking about our future," Babe answered.

The woman set her glowing cigarette on the bed stand. She turned to the Babe, slipping her arms around his thick neck and pulling him close to her once more. She kissed his mouth, kicking away the sheets and wrapping one long leg around Ruth's fleshy hip. She ran her hand down his spine, stopping at the small of his back to pull him against her until the folds of their white bodies pressed together like wet clothes in a washing machine.

He pushed her away.

"What the hell's the matter, Babe!"

"I got a decision to make," he said.

"About us?"

"About this," he answered, moving to the opposite bed stand. He opened a drawer and removed a white envelope, torn open at one end, on which was scribbled a message in blue ink. The envelope was thick with paper. He rolled back to the center of the bed and onto his back. He held the envelope to his forehead. Then he tapped it against the tip of his nose.

"What is it?" she asked.

"I'm leaving Chicago tomorrow," he said. "I could throw this thing away and it would be like I never had it. I'd be rid of the whole problem."

"You're not going to throw *me* away, are you?" she asked. "Not after all we've meant to each other."

"Of course not, doll."

*The tickets would prove worthless. The Yankees would sweep in four.

She slid her hand down his wide belly. Down, down . . .

"Or I could go to the police," he continued. "I could do my duty as a citizen. As an American. I mean, nobody's above the law, right? Nobody's without responsibilities to Truth. Right, doll?"

"*This* is truth," she said, grabbing Ruth.

"Then again, I know Capone *personally*," he continued, altogether absorbed in thought. "He's always treated me right. Drinks, music, women. He's real generous. Why should I hurt him? This stuff'll put him away for good. Why do I want to do that? Because he deserves it? Hell, I've always enjoyed the man. He's got great women around. Lots of 'em. Generous women."

"Generous like this?"

"Oh," the Babe said. "Oh. Yeah. But let it go for a minute, I gotta think."

"Damn, Babe, what's the matter?"

"I just gotta think. I gotta decide. I never done nothing like this before."

"You ever done *this*?" she asked, pulling the sheets over her head and disappearing beneath them.

He pushed her away and sat up in the bed. He held the envelope near his face. He shook his head. "Do you know what this is?" he asked.

"Don't you love me even a little bit?"

"This is a handwritten record of Capone's personal income," Ruth explained. "Al Capone. Scarface Capone. You heard of him, doll? It's in his own handwriting. Everything. Gambling, liquor, prostitution. All the profits he keeps quiet from the Feds. That he doesn't pay no taxes on. You know what I'm talking about, doll? This is Capone's suicide note, that's what it is. I don't know how he let it outta his sight."

"What?" she asked, looking up at Babe from the foot of the bed.

He nodded.

"Where'd you get it?" she asked.

"Somebody delivered it to me yesterday at the ballpark," he answered. "But I didn't look through my mail until this morning.

The envelope was sealed. There was just some scribbling on the outside. So I opened it. And I read Capone's own handwriting. And I knew I was in trouble. Because he's *really* in trouble. I don't know nothing else about it. Except that I got it right here. And I gotta do something about it."

She crawled toward him. "What are you going to do?"

"I could give it back to Al," Ruth said. He took a deep breath. "I could call him up tonight. He might be a little suspicious about how I got it, but he wouldn't do nothing to me. I'm a ballplayer. He likes ballplayers."

"You're the best ballplayer I've ever known, Babe," the woman said, reaching for the slugger once more.

"I imagine he'd do about anything to get this thing back."

The woman stopped. "Anything?" she asked. "Like give us whatever we want?"

"I already got whatever I want, doll," Ruth answered, standing up. He turned on the light and moved naked across the room. "I wasn't talking about blackmail. Christ. Blackmail Al Capone? Shit!"

"So give it back to him, Babe."

He sat down in an easy chair near the door. "But he ain't a nice man," Ruth explained. "I know. I seen him. I been with him. He's got a lot of money and power. He's generous. But he's a bastard. A real sonofabitch. I seen the way he treats people. Especially women. Like they were nothing. It's disgusting."

"*I* only sleep with gentlemen," the woman observed.

"Damn right," Ruth answered.

"But I'm no lady in bed. Right, Babe?" she asked.

"Damn right, doll."

"Thanks." She smiled.

"If I was a gentleman," Ruth mused, "I'd give the bastard what he deserves. I'd go to the Feds. Hell, I've seen him hurt people real bad and laugh about it. And I laughed with him just because we were famous together and it didn't seem right *not* to be his pal. But you want to know the truth? I never liked the bastard. It always made me sick inside. He deserves to rot."

"I don't want to hear anymore about it," she said, settling back among the pillows. "I ain't your lawyer, you know."

"No, you're not."

"I'm your girl," she concluded.

"No, you're not," Ruth said.

"What?"

But Ruth had risen from the chair and stood now with his back to the brunette. His wide, white body nearly blocked the whole closet as he removed and tossed onto the chair behind him a gray herringbone suit, a white dress shirt, and a red silk necktie. He dressed quickly (without underwear), slipped into Italian loafers (without socks), and said goodbye to the woman in his bed (without a parting kiss). He stopped at the door. "Thanks, doll," he said.

"Where are you going, Babe?" she asked. She had watched him dress without comment. She had not moved from the bed. "You want me to wait for you?"

"Sure, doll," he said. "After I get back from the Feds I'll go some more with you. We'll go till dawn. I swear to God. That's how good deeds make you feel. A regular gangbuster! That's what I am, doll. Goddamn right!"

"What will I do while you're gone, Babe?"

"Oh, hell," he said. He shrugged his shoulders. "Turn on the radio if you want. Listen to a story."

"There's nothing on at this hour."

"Then make up a story."

"What story?"

"Any story."

She smiled. "All right, lover."

He opened the door. Then he stopped. He turned. "I'm doing right, ain't I?" he asked.

"Well . . ."

He didn't wait for an answer. "Hey!" he said. "What's your name anyway, doll? I guess I didn't catch it. But you sure are a good kid. I want you to know that."

"My name?" She sat up in the bed, straightening her black hair with her fingers.

"Yeah."

"My name's Alice," she answered.

But Babe Ruth didn't hear. He was already gone: down the hall, halfway to the elevator, whistling the "Battle Hymn of the Republic," bound for the office of Eliot Ness, special investigator for the federal government.

■ WOODY'S STORY ■

Well, it was like a cyclone hit, what with the runnin' around and everybody's hollerin' mixin' together in the dark ballpark. You couldn't move 'cause everywhere you turned there was somebody in your way, and you couldn't stand still neither 'cause there was legs and arms and every manner of body parts just a-pushin' you this way and that. Just a mixed-up bunch of blurrin' shadows all runnin' back and forth into each other like they was bumper cars at an amusement park. And Capone wieldin' the tommy gun wailin' into the microphone for everybody to quiet down and stand still, which of course was the one thing in the world that nobody in that bunch was willin' to do.

So I done the only thing that made any sense at all. I started singin'. Makin' up a little tune right there on the spot. Bummin' around, seein' stuff, you get to where pretty soon your mouth is spittin' out songs before you even know it. Put together a little tune about the poor ol' Mothman. It came out all right. Had no guitar just then so I sang by myself and played the harp a little between verses.

Now, I've played in a whole lotta honkytonks and I've watched a lotta punches thrown and I've seen a lotta gory hide left on the tables and floors of them taverns. Men and women, bosses and workhands shoutin' back and forth to each other while I tried to play a tune to make my livin'. Serenadin' the oilers and greasers in Texas City and the marijuana smokers in flop towns and the soggy-smellin' old men along Fifth and Main in Los Angeleeze. None of them was in any real mood to be serenaded. And I throwed down my hat and pretty soon I had those gents singin' with me and even contributin' a buffalo nickel as a tip. But that dark night in the ballpark, with all them human bumper cars crashin' below me, I might just as well of been singin' to a brick wall. Nobody was in no mood. They was too busy bangin' and cryin' and yellin' that the world was comin' to an end. They was sure of it.

'Course the world ain't gonna end in no ballpark in Kansas where all the electricity is burned out. The Lord's got more sense than to waste the best show of all time on a place where you can't even see it happening. But there was just no convincin' the folks on that field. So I sung all that much louder. But I might as well of been playin' for a room fulla the deaf.

Poundin' and scufflin' down there in the dark, just a few feet away, and I couldn't see nothin'. Just heard their scratchin' words and felt their hot breath. People pushin' and shovin', all of 'em blind as bats. Then they started pushin' around *me* until there wasn't hardly no room to breathe. Which is a darn important thing for a man to keep hisself occupied with if he wants to go on livin'. 'Course with all the darkness and the gunshots and the sizzlin' body of the Mothman nearby, there had arose such a panic that keepin' alive was startin' to be a real consideration. Suckin' for air and keepin' from becomin' a doormat for all them folks was a real important goal. Lookin' back now I don't think I was ever closer to the 6 $\times$ 3 in my whole life as I was that night.

But it all come to an end. About an hour or so after it got started, things quieted down. Folks started findin' their way out the exits and into the dark streets where there was more room to wail and scream and carry on like a town fulla old women. I stayed in the ballpark 'cause I wanted to see the whole show. Pretty soon, enough folks had filed out that there was room to start singin' again:

"Takes a worried man to sing a worried song,
Takes a worried man to sing a worried song,
I'm worried now
But I won't be worried long . . ."

Between verses I heard this moanin' comin' from down on the field right near the stage. Real slow words just oozin' out like sap from a tree. Sounded pretty bad. I slipped my juice harp into my shirt pocket and started toward the sound.

Turns out it was a kid I met the night before on the train headin' outta Chicago. Buddy. He had rolled underneath the stage to keep from becomin' hamburger beneath the soles of the panicky folks. Looked like somebody'd got him anyway, though. He'd been banged up good from gettin' tossed offa the train that afternoon. But now he was worse. His forehead was swollen and bleeding from where it musta collided with what I judged to of been a pretty sturdy foot. Foot always wins that kinda collision. The kid was still woozy when I bent down to talk to him. His eyes was dancin' in their sockets. "You hear me, pardner?" I asked.

He slapped hisself upside of his own head like he was tryin' to shake off the rattle of some rotgut whiskey that was playin' a drum and a mean ol' standup bass right in there between his ears. I touched the side of his face real soft 'cause I know how sometimes the feel of another human being, 'bout any old body, can bring a fella back. He shook his head, tryin' to clear all them bad bass notes out through his ears. "Take it easy there, Buddy," I said to him.

After a minute, he come to. He tried to sit up but I pushed him back onto the grass to let him get his senses back. I seen a million people like this. Head all twangin' like a guitar string that's been tuned too high, too tight. Aside from lettin' 'em know they is still alive, which is sometimes questionable, you got to tell 'em not to go and prove it by jumpin' up off the ground and dancin' around like some idiot just to show their head's hard as a nail. 'Cause nobody's head's hard as a nail. Except maybe mine.

After a short spell I let the boy stand up and we made our way out of the ballpark together. Twasn't hardly nobody left inside that old hollow of a park by the time we finally left it. Just me and him and the poor ol' smokin' Mothman. We started through town straight in the direction of no place. Lotta folks headin' there these days. No place. Most everybody's headin' there. More popular than the Ritz-Carlton. Lot less expensive, too. That's the attraction, I guess.

The streets was pretty empty. Everybody was huddled up inside their houses, burnin' candles 'cause there still wasn't no electricity. The kid kept lookin' around. At first I thought he was just scared of the Mothman like everybody else, or maybe still scared of the gangsters. But after a while he told me he was lookin' for his two friends. The ones we'd rode with back on the train. I asked him how his friend Alice had got away from Capone this time, but he said he didn't know nothin'. Just that he had to find her quick to get to California in time.

Lotta people goin' to California. I didn't have to ask him why he was headin' there. Baseball or spaceship, it don't matter. He was goin' there for the same reason as everybody else, I guess. They's all lookin' for their piece of America. Lookin' hard and long.

We finally ended up at the train station, one square building 'bout the size of a schoolroom. All locked up. Wasn't nobody around. Wasn't no trains runnin' then neither or I'd of probably high-tailed it right there. Twasn't that I was scared or nervous in that town but just that I was gettin' mighty tired of all the darkness. All the hushed voices comin' out from inside the locked-up houses. I been in a lotta places where people was down and out, nothin' in their bellies or in their pockets, but still you could find among 'em a good friendly bunch getting a lot of laughin' and talkin' done and more than willin' to hear a song or two written just about them. But this town, least this one night, was different. Wasn't nobody around to hear music. Hell, me and the kid was probably lucky to be alone that night, way out on the edge of town where none of the gloom had reached yet. I know we was both thinkin' about other things than just bein' afraid. Fear ain't a worthy subject to think about. You might as well be thinkin' about nothin' at all. Fact, you'd be better off thinkin' about nothin'.

Well, just about the time I settled in, ready to rest my eyes, which was weary from seein' things that put such a strain on eyes, that overwork 'em—like the Mothman, the bright lights of the ballpark, Alice—just about this time, Buddy told me he was goin' into the wheat field to look for Alice. He said he had somethin' to say to her. That if they wasn't gonna be together no more he wanted to say goodbye. And some other things. He didn't care what I told him about his takin' care of hisself with that banged head or about how it was too late at night to be wanderin' through a wheat field. He was goin'. I called out to him to meet me here, by the tracks, when he was ready to head west. Then I guess I dozed off.

'Bout an hour later I was awoke by Buddy's return. He didn't say a word, but I could feel him settlin' in beside me. When I asked him what happened, he didn't say nothin'. He just looked away toward the wheat field—his eyes was far, far away. He was real sad. It made me sad too, but I knew it was time to leave the boy alone. I wanted to ask if Alice was all right. If she had got away from Capone. But I was afraid that to make Buddy answer those questions would just make him sadder. So I rolled over and pretended to go to sleep.

Coupla minutes later, he laid down right up against my back to keep hisself warm. He didn't say nothin' until about three hours later when a westbound train rolled past. But I don't believe neither of us caught a single wink of sleep. And when that train rolled in, all Buddy said was, "Let's get outta here."

■ ■ ■

Alice de Minuette was half awake. She had slept very little in the wheat field. Now the sunlight was too bright for her to open her eyes—even when she heard a voice call to her from directly above. Powerful and melodious, the voice was vaguely familiar. But it was not Loren's voice. Or Buddy's voice. It seemed to Alice a voice from a dream not yet burned away by the new morning light.

The dream was about God.

"Hey, you!" the voice called. "Down there!"

Though Alice had never before dreamed of God, she was not surprised or disappointed at the sound of his voice. His pronunciation was homespun midwestern, yet his cadence suggested a worldliness that one might expect of the Almighty. Subtle in tone, flamboyant in timbre and pitch. Vaguely familiar. In all, the voice of God made Alice de Minuette more secure with the state of the universe. She liked this dream.

"Hey! Wake up down there!"

She felt Loren Woodville stir beside her on the soft black soil. She heard him speak. "Jesus Christ," he said. She smiled to herself as she opened one eye. The light from above was blinding. Beautiful white. She lowered her gaze to discover her friend Loren—who wore only a T-shirt and boxer shorts—rubbing the glare and sleep from his eyes. He struggled to his feet.

"Would you grab this rope, please?" the voice called down.

Alice jumped to a sitting position when at last she realized that this was no dream. There *was* a voice coming from above the wheat field. She buttoned the top buttons of her wrinkled dress, ran her hand through her hair, and turned to the bright sky, jarred into wakefulness. She squinted her eyes against the harsh light.

"That's right, son," the voice called down to Loren, who had grabbed hold of the rope.

Silhouetted against the sky was a pear-shaped balloon the size of a large building, which hovered twenty feet over the tops of the wheat stalks. The surface of the balloon, made of the shiniest silk, shimmered in the morning sunlight. Written in huge letters across the balloon was:

"Morning, folks!"

Beneath the great balloon hung a wicker basket in which stood the mayor of Smallville, Professor Marvel. He wore formal, colorful attire—more flamboyant than he had worn the night before. In one hand he held an emerald-green top hat and in the other a gold-inlaid walking stick. He leaned out of the basket, waving the hat when he recognized Alice as a former beauty contestant. The great balloon shifted in the morning breeze. The old man's watch chain caught a ray of light and glistened in the sun.

"The mayor!" Alice whispered to Loren. "What will we say to him?"

"Good morning, Alice," Loren said to her as he slipped into his trousers. He held the rope in one hand though he seemed otherwise oblivious to the great balloon hovering above. He smiled at Alice. She noticed for the first time that he had lost a front tooth since last she had seen him in full light. "It is a good morning, isn't it?" he asked. "Alice? It *was* a good night, wasn't it?"

"Oh," she said. She looked at Loren Woodville. Though his face was swollen and discolored from his passage off the Denver Behemoth, there burned in his eyes a light Alice had not noticed before, not even when his dream of Martians had been most hopeful. Alice wondered if the same light glowed in her own eyes. She had not seen it before. But she had *felt* it. With Loren. Felt the light. Only hours before. It was soft. It was fiery. It had felt like fluffed down in an electrical storm. "Oh, yes, Loren," she said. "It's good. A good morning. Very good."

"Morning!" the mayor repeated.

"Good morning," they called up, unembarrassed by their impropriety.

"Quite a night, eh?" the mayor asked.

Alice was not sure how he meant his question. Did he refer to the terrors of the ballpark: the insects, the Mothman, Capone, the darkness? Or was he commenting on the wheat stalks leveled and the subtle reshaping of the soft black soil during Alice and Loren's more private night that followed?

"That's a beautiful balloon, Mr. Mayor," Loren answered.

"Call me Professor," Marvel answered.

"Nothing like a little ballooning to begin the morning on a high note," Loren continued.

"Ah," the Professor answered from above. "I'm afraid this is not recreational ballooning. It's escape, friends. You see, our great civic achievement has brought no joy to Smallville. It *has* brought grief and anger, crop damage, and disgrace to Edison himself." He sighed. "Not to mention me. I don't think I'm mayor anymore."

"Your lights were very beautiful," Alice said, brushing black soil from the folds in her blue dress. It seemed to Alice that her world was defining itself more and more by the particular quality of light at any moment. The way Clark's eyes consumed light. The way Loren's eyes radiated it.

Professor Marvel shook his head. "It's all right," he explained. "I'm a balloonist by profession. Also a soothsayer and powerful wizard. I'll get by."

"Wizard?" Loren asked.

"Terrible but beneficent," Marvel answered.

"Where are you going?" Alice asked.

"Wherever the winds take me, more or less," he answered. He held one finger to the wind. "This morning, I'd say that's west. Yes. Very good. West. Where a man is allowed a little mistake now and then."

"West?" Loren asked.

"I should be moving on," the Professor said.

"How fast does this balloon travel?" Loren asked.

"Depends on the winds," the Professor answered. "Now, if you'll just release the rope slowly. Nice seeing you again, miss. If we'd ever gotten around to judging the Miss Smallville contest, I'd have voted for you. Believe me. Some night, eh? Well, goodbye."

"Goodbye," Alice said.

Loren said nothing. Rather, he jerked *down* on the rope, forgetting how delicately balanced is a lighter-than-air balloon. The great envelope tipped precariously to one side, swinging the wicker basket beneath it like a thrill ride at a carnival. The Professor grabbed onto the basket with one hand to keep from falling out. With the other hand he waved his top hat in lurching, awkward circles above his head. With his godlike voice he murmured obscenities (audible only as the wicker basket swung—first one way, then the other—past Alice and Loren).

At last the basket slowed above the wheat field and the great envelope of air righted itself in the sky. The Professor leaned out of the basket and spoke more calmly. "Despite the size of this device," he said to Loren, "it is important to remember that you are *not* pulling about a stubborn mule! It's only a lot of hot air up here. Delicacy, my boy. Delicacy!"

"Sorry," Loren said as he pulled the balloon more delicately toward the ground.

"Which is not to mention the fact that I believe I asked you to release the rope rather than pull on it in the first place," the Professor continued.

"I have a proposition for you," Loren explained.

Alice stepped back as the great balloon came to rest in the wheat field. Professor Marvel stood in the basket, tapping on the wicker with impatient fingers. The great balloon shifted and pulled in the wind above him like a barely restrained animal. The Professor shook his head.

Loren held tightly to the rope.

"I could simply untie one or two of these sandbags," Professor Marvel said. "And this contraption would not only lift me, it would lift you, dangling by that rope, into the air."

"That's not far from what I had in mind."

"Which is not to say that I'm a man ill prepared to entertain a worthwhile proposition now and then," the Professor said. He placed the green top hat on his head. He turned to Alice. "My, you are beautiful, miss."

She shook her head. "I'm a mess," she said.

"Ah," Professor Marvel answered. "If only all womankind looked such a mess!"

"I'm a scientist—" Loren Woodville started.

"And so am I!" Professor Marvel interrupted. "Alchemy. You?"

"Well, physics," Loren answered. "But what I'm working on these days probably has as much to do with alchemy as it does with conventional physics. I'm certain you could help me."

"Yes?" the Professor of Alchemy asked.

"I'm in the midst of a breakthrough that will change the world forever," Loren explained. "It will change our concept of the whole universe! But I've run into a little trouble."

Professor Marvel looked at Alice. "She's your laboratory assistant?" he asked.

Alice nodded yes.

Loren shook his head no.

"Well?" Marvel asked. "Which is it? Is she?"

"She's my partner," Loren answered.

"I see," Professor Marvel said. "Continue."

"Partner," Alice whispered to herself. The common word sounded inexplicably strange to her. It sounded foreign. Or like a word she had only seen written but had never heard pronounced. Though neither of these things was so.

"We need to cover a great deal of ground in a very short time," Loren explained. "But neither of us is very good at hopping freights or thumbing rides. At least, not yet. And we have no money. So you see we're in a bind. But your balloon—"

"Where do you need to go?" Professor Marvel asked.

"Away," Alice said. "Just *away*."

"From here?" he asked.

Alice nodded.

"From those gangsters?" Professor Marvel continued.

She nodded once more.

"Well, that's easy enough."

"No," Loren said, "California. We need to go away *to* California."

"Oh, that's right," Alice added. "That's what I meant."

"Well. That's another matter entirely," Professor Marvel said. "California is very far away, though this balloon *has* traveled to more distant places. I suppose it could be done. If the incentive was great enough."

Loren nodded. He stepped toward Professor Marvel. He held his right hand over his heart. "If you take us to California you will become an enduring part of history," he explained. "I promise you, Professor. Schoolchildren will speak your name."

"In some places," Professor Marvel answered, "little people already speak my name. There, I already *am* an enduring part of history." He held his finger once more to the wind.

"Well?" Loren asked.

"Due west," Professor Marvel answered.

"California."

"Yes."

A more powerful gust of wind rose from out of the east. The moored balloon pulled and strained against Loren's grip, bucking and jerking. The great envelope leaned dangerously near the tops of the wheat. The wicker basket in which the Professor stood bounced on the black soil, and the roped bags of sand tied to the basket swung in arrhythmic jerks. The balloon moved as if angry.

"To the balloonist," the Professor shouted, "the wind is a strange and powerful friend."

"All friends are strange and powerful," Loren answered. He looked at Alice. "That's why we need them."

"Climb in," Professor Marvel said.

"I don't know," Alice answered, backing away from the shuddering basket.

"What!"

"I've never flown in a balloon before," she said.

"Alice," Loren answered. "This is no time for hesitation. Besides, it's not like you."

"I know," she said. "But this is different. Actually climbing in. Flying away and all."

"There's nothing to it, miss," Professor Marvel said. "The balloon does all the work. The air. The sky."

"We're not safe here," Loren added. "*You're* not safe."

Alice looked up at the great balloon, towering in the morning sky. It was bigger than some of the buildings along Lake Shore Drive. "I don't know," she said again. She rubbed her hand across her eyes. "What about Buddy? We can't just leave him."

"We already agreed," Loren said. "He's safer without us. He's just a kid. He shouldn't have to live so dangerously."

"Maybe we should wait until afternoon."

"We don't have *time* to wait," Loren said. "There are people looking for you, remember? And history is soaring farther away from us with every passing second. Right? This is our chance. We won't get another in our whole lifetime, Alice."

"Yes, " she said. "I know."

"Partner?" he asked.

"Maybe you should go without me," Alice said.

The balloon bucked once more in the wind.

"What?" Loren stepped toward Alice.

She looked away. "Maybe it would be best."

Loren shook his head. "It would *not* be best."

"Please, folks," Professor Marvel said. "I'd really rather not have to face my constituency this morning. Let's just go. If you're going."

"Is it me?" Loren asked her. "You don't want to go with me?"

Alice shook her head. "It's nothing, really. It's ridiculous."

"Because if it's me, just say the words," Loren continued. She did not look at him. "I won't ask why. There are some questions that can't be answered. Some questions that shouldn't be asked. I won't ask, Alice. Just say the words."

"It's not you, Loren."

"Because I'll stay behind," he continued. "You're the one who needs to get out of here. You can't go into town. You can't go back to the railroad station. And you can't stay in a wheat field for the rest of your life. Is it me?"

"No!" Alice answered. "It's not you. I'd *like* to be with you. Just not in a balloon. I'm sorry. I'm afraid of heights, if you want the truth."

"Heights?" Loren said. He breathed deeply.

"I don't even like to ride in elevators," Alice explained.

"That's all?" Loren asked.

"That's all," she said. "But it's enough if you're riding in a balloon."

"Please, please." Professor Marvel held up one finger to halt Alice's fears. He bent and disappeared within the wicker basket. When he straightened he held a small suitcase upon which was painted, in bright colors, PROFESSOR MARVEL. He leaned the suitcase on the wicker edge and flipped it open with his thumbs. "Something perfect for you, miss," he said. "Something to make even the most frightened traveler of that great blue yonder feel confident and secure. As if we had all been born to fly."

Loren and Alice moved toward the basket.

Professor Marvel cleared his throat and struck a proper oratory position. "Being a man who has spent the better part of his life hovering, drifting, flying through these vast skies, I have quite naturally come into contact with a great many aviators with whom I have shared experiences, souvenirs, and recollections," he explained, digging with nimble fingers through the open suitcase as he spoke. With the backs of his hands, he pushed aside small boxes painted bright colors and tiny velvet bags drawn closed by golden string. At last, he withdrew a small wooden box. He handled the box with great care, as if it were made of the finest bone china.

Alice and Loren leaned nearer the basket.

"One of the aviators with whom I was acquainted," he continued, "was a Mr. Wilbur Wright."

"Of the Wright brothers?" Alice asked.

"The same," the Professor answered. "A nice fellow. He gave me this medal as a little token of his friendship." Professor Marvel opened the wooden box and removed from it a shiny, circular lapel pin. He held it out to Alice. "It was awarded to Wilbur in 1906 by the President of the United States in recognition of the great contribution made by the Wright brothers. This medal is the symbol of excellence in aviation."

Alice took the pin from the Professor. Inscribed across the front was the word Rotary. Alice narrowed her eyes. "Wait a minute," she said. "I've seen pins like this. It's a Rotary Club pin. Lots of men wear these."

"Not *this* one," the Professor said, grabbing the pin from Alice. "This is a very elite Rotary Club. The club you refer to is loosely *based* on this organization."

"Oh."

"This is the *Rotary* Club," the Professor continued. "You know, rotary. Like propeller. That's where the name came from. This very medal!" He pinned the aviation award on Alice's blue dress. "Only great aviators may possess it. And so, by the authority vested in me—and at no charge—I honor you, Alice, with this Distinguished Award and bestow upon you all the privileges and obligations that go with it. All right?"

"I can't accept this," she said.

"It's already yours, dear," the Professor said.

"But I haven't done anything," Alice said.

Professor Marvel nodded his head. "Ah, but you will. You *will* be a great aviatrix. Otherwise, you'd not be wearing an award for aviation. It's really very logical. Undeniable."

"Logical?" she asked.

"Indeed."

"But this *is* a Rotary Club pin, Professor," she said.

He shook his head. "*The* Rotary Club pin."

"Oh."

Another gust swept over the wheat field. The great balloon jerked once more against Loren's steady grip. The envelope leaned and billowed. The ropes strained.

"Alice?" Loren asked. "Will you come with me?"

She touched the pin with her fingers.

"If we hold tight we won't fall," he continued.

She nodded her head yes.

"Indeed," the Professor said. "It was the award that convinced you, wasn't it? The award that pushed you over your fear. The honor and obligation."

Alice nodded to the Professor as she climbed into the wicker basket. "Indeed," she said.

When she looked at Loren she smiled and rolled her eyes.

"Do *you* have any crippling insecurities?" the Professor asked Loren Woodville.

Loren shook his head. "Not anymore," he answered, climbing into the basket as the lighter-than-air balloon rose from the Kansas wheat field. The great envelope of air pulled the basket into the same sky through which had recently traveled beings and objects even more marvelous than itself. The Professor tossed a sandbag to the ground and the balloon leaped into the wind.

"California!" Loren shouted happily.

Alice pressed against him. But she said nothing. She was away from the wheat field, away from the darkness, away from Capone. *Away*. Just away. Which is where she had hoped to be. But she could not celebrate with her friend Loren Woodville. She liked him very much. She was pleased to be with him. But she was still not altogether unalone. She looked down, holding tight. The wheat field waved in the breeze as if to say goodbye.

She thought of Buddy Easter.

By midafternoon, the train upon which Buddy Easter and Woody Guthrie rode (a highball out of Topeka due into Los Angeles the next afternoon) was somewhere on the cold high plateau of central Colorado. The boxcar was crowded with men of all shapes and sizes, all colors and dispositions. Some sat. Some stood. Some were too weak from hunger to do either. These men leaned against the vibrating wooden walls like packing crates. Some men hung out the open boxcar door, their hair blown in the chill wind, their shouts lost in the thunderous rumble of the train upon the tracks. Other men slept as peacefully on the hard floor of the boxcar as ever did John D. Rockefeller in the Ritz. Some men smoked, some men drank rotgut whiskey, some men told stories about the riches to be found in the green valleys of California.

Buddy Easter just wanted to be left alone.

"You all right?" Woody asked the boy.

Buddy had claimed a comfortable spot in one corner of the boxcar, spread a newspaper across his lap, and lapsed into a cold silence that chilled and worried Woody Guthrie. He had said barely a word since they jumped the train the night before near the deserted station in Smallville.

"You all right?" Woody repeated.

Buddy nodded.

"Good," Woody said. " 'Cause you're ridin' with some real fine company in this boxcar. It'd be a damn shame to make a trip like this and not say a thing or two to some of these fellas."

Buddy pulled the newspaper up nearer his chin. "I'm all right," he said. "Don't worry."

"Your face sore?" Woody asked. "You been banged up pretty good. But it's all right. 'Cause when somebody asks you about all that black-and-blue you just say, 'Yeah, but you should see the other guy!' Right? Huh, Buddy? You tell 'em that."

Buddy nodded.

"Some illustrious ramblin' men in this boxcar," Woody continued. "Like that man who bandaged up your hand. That was Dr. Benton Sheridan. He's a real doctor. College educated. But the crash took his practice, and the whiskey took his nerves. So he rides the rails attendin' to the boys he meets here. Boys like you and me. Boys who don't turn away from a man just because they smell whiskey on his breath. Boys who don't walk away from a man just because he's seen some bad luck or had some hard travelin'. You know, guys like us, right?"

Buddy nodded and looked away.

On the far side of the car stood two men toe to toe, a tall man in a cowboy hat and a short man with a cigarette. They shouted at each other and turned red in the face. They pushed each other. Their angry words jumbled among the rumbling and clanking of the train, the conversations of the other men, and the stamping of their own heavy feet on the floor of the boxcar. Only the anger was audible from where Buddy sat.

The short man with the cigarette threw a punch. He missed. Others gathered around the angry pair, shouting encouragement and shadowboxing with the movements of the real combatants. The tall man punched the other square in the mouth. Luckily for the short man, he had no teeth to begin with. Unluckily for the tall man, the glowing end of the cigarette lodged between his fingers and burned the palm of his hand. The tall man stepped back, shaking his hand, blowing on the palm. Dr. Sheridan moved between the men. He looked at the burned hand while the small toothless man paraded the boxcar victorious.

"The littly guy's named Jackson," Woody said, pointing. "He had a real bad runna luck last year. See, he was workin' as a midget in the Ringling Brothers circus. Then, as you can see, he grew. Thirty years old. And he grew almost a *foot* in one summer. Just like that, his career was down the ol' drain. He don't know nothin' else but bein' a circus midget. Don't know no 'big clown' tricks. And he says he's damned if he'll learn. That they just ain't him. So he's been real mad. Pickin' fights with guys twice as big. Thinkin' he's a regular heavyweight. One of these days somebody's gonna knock ol' Jackson back down to size."

Buddy nodded, his thoughts far away.

"And that man over there is Anderson McCrew," Woody continued. He pointed to a black man who sat in the center of a ragged crowd. Each man listened to McCrew's words as if listening to a radio broadcast of the final game of the Series. Attentive, involved. His black face was lined but not old. On his head was a tattered trilby. "He's a sort of soothsayer."

"He knows the future?" Buddy asked.

Woody was encouraged by the boy's interest. "Not exactly," he said. "He's a *sort* of soothsayer. See, ol' Anderson don't know a thing about the future. But he knows everything about the past. Everything! Every little detail. He knows about all the trees that ever fell in the forest when nobody was around to hear 'em. He knows about your childhood and before. He knows."

"Everybody knows about the past," Buddy said. "You study it in history class."

"Not the way Anderson knows," Woody answered. "Why, Anderson knows what color the sky was on the day Columbus discovered America."

"It was blue," Buddy said.

"But Anderson knows what *shade* of blue," Woody continued. "And there's 'bout as many shades of blue as there is people."

"Yeah," Buddy said. "That's true."

"He knows like he was there hisself. He knows what Columbus had for supper the night before and how Mrs. Columbus felt when she heard the good news that they was namin' a town in Ohio after her old man!"

Buddy leaned back into the corner.

"He knows things about you that *you* don't even know," Woody said. "Long as it's already happened. He knows everythin' about the past, but he don't even pretend to know what's comin' next."

Buddy pulled the newspapers up once more to his chest. "If I want to know what happened yesterday," he said, "all I have to do is buy a paper."

"It's a sad gift sometimes," Woody said.

Buddy nodded. "Lots of times the past is the saddest thing in the world."

"What the hell happened last night, Buddy?" Woody asked.

"Nothing," Buddy said.

"Is Alice all right?"

The boy shrugged. "I guess."

"Did you see her?"

He closed his eyes and nodded.

"Was she with Capone?" Woody asked.

"No, she was all right."

Woody nodded and looked away.

The train blew its whistle. The long, lonesome call cut through the thin Colorado air. Outside passed fields of blowing grasses, yellow in the afternoon sun. In the distance rose the great peaks of the Rockies, all shades of purple and blue like the sky turned inside out. The men who stood at the door spit out of the train toward the passing country.

"They're showin' how they love it," Woody explained. "Spittin' at the goddamn beauty of it all. Reachin' out to it. Tryin' to touch it. But it's too big, too beautiful. So what else can a man do but spit? How else can you acknowledge it but by touchin' it any way you can? 'Cause it's too goddamn beautiful not to touch."

Buddy's eyes remained closed.

"You understand?" Woody asked.

Buddy said nothing.

"Sometimes you see things like that," Woody continued.

Buddy nodded.

Woody grabbed the newspaper that had lain open across Buddy's chest. It was today's paper—a rare commodity aboard a flatbed. New news. He glanced down the headlines. "Have you seen it?" he asked his partner.

"Go ahead," Buddy said, opening his eyes. His face was swollen. His eyes black and his forehead distended, he looked like Dr. Frankenstein's second, and last, try. "I don't care."

Woody stopped. He folded the *Garden City Gazette* along the seam and held it for Buddy to see. "Look here," he said. He pointed to a small article. "You'll care about this."

Buddy sat forward to read.

Soaring Object Sighted in Local Skies

GARDEN CITY—An unidentified heavenly object was sighted last night moving across local skies by Garden City resident William Norton. Norton, a retired fireman and amateur astronomer, reported the object to *Gazette* offices at 7:45 P.M..

Norton first described the object as a new star in the eastern sky. Further observation, however, indicated that the object is moving across the heavens in a manner inconsistent with the normal shift of the stars.

Dr. Ellis Hunt, astronomy instructor at Garden City High School, confirmed that the object could be no star when contacted at his home by the *Gazette*.

"But it isn't a meteor or comet either," Hunt said. "My observations indicate that not only is it moving against the background of stars, but it is moving heavenward rather than earthward. As if launched like a skyrocket on the Fourth of July."

Neither Norton nor Hunt was able to offer a conclusive explanation for the strange sighting. Both, however, have their theories.

"I believe it is a red hot stone spewed from a volcano somewhere on the planet," Hunt said. "Nothing else explains the speed and height at which it moves. Surely it is not the product of mortal man."

Norton, who is of American Indian background, suggests that it might be something beyond our understanding. "When I was a boy I was told about the phoenix," Norton recalled, "a great bird that rose, glowing, from the ashes of a consuming fire to soar about the earth. I know the idea is outdated. Belief in such things is dead. But then, the nature of the phoenix is one of rebirth. So who knows?"

The Federal Weather Bureau has assured the *Gazette* that the object is of natural origin and poses no threat to the general public.

"You're still planning on catching it, aren't you?" Woody asked. "Shagging it and catching it? That's what this is all about, right?"

"Damn right," Buddy said. For the first time since leaving Kansas, Buddy Easter smiled. His swollen cheeks, fat lip, chipped front tooth—all participated. He nodded. "In fact, when we get to California—"

He stopped, distracted by another violent movement on the far side of the boxcar. He turned. One of the men gathered around Anderson McCrew (soothsayer of the past) had leaped off the floor, stepped awkwardly over the two seated beside him, and stood now with hands clenched in fists over the black man. McCrew remained seated on the wooden floor. The angry man's words were as audible as a conductor's call on a silent night.

"Nigger!" he yelled.

McCrew did not move.

"Goddamn nigger!" the man repeated, kicking at the black man. "You call *me* a bastard? You black sonofabitch! You tell me *my* mama was a whore? Shit! I'll break your goddamn head. Now stand up! Lyin' nigger!"

Woody stood up beside Buddy. He patted the boy on the head and moved toward the crowd, his right hand anxiously tapping the side of his leg. He stood on his toes to see over the other men.

"Stand up, sonofabitch!" the angry man yelled.

"Leave him be," Woody replied. The crowd of men turned to face him. They parted as Woody pushed his way into the circle. "You asked for the truth, buster," he said to the angry man, "and Anderson gave it to you."

McCrew stared at the floor.

"He called me a bastard!" the angry man continued. "No nigger calls me a bastard."

"Settle down, Charlie," a man in a red bandanna suggested, touching his friend on the arm.

Charlie pushed him away. "He called me a bastard."

"Then that means you *is* a bastard," Woody answered.

"Fuck you," the angry man said, pointing at Woody. His hand shook with rage. His face was red. "You're the second one I'm throwing off this goddamn train."

"I'd like to see you try," Woody answered.

Charlie turned back to McCrew. "But you're first," he said. "Now stand up!"

Anderson McCrew nodded. He reached behind him for a wooden crutch set on the boxcar floor. He leaned against the crutch as he pulled himself to a standing position. He slipped the crutch under his arm. Anderson McCrew had only one leg. "Won't be the first time I been throwed off a train for tellin' the truth," he said.

"The nigger's crippled," Charlie said, stepping away from McCrew as if the man's condition was contagious.

"*I* ain't though," Woody said.

Charlie's face had gone white.

"Have a little nip of this, Charlie," the man in the red

bandanna said, holding a bottle out to his friend. "Calm you right down."

Woody stepped forward. He raised his hands to chest level, clenched in fists (more like John L. Sullivan than Joe Louis). "Come on, buster," he said.

"How'd the nigger know?" Charlie asked.

"It's a gift," Anderson McCrew answered, laughing. He turned away. "A blessing from the Lord."

"Have a nip of this," the man in the red bandanna insisted, pushing the bottle up to Charlie's face. "Come on, it's store-bought. Cost me two bits. Go on."

Charlie obliged. He smacked his lips. "You know," he said, handing the bottle back, "I really *am* a bastard."

"Don't need no soothsayer to see that," Woody said, his fists still raised.

"Let it be, Woody," Dr. Sheridan said.

"Yeah, have a nip of this," the man in the red bandanna said, passing the bottle.

Woody obliged. He smacked his lips.

"Mind if I join him?" Dr. Sheridan asked, taking the bottle.

Charlie walked to the boxcar door. He sat with his back to the others, his feet hanging over the side.

Dr. Sheridan smacked his lips.

The terrible moment had passed.

"Talk about medicine," Dr. Sheridan said, passing the bottle. "You take a moment of anger and prescribe aspirin or plenty of rest or castor oil and what do you get? Blood. But if you prescribe a little nip of this? Hell, name me a better medicine."

"Better medicine?" Woody asked. "Truth."

Dr. Sheridan shook his head. "Too much of that'll kill you," he said.

When the bottle was empty, Woody patted the doctor on the back and turned once more toward the quiet corner of the boxcar in which Buddy sat. But Buddy was not alone. Anderson McCrew had moved across the car to settle in beside the bruised boy. The two were engaged in conversation.

"Hello, Woody," McCrew said, extending his hand from where he sat on the wooden floor. His skin was leathery and his grip strong.

"Hello, Anderson," Woody said, taking his hand.

"You told him, Woody," Buddy said.

"Told him what?"

"My name," the boy answered. "And all about the baseball. You told him. But I'm no sucker, you know."

"I know you're no sucker," Woody said. "But I didn't tell him nothin'."

"I don't believe you," Buddy said.

"So ask him somethin' I don't know," Woody suggested, sitting beside them. "I told you he knows things. Ask him somethin' secret. 'Cause if it happened, he'll know. Like he was there hisself."

The black man nodded.

Buddy turned to Anderson McCrew. The man's eyes were as black as a well. Deep. Buddy imagined that light must echo in them as it descends and is consumed. For Anderson's eyes did not seem empty of light but rather filled by it. Insatiably hungry for it. Consumptive. Buddy remembered how Alice's golden hair seemed to *produce* light. He imagined being in a room with Alice and Anderson at the same time—one glowing, the other consuming light. They would, as in short division, cancel each other out. And it would be like being with neither of them. Like being alone.

"All right," he said. He moved nearer the black man. "Tell me this, Mr. McCrew. Where did I find Alice after I left Woody last night at the train station?"

McCrew answered without hestitation. "In the wheat field."

Buddy gasped.

"Making love with Loren Woodville," McCrew continued. His eyes grew blacker. He smiled. "They didn't see you 'cause they was holding on to each other like frightened children in a thunderstorm. You understand? Comforting each other. Being human beings *together* instead of always apart. It was the only thing they could do to remind themselves that they was still alive. And that their lives was still worth living."

Buddy closed his eyes.

"But you was confused," McCrew said. "And hurt."

"All right," Buddy said. "I believe you."

"You was feeling betrayed," McCrew continued. "But it don't have nothing to do with you, son. You and Alice share something real different. You know that. You've known it all along. But you haven't understood *why*—"

"All right," Buddy repeated. "That's enough. I believe you."

Anderson McCrew stopped. He nodded. "Don't help me none at the horse races," he said.

"I believe you," Buddy said.

Anderson McCrew leaned nearer the boy. Their foreheads almost touched. McCrew put the hard tips of his fingers on the boy's bruised face. "Don't help me none with the numbers," he said. He closed his black eyes. "But sometimes I do come across the most wondrous things. . . . ."

■ PROFESSOR MARVEL'S STORY* ■

Light air is my companion. The earth beneath my feet has always seemed to me a nagging wife, while the sky has beckoned as a loving mistress. How might I ever have kept my head when above me I beheld wonder on each clear morning of the year? Always, the prospect of ballooning from the black and white of one world into the vibrant color of another. It is show business. Carnival chicanery. The political life. Triumphs transformed into tragedy. Setbacks seduced into success. Ladies and gentlemen, illiteration fails me. My life has been a marvel.

*Excerpted from Marvel's autobiography, *A Life of Hot Air* (New York: Grassi Press, 1938).

Because the details of the "Mothman Incident" are recounted in many contemporary publications, they need not be repeated here. The tragedy of the entomological invasion is already well enough documented (perhaps too well!). Besides, it is difficult for me to recall the night impassively. After our moment's luminous triumph, the terror of the darkness that followed is heightened in my memory until its proportions become as wide and sweeping as the Mothman's wings themselves. This much I will say: I did not despair for long. By the next morning I was once more optimistic. I knew my term in Smallville had come to an inauspicious end, yet I sensed the distant strains of a triumphal march beckoning to me from *someplace else*.

As in the past, I prepared my balloon.

The town was still as I ascended. The morning was clear and quiet. I thought it ironic that my leave of Smallville should be so different from my arrival. Brass bands had played Sousa marches two years before when I landed ceremoniously—albeit accidentally—atop the City Hall. Red, white, and blue bunting was draped from the eaves and lightposts. It was election day. There was no leading candidate for mayor. The field was open. I seized the moment, quickly convincing the voters that my background was rich in civic leadership (after all, most of good wizardry is simply the competent administration of routine tasks). More, I allowed—perhaps even encouraged—Smallville's citizenry to believe my arrival fated, omnipotently planned. But the truth? It was only the wind. An accident. I had intended to land in my nephew's cow pasture in Omaha, Nebraska. I didn't even know I was in Kansas until after I was elected mayor.

Of course, it *might* have been omnipotently planned. Who can say?

I drifted past the edge of town and over the first stalks of the great wheat field that stretches west to the high plains of the Rocky Mountains. All was still. Untying another sandbag, I prepared to ascend higher—into the white, heady clouds—when I noticed something unusual on the black soil below. Figures. Bodies. Prostrate. Sleeping. I released a burst of light air and descended until my basket brushed the tops of the tallest wheat stalks. I called to the sleeping pair.

"Good morning!"

A man and a woman. They lay beside one another on the soft soil. Propriety forbids any detailed description of their position. Suffice it to say that they reposed tranquilly in an affectionate embrace. I regretted having awakened them. I wished immediately I had simply floated past. But I had been made so anxious by the circumstances of my departure that the impropriety of my stopping was not immediately clear. They stirred on the soil below. They were awake, and I was committed to the awkward moment. I threw down a rope and engaged the couple in conversation.

■ 3 ■

The woman's name was Alice de Minuette. She had awakened with a startled, confused look when I called down to her. Yet as she turned to the sky, I was greeted by the most radiant glimpse of morning I have ever seen. She was familiar to me. Alice had been a Miss Smallville contestant only hours before. I had felt, even then, a particular attraction to the woman. After all, the timing of *her* arrival (the very night of the beauty pageant) had seemed as fated as my own. But Alice had not been as fortunate as I. There was no Miss Smallville crowned that infamous night. No all-expense-paid trip to Denver, Colorado. The "Mothman Incident" dashed Alice's hopes as it dashed my own. All of which made me feel even greater attachment to the woman. And greater regret that she should be embarrassed by my awkward aerial invasion. Still, Alice was too steadfast to remain long shaken by social impropriety (mine *or* hers). As I was too steadfast to allow my curiosity to remain unsatisfied.

The man beside her was named Loren Woodville. He was tall and spoke with a quiet intelligence that held up his whole being as helium holds up a balloon. One couldn't *see* his intelligence; one could only see his spirit soar. He was anxious, but he seemed quite happy. And why not? Alice obviously felt great affection for him, though the precise nature of this affection remains unclear to me even now (to call it "love" *feels* inaccurate, yet to call it anything else seems an understatement of its significance).

■ 4 ■

Who might have imagined that something as insignificant as a Rotary Club pin could turn a woman's whole life around? Yet such things happen. The miracle of Alice's transformation in the wheat field stands as evidence. She was no longer afraid of heights when I pinned the tiny medal upon her dress. She *became* an aviatrix. I have used this psychology before. Fake diplomas, testimonials . . . I've given intellectual confidence to men with straw for brains, compassion to men with hearts of tin, and courage to men who once were frightened by their own shadow. For I discovered that by filling the gaps in one's personality with the proper symbols, one can be made whole. The trick, of course, is recognizing the proper symbol. I don't believe I ever discovered a more clever or unlikely tool for such therapy than the blessed Rotary Club pin. I don't believe I ever achieved greater success.

Which is not to suggest that Alice de Minuette was any simpler of mind than past acquaintances. Rather, she was an intelligent and worldly woman. Which counts for nothing in this regard. For I believe everyone is essentially simple *regardless* of intelligence or sophistication. We are simple creatures. That's all. Manipulating this single fact is what makes possible the election of a stranger as town mayor, the beatification of an ordinary man as a wizard, the installation of a novice as a movie studio executive. This knowledge is the secret to every magician's trick, every salesman's patter, every soothsayer's truth.

It is the only secret worth knowing.

Yet some call me a charlatan—a liar, a fake, a fraud, a criminal—simply because I know this secret and exercise its powers. Simply because I eat of this forbidden fruit. Yet always I have shared my delicious apple of knowledge. For every scheme in which I used my special understanding to gain profit or position, there were three other schemes or mistruths used to help other human beings. Alice de Minuette is an example.

Was it wrong to have misled her regarding the Rotary Club pin? Was it wrong to have liberated her from fear? Would she call me a charlatan if she learned the truth about her aviation award? I think not. For I saw in her eyes, which she rolled heavenward as if thanking the gods for her deliverance from anguish, that she was grateful to me. Her respectful demeanor during the trip west further demonstrated her gratitude. The kiss she gave to me when we eventually parted company beneath the HOLLYWOOD sign was a final symbol of her devotion. Would a woman of such distinction react this way to a charlatan?

■ 5 ■

A balloon is not "steered." It is directed by ascending or descending until the balloonist finds a wind that coincidentally moves in the direction he wishes to travel. Up or down are the balloonist's only choices, while east or west, north or south, are his aims. Airplanes are far more reliable. But they are never magical.

Ask any balloonist and he will tell you this truth: sometimes the wind understands a balloonist's wishes. Perhaps the wind *always* understands our wishes but chooses to grant them only occasionally. In any case, there are days when the wind blows a balloon on a course more perfect than Charles Lindbergh might ever steer with his airplane rudder and flaps. It is beyond explanation, yet surprisingly common. The wind simply understands and cooperates. One hundred miles per hour in precisely the direction a balloonist wishes to travel. A straight line. It is almost enough to make a person believe in beneficent wizards!

The day we launched from the Kansas wheat field was such a day. The wind blew west.

■ 6 ■

The Midwest of America looks beautiful from a balloon in the same way the surface of a perfectly still lake is beautiful when viewed from under the water. Silent, luminous uniformity. Crossing over the mountains that divide the continent, however, is like looking up at the same surface on a stormy day. Splashes of white violence, undulations, peaks. Yet still submarine silent (for the cold upper reaches are as foreign in their way as a world made of liquid). While the desert that stretches west from the Rockies is marked by tiny waves that ripple the surface like silent music.

■ 7 ■

11:00 P.M. October third.

After soaring for almost seventeen hours, we landed in Culpebble, California, a town so small that Smallville, Kansas, seemed a metropolis by comparison. The Mojave Desert loomed on the edges of the town, straining to swallow up the general store, the gas station, the post office, and the half-dozen wooden shacks that clustered around a single deserted crossroads—straining to creep, like windblown sand, into the town and over it. finally burying the sun-bleached wood forever. Or so it seemed to me at the time. But I was very hungry, and the world itself always looks ravenous to me when I am hungry.

We stopped for food. Alice had insisted. Actually, Alice had *been* insisting for several hours before we came upon the dark scattering of buildings in the moonlit desert. The vast emptiness of the Mojave is awesome. Particularly when you are hungry. Or, like Alice, do not enjoy the same ease with which Loren and I were able to relieve our most urgent bodily callings (the faceless far below must have thought the patter on their roofs the first sprinklings of a storm that would never arrive).

We moored the balloon behind the gas station and began knocking on doors. As I alone in our group carried cash, I graciously volunteered to buy dinner for the others on two conditions: first, that Loren mention me in his autobiography (which he talked of writing after his scientific theory made him famous); and, second, that Alice kiss me upon our landing in Los Angeles (which, I am confident, was not against her sincerest wishes anyway). They readily agreed to my conditions.

But finding food was not so easy. The town was deserted, literally deserted. Loren described the scene as vaguely familiar.

After some deliberation, we broke the rusted lock on the door of the general store and stepped inside. A million particles of dust crossed the streams of moonlight that coursed the deserted store. On one wall was a shelf littered with old books, many bound in leather with genuine gold leaf, others but cardboard editions of Zane Grey or Edgar Rice Burroughs. Another shelf was piled with empty wine bottles and whiskey flasks. Candlesticks were strewn about the corners of the store and rings with rhinestones the size of bottlecaps were neatly arranged in a glass counter. A rack of men's clothing stood near the window, a clarinet served as a doorstop to a back room, and a dozen purple dresses lay folded atop a broken Victrola.

Silence. And no food.

I turned to discover Alice looking into a wicker baby carriage in which lay a china doll perfect but for a hideously shattered face. She stared for some time. Loren moved to her. He touched her hand. She grew pale. I don't understand why, except that the bashed doll had blond hair and blue eyes almost as luminous as Alice's own. After a moment, I noticed that Loren's hands were shaking too. The silence was terrible, but expressive. Finally I understood that the Rotary Club pin had not alleviated *all* the fear and sadness in the hearts of my companions. I resolved to rummage through the general store for some other talisman to help fill the gaps yet undefined in my friends' personalities and pasts. I picked through the junk, finally filling a paper sack.

Then a coyote howled nearby. Alice and Loren turned to me with eyes as wide as a rabbit's. They were not hungry anymore. We returned to the balloon and, without looking back, flew away from Culpebble, California.

■ 8 ■

It was midmorning when we drifted over the San Gabriel mountains and landed in the Hollywood Hills. We knew where we were because of the great white sign that advertises the city to the world: HOLLYWOOD. The very word seems inappropriately presented in anything but capital letters. Yet the city itself is composed more of single-story bungalows than of imposing skyscrapers. It is not architecture that necessitates uppercase. It is powerful myth. As was true in ancient Greece, where once there stood a similar wooden sign in the hills above *their* city of mythic show-business promise; ATH-ENS, their sign read. Uppercase—regardless, heedless, unconcerned whether the city's architecture and political structure might one day crumble.

"Civilization is not eternal," a wealthy Athenian producer once said. "But stardom? Ah, yes."

We were in Hollywood! From the moment we landed I knew I had never been more at home.

■ 9 ■

The three of us stood for some time on a bluff overlooking the city. The day was very clear. The sun shone above us, palm trees swayed beneath us, and mansions sprawled around us—a picture postcard come to life. The air smelled of jasmine. An orchestra rehearsed Mozart somewhere over the hill (I would later learn of the newly completed Hollywood Bowl). A gentle breeze blew across the valley from the Pacific Ocean. I have seen cities of emerald and poppy fields the color of bubble gum. But nothing like this. If more hearts are broken in Hollywood than in any other place on the planet (true), this interplay of myth and beauty and sunshine makes their demise almost worthwhile.

I speak, of course, as a man who has made his fortune in this town. Perhaps my perceptions are colored by success. But then, perceptions colored by failure are no less biased. True? Cynicism is no guaranteed pathway to Truth. And if perceptions are without color altogether, then what in heavens is Technicolor for?

I understood this even as I surveyed the city for the first time. But my companions were serenaded by another muse. They were unmoved by the mythic possibilities of the place, resolved to complete a journey I do not fully understand to this day. They might have gained a fame equal to my own if we had remained together. I might have done for Alice what I subsequently did for so many others—I might have made her a star. After all, she was beautiful, bright, and filled with a vague sadness that translates on the screen as pathos while remaining in real life the very resolve that makes survival possible. And Loren (creator of the Woodville Theory) surely belonged in pictures as a creator of implausible plots. Hollywood *loves* fantastic impossibilities.

Hollywood would have loved them both.

■ 10 ■

We parted company beneath the HOLLYWOOD sign. Loren and Alice offered to help me deflate and dismantle my balloon, but I knew they were anxious to make their way across town. Besides, I was not finished with the vehicle just yet. I suspected that a genuine public "event" (such as an illegally parked balloon) might serve my career more fully than the perfect but private landing just completed. I needed drama. A crowded place. The courtyard of Grauman's Chinese, for example. Press coverage. Notoriety. It had worked for me before.

Loren Woodville claimed *he* wouldn't be needing publicity stunts to gain press coverage. He waxed eloquent about "the real thing." History. Of course I never believed him. Martian space spheres? Yet Loren entertained no doubt. I have always thought disillusionment the ugliest of experiences in a man's life. So I refrained from relating to Loren Woodville a disturbing observation *I* had made some years before through a small telescope while ballooning near the top of the stratosphere. My observation: the explosive spaceships come not from Mars but from our sister planet, Venus.

There are some things a man must learn for himself.

For all Loren Woodville's eloquence (and arrogance), I nonetheless sensed in him a growing fear as we shook hands beside the balloon. It was not a fear of failure. He remained confident. After all, he was in California and would be waiting on the beach when his "space sphere" landed. Neither was it a fear of success. I have seen many turn the corner from obscurity to renown, but I have never known a man more well prepared for recognition. Rather, Loren's fear must have come from the frightening realization that his life's work would soon be *neither* a success nor a failure but reality. His life's work would be altogether independent of his life, one way or another; it would simply *be*. And Loren Woodville would be alone.

At last I understood Loren Woodville. He was a frightened man. Not frightened of the gangsters. Or the Mothman, or the dizzying heights of my balloon. Rather it was the dizzying heights of his own imagination and desire that set him reeling. Loren Woodville was no adventurer. He was a missionary. His were not material aims. His was a rethinking of the whole universe. Loren sought no academic explanations. He sought salvation.

Of course! I dug through the paper sack filled with items taken from the deserted store in Culpebble. I *knew* there would prove a truthful talisman among them. I removed an item as perfect in its importance to Loren as the Rotary Club pin had been to Alice. An acknowledgment of his place in the world, his purpose. A license more true than any of his advanced degrees. I slipped the worn cap—blue felt, red ribbon, black brim—onto his head.

"Salvation Army?" he asked.

"Of course," I said in my most practiced, reverential voice. "With what better militia might we greet our stars incarnate?"

He adjusted the old Salvation Army cap on his head.

"It looks good on you, Loren," Alice said.

She was right.

The pair thumbed a ride in a passing Packard. Loren waved the Salvation Army cap to me through the window, and Alice blew a kiss as the car drove away in a cloud of dust. It was the last I saw of them.

■ 11 ■

The last I *heard* of them was later the same evening. I had bought a newspaper to read about my spectacular balloon landing atop the Hotel Roosevelt's roof. I was disappointed, however, to discover that my aerial accomplishment did not make the front page. This is because there was a bigger news story that day. A national story: Al Capone had been arrested on charges of income tax evasion. The article quoted a policeman named Eliot Ness who claimed to have received documentation of an "irrefutable nature" from a source he refused to name. Capone had returned to Chicago without comment.

To this day I believe Alice de Minuette was somehow involved.

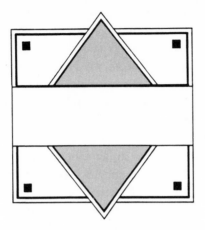

It was evening in Long Beach, California. The lonely strip of beach upon which Loren Woodville awaited his rapidly descending space sphere was lit only by a glow from the Pike, a seaside amusement park half a mile distant, which boasted the greatest roller coaster in the western United States. Above, the sky was blanketed by thick clouds. No moon, no stars, no sight of the sphere as it descended toward the coast. But Loren Woodville did not need to *see* the sphere to know exactly where it was. Geometry served to chart and predict its course more efficiently than the naked eye. Whispering mathematical equations, he ran the toe of his shoe through the damp sand to outline a thirty-foot-wide square into which the sphere would shortly land—a stone's throw from the foamy waves of the Pacific Ocean, a million light-years from his lonely room in Chicago.

Distant sounds from the Pike drifted like invisible balloons in the ocean air—children's callings of wonder and awe, screams from the steepest dips of the infamous roller coaster, and barkers' voices (colleagues of Professor Marvel) extolling the romantic possibilities of "winning one for the little lady." The clatter-clatter of machinery. A calliope played Bach while the carousel glockenspiel hammered out "Yes, Sir, That's My Baby." All audible half a mile distant, carried on the ocean breeze as messages in bottles are carried on the sea's currents. However, it was not the cacophonous amusement park that threatened the clarity of Loren Woodville's practiced words. Rather, it was the steady roar of the surf that demanded he pronounce his speech as self-consciously as Diomedes.

"Welcome, friends." His voice was strong, his gestures gentle. "We greet your arrival with respect and pray humbly that together we may find the Truth and Joy which is denied to those who remain forever apart."

He looked at the ocean as if to elicit a response. Nothing. No crashing ovation. No contemplative ceasing of the rhythmic lunar clock. Only the steady surf (creeping, creeping) as it consumed the edge of the American continent foot by foot. In the hour Loren had waited on the sand, the waves had grown close enough that mist from the tumbling gray hung now in the air around him like particles of steam spewed from the Denver Behemoth. The tide tables, however, indicated that the waves would never quite reach his square in the sand; they would never dampen the Martians' "landing pad." Like Alice de Minuette, he thought, the waves would turn away at the last moment.

He and Alice had stopped at a drugstore soda fountain on Sunset Boulevard some hours before. He wished now he might forget. He wished they had never stopped. They had sat at a counter—swiveling onto the patent leather stools like children—and had ordered syrupy concoctions with a relish impossible for all but the parched of spirit as well as throat. Their flight had been a long one. With the first fizz of cherry soda, however, they slaked the thirst of the dry stratosphere through which they had traveled. Loren remembered the moment fondly, the fizz. They delivered the same message to their taste buds that together they had sent to each other's hearts two nights before in the silent wheat field: the long wait is over; you are not forgotten.

But the moment had not lasted as long as the fizz. . . .

Loren Woodville returned to his solitary work on the dark

beach. A box camera and tripod borrowed from Professor Marvel needed arrangement on the sand. Loren pointed the camera toward the square into which his Martians would shortly land. He placed his tweed jacket—which only two nights before had covered Alice's shoulders as she slept—at the center of the square and ducked behind the black curtain to adjust the camera's focus. Loren had only a passing knowledge of photography. But he believed that whatever his pictures might lose in technical quality (as compared to the work of a professional) would be more than compensated for by the spontaneity and candor on the tiny faces of the Martians.

Besides, Loren hoped for a moment alone with them.

He focused on the tweed jacket. In the background glistened the lights of the Pike: reds and blues and greens, like thousands of colorfully lit ballparks viewed from great height through a moth's-eye view. The ocean ran up to the amusement park. Deep and dark, the rolling of the water was barely perceptible through the camera. The shifting and pitching of the waves seemed to Loren a frightening power only precariously restrained. That seaside communities like Long Beach were built so near repositories of almost unearthly force, and that residents actually *slept* at night with such knowledge, seemed to Loren a far more unlikely reality than his maligned Woodville Theory. Millions of people resting peacefully beside oceans whose deadly waters are restrained only by an orbiting rock 240,000 miles away? What would the "rational" detractors of his theory say to that one?

In truth, he didn't much care anymore.

A man had approached Alice at the soda fountain. He had sat beside her. His name was Monroe Stahr: well-tailored and handsome, he worked as a movie studio executive and talent scout. Stahr was not interested in Martian spheres, cherry sodas, or lighter-than-air balloons, but he claimed to have been professionally impressed ("almost overwhelmed") by Alice de Minuette's natural presence, personality, presentation, possibilities. Screen possibilities. Star quality. He spoke to her of Garbo. He was quite convincing. Alice *was* special. Just not special enough, Loren thought. She left with

Monroe Stahr even before she finished her soda. Loren Woodville knew this, though he wished he might forget.

He stood up from behind the camera. He had discovered that the weight of solitude is even greater in triumph than in defeat.

He looked once more into the sky. Cast upon the underside of the clouds was an illuminous disk beamed from a powerful searchlight at the entrance to the Pike. The circle of light raced about the clouds like a firefly in a fog. Almost otherworldly. But altogether practical. Like the great lights that heralded premieres at Grauman's Chinese, the beam searched not for enemy aircraft but for customers lured like moths to the promise of glamour or excitement at its brilliant source. Loren found such lights interesting for another reason—the Woodville Theory. The projected disk of light moved about the sky in a manner similar to that which Loren had once associated with the movement of Martian spacecraft. He considered it possible (even likely) that Martians often disguised their vehicles to *look* like these luminous advertisements so common to big-city skies. What better way to conceal their presence? Which is why anomalous flying objects are most often sighted in the country. There *are* no searchlights in rural areas and so no basis upon which a Martian craft might be mistaken for mere light. Loren thought the argument promising. But promising arguments were unimportant now. In twenty minutes, a Martian space vehicle was due to land on the square of sand directly before him. Before his waiting camera and all the world.

He took a deep breath. He was weary. His triumphant moment was altogether unlike the way he had expected it to be.

Then something else unexpected: "Hello," Alice said.

Loren Woodville jumped at the sound of her voice.

"Alice?" He turned.

She had approached from behind. The odd footprints of high-heeled shoes stretched into the darkness behind her. She wore new clothes (a white silk evening gown, cut low in front and slit up the side), and she carried a white beaded purse. Her step was graceful even on sand. Her hair shimmered. Her eyes were bright. She glowed on the dark beach like an angel.

"Alice," he said.

"Hello, pal," she answered.

Loren Woodville felt his breath catch in his chest. It was not that he was short of air but that he was pumped up by too much of it. He felt as though he would burst like a toy balloon. Alice! he thought. Yet he could not exhale, for he feared that the expended air would propel him into crazy loops above the ground. He did not know what to do. So he held his breath until Alice spoke again.

"I told you I'd be here," she said.

"I wasn't sure I believed you," he answered, struggling secretly to gain his breath.

"This is an historic moment, right?" she continued. "One way or the other. How could I have missed it?"

"Everything's history," Loren answered. "One way or another."

She smiled. "Even the movies," she said.

"Oh, yes, the movies." Loren looked away.

Alice stepped past him. She touched the box camera with the tips of her fingers. She turned back to him.

"Pictures?" she asked.

"Pictures," Loren answered.

"It's very dark here," she said. "Too dark for pictures, isn't it?"

"The landing will brighten things up," Loren explained.

"Why don't we find some wood and light a bonfire?" Alice asked. She turned in a circle on the sand, surveying the beach. "Why don't we brighten things up right now? Just the two of us. And the land and the sea."

Loren slipped his hands into his pockets. He looked at Alice. She was frighteningly beautiful. He thought of an old song, "How you gonna keep 'em down on the farm after they've seen Par-ee." She was his Paris. Even a Martian princess would not dazzle him now as once he might have been dazzled.

"You should have known I'd be back, Loren," she continued.

"I wasn't sure."

"It was only business," Alice explained. "Stahr's a real producer. In fact, he's the president of the studio. A nice man. But that doesn't change anything between you and me, right? I asked you to join us. I told you it wouldn't take long. That we'd make it back here in time. What were you thinking? You think too much. There are nice people in the world. There always will be. You're one. Stahr's one. But you're special to me, Loren. Special in ways that he could never be. Still, I might *work* for him. Right?"

"You look beautiful," he said.

She turned away.

"I mean, you're all dressed up," he continued.

"You scientists are observant, aren't you?" she said.

"Of course you should work for him," Loren answered, "if you want to work for him. If you *want* to work in the movies. If you want that kind of life."

"What are you talking about, Loren? Do you know something about all this?"

He shook his head no.

"Then what are you talking about?"

"I'm glad you've come," he said.

Alice looked into the overcast sky above them.

"I missed you," he continued.

"I have a thing or two invested in this moment too," she answered. "I was along for the trip."

"So you believe in the Martians?"

"Why are you being so difficult, Loren?"

"Do you?"

"Believe?" she asked. "I don't know. Why is it so important? In a few minutes it won't matter who believed what. Baseball, spaceship . . . the truth will just *be*."

"But it is important."

Alice picked up Loren's tweed jacket from off the beach. She brushed it clean of sand and folded it neatly over her arm. She moved behind him and slipped the jacket onto his shoulders. "It's chilly," she said, touching the back of his neck with her palm. Her touch was warm. "It needn't be. You should take care of yourself."

Loren turned to face her. "Since we arrived in California this morning over four hundred women have been abused and misled and disappointed in their efforts to become movie stars." He touched her cheek with the back of his hand. He shook his head. "And yet you've succeeded on your first attempt. Heck, it wasn't even an attempt. It was an accident."

"Four hundred, Loren?"

"Statistics," he answered. He shrugged his shoulders. "I stopped at the library on my way over here. After you left the soda fountain. I was a little concerned."

"Four hundred broken hearts?" she asked.

He nodded.

"Am I supposed to feel guilty?"

Loren shook his head no. "You're supposed to feel special," he answered. Then he looked into the sky. Clouds. Darkness. Nothing more. Not yet. But soon . . .

"Well, thank you Loren Woodville."

Soon . . .

She pressed against him.

Now . . .

He kissed her.

Except for the carnival music and the steady crashing of the waves, all was quiet beside the thirty-foot-wide square in the sand for some time.

"The spaceship will glow as brightly as a comet," Loren whispered at last, still holding Alice de Minuette. "It will trail behind it a fiery tail of celestial refuse. When it bursts through the clouds, the world will be illuminated almost as brightly as in the day."

"The dark times are over?" she asked.

He nodded, slipping his coat over her bare shoulders.

"The dark times are over," she whispered.

The coat was too big for her. The sleeves reached below her hands. But she brought a graciousness to the wearing of the tweed that made Loren's blood rush in his body. Her slender form, outlined by the white silk, moved beneath the coat as she turned toward the sea.

"Across it lie other worlds," she said, pointing toward the

rolling waves. "The same waters that break on this shore break on the shores of China and Russia and Australia. I've never seen the ocean before. It *is* something, isn't it? It's better than lunch at the Brown Derby. Better than Max Factor. It's real. And if I threw a bottle far enough out into the ocean—" She stopped. She watched the tide move inches nearer with each pulse.

"So you're going to be a movie star?" Loren asked.

She turned back to him. "That's what they say."

"A movie star needs a movie."

She nodded. "They have one for me. It's about a giant gorilla that attacks New York City. He fights airplanes and climbs buildings. It sounds crazy, but they think it'll be a big success. They were casting today. See, the gorilla has a soft side. He falls in love with a blond-haired woman."

"You?"

She shrugged her shoulders. "You have to start somewhere."

"That's right," Loren answered. "But 'somewhere' isn't the same thing as 'anywhere.' "

"This isn't just 'anywhere,' Loren."

"Do you *want* to be a movie star, Alice?"

"Everybody wants to be a movie star."

"I don't," Loren said.

"That's because you're happy with what you are," Alice said.

"Well maybe *that's* what you want to be," Loren answered. "Happy with what you are. Happy because you're doing something that's important to you. Which may not be playing second banana to a giant gorilla."

"Second banana?" Alice said. "Very clever, Loren."

"People will use you," he said. He jingled change in his pockets. "It happens. People mistake a tiny reservoir of beauty for a bottomless ocean of giving. So they take. And they take some more. Because they can't believe such beauty might ever run dry. They take your light and joy to use for themselves. And once it's gone, they don't give it back. They can't. Taking from you is what keeps them alive. Taking from people who are at once more beautiful and more tragic than themselves. Beautiful *and* tragic. They don't want one without the other. It's a package deal. That's Hollywood talk, right? Package deal? That's what they want."

"Loren," she said. "What's gotten into you?"

"I don't know," he said, suddenly calm.

"I'd just like to be an actress," she explained.

He stopped. "An actress?" he asked. He took a deep breath and smiled. "Ah, now, that's something different, Alice. You might be a fine actress. You might add Truth to the world. Truth! I would love for you to try. I would love you for trying. I would help you. It's just this 'movie star' business that frightens me."

"I don't know about the gorilla picture," she said.

He shrugged his shoulders. "Maybe there's something in it for an *actress* as well as for a blonde," he said. "I don't know. Maybe I've been unfair. Maybe there's more to it than there seems."

"You *have* been unfair," she said. She shook her head and turned back to the sea. "But you're not wrong."

"Twelve minutes," Loren said.

"What?"

"Till the space sphere lands," he explained. He pointed to the square of sand. "Right here. Tonight. Then we'll *both* be famous. We'll be celebrities. For a time. Then we'll be whatever we want. Maybe recluses. We'll disappear. We'll lead lives of solitude. To-gether. In a new world."

"You are quite crazy, Loren Woodville."

He looked at her. He did not smile. "I know," he said. He looked down. He etched a small circle in the sand with the toe of his shoe. "I've known for a long time, Alice. But it doesn't help to know. It doesn't make any difference. Madness. The knowing is like being aware of your own breathing. It's there. But you can't *do* anything about it. You can't stop it. Because it's just something you do to stay alive."

"I'm glad you've stayed alive, Loren."

"Eleven minutes, Alice!" he shouted, turning to the sky.

Alice looked down the beach.

Silhouetted against the lights of the amusement park was the approaching figure of a boy.

"Buddy?" she whispered.

Buddy Easter waved as he neared the thirty-foot-wide square in the sand beside which Loren Woodville and Alice de Minuette stood. He walked with a limp. His left shoulder hung lower than his right. Yet there was cheer and relief in his step—like a battered soldier returning from a long, bloody war. Victorious.

"Buddy!" Alice called.

"Buddy?" Loren asked.

Alice moved across the sand to meet the boy.

"Hello, Alice," Buddy said. He smiled. His face was bruised but his eyes remained bright and hopeful. He extended his right hand (his unbroken hand) to shake. His greeting was formal but warm.

Alice held his hand for some time. She fought the urge to take him in her arms. "You have never been far from my thoughts," she said.

Loren joined them in the sandy square. "Hello, Buddy."

Buddy shook Loren's hand, then stepped back. He smiled and motioned with a sweeping of his palm to the empty space beside him. "Look who's come with me," he said. He turned and winked to the empty air. "This, friends, is Abner Doubleday."

Loren and Alice looked at the empty space. Then at one another. Then at Buddy Easter.

"What did you say, Buddy?" Alice asked.

"Right here," the boy answered. "My friend. Abner."

"I don't understand," Loren said.

"Are you all right, Buddy?" Alice asked.

"Oh, yes," Buddy answered. "Alice, it's wonderful to be with you again. All of us together. I'm *fine*. After all, here's Abner. And you. And me. How could I be anything but all right? This is what I've always wanted! Right this minute. You and me and Abner." And then, as an afterthought, "And Loren."

"Who is Abner?" Alice asked.

"He's my friend," Buddy answered, turning to his invisible companion. "Abner Doubleday. Civil War hero. Inventor of baseball. You can say hello, if you want. He can hear you, even if you can't hear him."

Loren and Alice looked at the empty space beside Buddy.

"Hello, Abner," Loren said. "It's a pleasure to meet you."

"Am I missing something here, Loren?" Alice asked.

"Maybe," Loren answered. "Though I can't say for sure."

"Are you all right, Buddy?" she asked.

"I told you I'm great," Buddy said.

"How did you get here?"

Buddy turned back to the empty space beside him. He listened. Silence. "No, Abner," he said, after a moment. "I haven't forgotten how difficult it is for them."

"How did you get here?" Alice repeated.

Buddy smiled. He looked into the cloudy night sky. "We lost track of the baseball this afternoon near Redlands," he said. "Until then we'd been traveling right under it for some time. Then these darn clouds rolled in. But I remembered your calculations, Loren. Long Beach. And you said it would land here whether it was a baseball or a spaceship. You said that gravity's gravity."

"That's right, Buddy," Loren said. "Eight minutes more. But it's not a baseball."

"Abner says it's a baseball," Buddy answered. "He saw Ruth hit it. He *invented* the game. He ought to know what's up there, right? And Anderson McCrew says it's a baseball. He's never wrong. I'm sorry, Loren."

"Who is Anderson McCrew?" Loren asked. He looked around the sand. "Is he here too?"

Buddy shook his head. "Of course not," he said. "Do you *see* Anderson McCrew?"

"How did you get here?" Alice asked.

"Boxcar, mostly," Buddy answered. "I traveled with Woody as far as Bakersfield. He stayed there when he met some friends of his. He said I could stay too. But of course I had to be here. Woody's all right. We had a real good ride. I met some interesting people. I learned a thing or two about the state of the world while I was at it. Oh, Alice. I learned a thing or two."

"When did Abner come along?" Alice asked.

"After Woody left," Buddy answered. He kicked sand at the empty space beside him, laughing and turning as if in anticipation of a playful reprisal. "He was waiting in the boxcar when I got on in Bakersfield," Buddy continued. "Believe me, he was the last guy in the world I expected to run into! Right, Abner? All along I was thinking I'd have to prove myself by catching the baseball. I didn't think he'd come back until I did something great. But that's not the way it is. Right, Abner?"

Buddy turned to the emptiness and waited for an answer. After a moment, he nodded and smiled in response to an invisible communication.

Loren and Alice merely looked at the empty space.

"So you're not going to catch this baseball?" Loren asked at last.

"Sure I'm going to catch it!" Buddy answered. He looked into the sky. "That's why I left Chicago. It's something I have to do. It's just that I'm not doing it for Abner alone. I don't have to. I don't have to prove anything to my friends. But that doesn't mean I can't still do things for them. Right, Abner?" Silence. After a moment: "I'm still going to catch it. For myself! And for you, Loren. And Alice. And everybody in the stands on the day of the Winter Game! Because I'm supposed to."

"Your face," Alice said. She touched the boy's shoulder very softly—as if approaching a wild animal—before moving her hand to his neck and then gradually up to his bruised cheek. She stepped back. "Your hand," she said. "All bandaged. What happened, Buddy? Did Capone find you? Or did all this happen when his men threw you off the train? Loren told me about the train. Did you bump your head? Is that what happened? I'm sorry, Buddy, I didn't want you to be hurt. That's why I left you behind. I was too dangerous. You understand, don't you? I was afraid I might never see you again. I just wanted you to be all right. Are you all right?"

"I'm all right," he said.

"I should have stayed with you," Alice answered.

Buddy shook his head no. "Dr. Sheridan's taken care of

□ 200 □

everything," he said. "I'm all right. Just bruised, that's all. I got stomped a little in the ballpark back in Smallville. But I'll be just fine."

"I shouldn't have left you alone," Alice said.

"It was good that you left me alone," Buddy said. "Besides, I left *you*. Woody and I hit the old lonesome go long before you and Loren ballooned out of the wheat field."

"How did you know we were in the wheat field?" Alice asked.

Loren stepped toward the boy. "How did you know about the balloon?"

"What's more," Buddy continued, "if we hadn't split up I'd never have learned about—" He stopped. He turned to the empty space beside him. He nodded and swallowed hard. He turned to the waves. When he looked once more at Alice he was smiling. "About the things I learned about," he said.

"What did you learn?" Loren asked.

"I learned about you, Loren," Buddy answered. "I learned about the foul ball at the White Sox game a few years ago that put you in the hospital. And I learned about your friend Edwin Hubble who wrote to you after you published the Woodville Theory to ask that you never visit him again. And I know about Astra Hubble. Her flaming red hair. And the lonely nights you suffered after she was gone. And the nights she missed you, too. You didn't know about that, did you? But she did miss you. Not that it matters anymore. Because she's all right now. And you—you're all right, too. You're in love again."

Loren Woodville said nothing.

"That's the most amazing thing about Anderson McCrew," Buddy continued. "He knows things about people they don't even know themselves. It's not like he reads a person's mind to learn a person's past. It's like he reads the mind of God."

"Anderson who?" Loren asked.

Alice turned to Loren. "Is all of that true?"

"Anderson McCrew," Buddy said. "I met him on the train. Woody introduced us. He's a soothsayer of the past. He knows everything that's ever happened. He knows about you, too, Alice. And me. And both of us together."

"I already know about me," Alice said, looking toward the surf. "I haven't forgotten. Things are good, Buddy. At last. I don't need to be reminded that they haven't always been good."

"He knows," Loren said. "All of it. But how could he know?"

"Anderson knew," Buddy answered. "He told me."

"I'm all right as I am," Alice said. "Thank you very much."

"But there's something you don't know," Buddy answered. "Something you *should* know, Alice. Something you have to know."

Alice moved beside Loren.

"I *have* to tell you," Buddy continued. "We can't go on otherwise, Alice."

"Buddy, can't we just be happy?"

"It's as important as the baseball itself."

"But this soothsaying business worries me," Alice said, slipping her hands into the pockets of Loren's coat. "I mean, if this McCrew only knows what I *did* and not what I felt, he might have told you terrible untruths. Because sometimes what I did and what I felt were two different things. And sometimes what I felt was more true than what I actually did. That's the way it is for almost everybody at one time or another. Right?"

Buddy turned to the empty space beside him. He listened.

Silence.

"No, she's not," he said at last to the empty air. "She's got nothing to make excuses *for*."

Buddy listened. Silence.

"All right," he said. He turned back to Alice. "There's nothing about the truth that should worry you," he explained. "Abner wants me to tell you. He's an adult and he knows the whole story. He wants you to know. He thinks you're quite wonderful."

Alice looked at the empty space.

"Anderson McCrew told me something important," Buddy said. "The most important thing in the world."

Alice nodded. "What did he tell you, Buddy?"

Buddy Easter took a deep breath.

"Six minutes," Loren Woodville said.

"Once there was a waitress who worked in a café on the South Side of Chicago," Buddy Easter began. "She was very beautiful but poor. She lived on her own. Her mother had been unkind to her because she thought bad things of her. So the waitress worked long hours and had none of the pretty things that make a sixteen-year-old girl happy. Then she met a young man who traveled regularly through Chicago. He had stopped at the café to buy a piece of apple pie. He was charming and cheerful and though he was barely older than the waitress, his pockets were full of money. And he was famous too. A big league ballplayer. A pitcher for the Boston Red Sox."

"How did you know that?" Alice asked. "I didn't tell you *that*."

"Anderson knew," Buddy answered.

"You don't have to go on," Alice said. "I know what happens from here."

"No, you don't," Buddy answered.

Alice turned away.

"The ballplayer gave to the waitress's life excitement and joy she had never known," Buddy continued. He spoke with an authority altogether independent from his youth and inexperience. He spoke with the borrowed wisdom of the ages. "Anderson stressed to me how sincere their feelings were. They loved each other. And he said I should tell the *whole* story so that you'd know I understand. So that you'd know I could never think badly of you."

"Buddy, why are you doing this?" Alice asked, turning back to the boy. There were tears in her eyes as salty as the air around them. "I never meant to hurt you."

"I *have* to tell you," Buddy explained. "It's fate. It's why we're here. Besides, it's wonderful, Alice. Trust me. More wonderful than you can imagine."

"All right," Alice said.

"The waitress had a baby," Buddy said. He closed his eyes and pronounced his words as if reciting from memory. "But she never told the ballplayer because she feared he might hate her. She was wrong. But she couldn't know. She was too young. She should have asked. But she was too innocent. So she disappeared from the café. She went back to live with her mother. What else could she do? She didn't have any money. And though the ballplayer looked for her, he never found her. He thought she had run away with another man."

Alice gazed into the dark ocean. She pulled Loren's coat tighter around her.

Buddy continued. "Three months after the baby was born, Chicago was struck by an influenza epidemic. Everybody remembers it. Everybody who was there. Everybody who made it through. The waitress fell victim and spent three days in a feverish delirium. Her mother cared for her. The waitress made it through the fever. But when she regained her senses, her baby was gone. Taken by the influenza, her mother told her; there was nothing she might have done. The waitress was alone."

Alice turned around. She wiped her eyes. "What's the point of this, Buddy Easter!"

"Your mother lied," Buddy answered without hesitation. "The baby didn't die. You don't know this, Alice, but it's the truth. I swear. Anderson knew. *You* should know. Don't you feel it? Your mother gave the baby away. To an orphanage. She thought badly of the baby because she thought badly of the ballplayer. And of you. Alice . . . oh, Alice. The baby grew up never knowing his name, or he'd have found you before now. Somehow. I swear!"

Buddy stopped. He wiped his eyes with his bandaged hand.

"Buddy?" Loren whispered.

A tiny smile spread across Alice's red lips. She moved to Buddy Easter. She touched him gently on the cheek as she had touched him three days before on the sidewalk outside the Parkview. In his welling eyes was a depth and sharpness of color she had seen before only in the looking glass. Also a fire she remembered in the eyes of the Babe that burned as clear and unwavering as a lamp on the dark side of the moon. She wondered how she might ever have missed the resemblance. Except that—before this moment—she'd have considered such a truth too good to be true. She'd have considered it impossible that real life might offer coincidences so ripe as this. But that was *before* this moment. That was when she still believed that such a thing as *coincidence* existed. Before she understood that the greatest triumph in the universe is the daily triumph of Truth over fact.

Alice opened her arms. Buddy fell into them.

"George Herman Ruth, Jr.," she whispered into his ear. She held him close. "How I've missed you."

Loren Woodville had lost all track of time.

From out of the sky: *Boom!*

Thunderous waves of sound shook the old buildings along the waterfront to the strained limits of their salt-rusted nails and screws. The sonic boom rattled the roller coaster at the Pike and shattered the glass in countless popcorn machines, sending flying kernels all over the crowded grounds.

"They're here!" Loren cried.

"See it, Alice? See it, Abner?" Buddy shouted.

A strange light illuminated the clouds directly above the thirty-foot-wide square in the sand. The powerful glow shone through the thick cover, casting moving patterns on the clouds. Growing brighter, the glow (like a light bulb held behind a rice-paper watercolor) highlighted the movement and texture of the clouds until the sky looked like a living organism, rippled with fluffy muscles. And still the light grew brighter.

"We've done it!" Loren said. He took from his back pocket the Salvation Army cap that Professor Marvel had given him earlier in the day. He pulled the brim low over his eyes to shield them from the light.

"There it is!" Buddy said.

Bursting through the clouds was a tiny ball of fire, bright as a star, which sent brilliant rays of red and orange in every direction—the city of Long Beach became as bright as the ballpark in Smallville on its night of Edisonian glory, the Pacific Ocean glistened in colors more vibrant than even the reflection of the most picturesque sunset had ever produced, and the underside of the clouds grew bright with stripes like a fluffy quilt knitted by God's most extravagant handmaiden.

"Alice! Buddy!" Loren called. "Get away from there. Get back. Over here!"

The waves pounded against the beach with an anticipatory fury as the heavenly body drew nearer. A high-pitched, whirring sound filled the air, silencing (negating) the music of the nearby carnival as Einstein's antimatter negates star stuff. This *was* the sky come to Earth.

Buddy could see the spinning red laces on the baseball.

Loren ducked behind the box camera, checking the focus once more, preparing to record the moment for posterity. For history. For suitable framing. The beach was lit as brightly as in the day. Alice and Buddy had moved beside him. He stopped. Through the camera's viewfinder, Loren Woodville caught sight of a strange man in a blue army uniform and odd baseball cap standing in the center of the thirty-foot-wide square. From nowhere. Loren stood up from behind the camera. But the strange man was gone. He ducked once more behind the camera. Nothing. He didn't understand. But there wasn't time. He glanced at his pocket watch. He bounced on his toes. Two thousand miles—heck, forty million miles! he thought. Ten seconds. he counted aloud: "Nine, eight, seven . . ."

He stopped at six.

Buddy Easter ran once more into the thirty-foot-wide square. Buddy held his swollen, bandaged hand above his head as if to catch a routine fly ball in a snow-white baseball glove. The boy drifted and staggered, calculating his position. Three steps forward, two steps back. He settled at the center of Loren's marked square, weaving subtly beneath the last gyrations of the approaching baseball. His bruised but hopeful face was illuminated by the glow of the speeding sphere.

"Buddy!" Loren called, jumping out from behind the camera.

The boy shaded his eyes from the approaching brightness.

"Buddy!" Alice called. She moved toward the thirty-foot-wide square. Loren rushed past her, pushing her aside and onto the soft sand, where she toppled near the camera. He raced toward the boy, hoping to pull him out from beneath the path of the sphere. He reached for the boy. But it was not meant to be.

Buddy Easter caught his father's baseball on the fly.

A blinding flash of light. A thunderous crash that shook the Earth. Alice covered her head where she lay. The Earth moved beneath her, the beach pitched and rolled like the sea. When she tried to stand, the ground slipped once more from beneath her feet and sent her again to the sand. The waves raged, spewing foam and froth and crashing in madness upon the shore. From the center of the thirty-foot-wide square glowed a brilliant light that faded only gradually as the seismic tremor—remembered today as the Great Long Beach Earthquake—passed.

All was terrible silence.

Alice sat up. Her head spun, her eyes felt swollen. She stood. The lights of the amusement park were dark. The lights of the city were dark. There was no phosphorescence in the heaving foam of the waves, only the glow from the thirty-foot-wide crater in the sand. All was still. Alice moved toward the crater. She peered over the steaming edge.

"Buddy?" she called.

Silence.

"Loren!"

Loren Woodville lay face down near the top of the crater. A tiny trickle of blood ran from his ear. He did not move. Alice ran to him. She knelt beside him. His eyes were closed. She touched his face, put her fingers to his lips. His head was heavy. She stroked his forehead.

"Wake up, Loren. Wake up!"

His Salvation Army cap lay shredded as if by a razor blade beside where he lay.

"Buddy?"

She turned back to the crater.

"Buddy?"

She scrambled deeper into the sandy crater.

"Buddy!"

Buddy was gone.

The baseball, white hot, spun like a top at the bottom of the crater. It spit sand, digging deeper into the Earth. The baseball Buddy had pursued so purposefully, glowing now like a star. But Buddy Easter himself had disappeared. Literally disappeared. He was gone. Not a piece of bandage from his broken hand. Not a scrap of his shirt. Nothing. Not a shoe. Not a lock of hair.

"Buddy!" Alice cried, falling to her knees beside the steaming baseball. She dug through the hot sand. Nothing. She threw handfuls of sand over her shoulder. Nothing. She ripped and tore at the sand. Nothing. She pounded her fist on the sand and finally dropped her head onto the warm grains. She stopped digging. Her fingers were raw. She could barely catch her breath. her eyes streamed. It seemed to her there was no point in ever climbing out. The tide had begun moving out, the waves breaking farther and farther away. Buddy Easter was gone altogether.

All was silence in the world. Emptiness.

Alice de Minuette might have remained in the crater all night had she not felt a gentle tap on her shoulder. Then another. And another. She looked up.

From out of the sky rained baseball cards. Hundreds of cards— perhaps thousands—some in blue-chip, mint condition. Carried in Buddy Easter's pockets, they had been liberated at the moment the boy caught the baseball: thrown, like confetti, as the greatest home run ever hit returned at last to Earth. Now they covered the silent sky, fluttering down upon Alice de Minuette like countless butter- flies drawn to the light at the edge of the American continent.

Alice stood. The sky was alive with baseball cards, tossing and falling, flipping and sailing on the ocean breeze. They were illumi- nated by the starlight that slipped through a hole in the clouds made when the descending baseball passed fiery through them. When Alice looked through the hole in the clouds, she gasped.

"Buddy!" she called.

A constellation, she thought. For the first time in her life she remembered the astronomical term without the sort of prompting Loren had provided so long before on the Denver Behemoth.

"He's a constellation," she whispered.

In the heavens above America had been born a new star. A point of light on the black background of night, the star provided—like a missing letter in a word—the single element necessary to give meaning to what would otherwise appear a random pattern. Though scientists would later name the new star NGC 8752 and dismiss it as unexceptional, Alice knew that its purpose was anything but ordinary. For the star composed in part the outstretched hand of Buddy Easter as he reached across the night skies for the baseball of his heart and dreams. The baseball he had caught. The image was as clear as any Alice had ever seen on the slick pages of a magazine. It needed no dotted lines drawn from star to star. It *was* Buddy Easter in the sky.

Alice scrambled out of the hole. She moved beside Loren Woodville. She knelt. "Look up!" she said, taking his heavy head in her lap. She stroked his eyes. "Look up, Loren. Look up!"

Loren did not stir. He could not look up. Alice would have to describe the sky to him. But she did not know what to say. Then she remembered. Monroe Stahr had earlier asked her to read a passage from *Romeo and Juliet*. She remembered now.

"Listen, Loren," she said. "This is what it's like.

"Take him and cut him out in little stars,
And he will make the face of heaven so fine
That all the world will be in love with night,
And pay no worship to the garish sun."

She kissed Loren's forehead. "Do you see, my love?" she asked. She turned back to the sky.

In the new constellation, Buddy Easter of Chicago, Illinois (through whose veins ran the most noble of American blood), smiled triumphantly.

EPILOGUE

Loren Woodville did not die in the great impact of the landing baseball. But neither did he awaken for many years. Cast into a deep coma, he slept as the decades passed without him, and in time both his disgraces and his triumphs were lost in the pages of history books and in the deepest recesses of Anderson McCrew's crowded brain. But Alice de Minuette never forgot him.

For forty years she paid his hospital bills and visited him weekly, sitting beside his silent bed, stroking the thinning hair on his head, telling him her most intimate secrets. She was a famous stage actress. Her social life was active. But she never married. She never bore another child. Her family lay silent in the hospital bed and silent in the night skies.

Then, without warning, Loren Woodville awoke. The world was a different place, but his spirit remained essentially unchanged. Alice, whose blond hair had long since turned gray, was at his bedside when he opened his eyes.

"How do you feel?" she asked.

In the reverie of the unconscious (his second extended stay) Loren Woodville had again been visited by profound revelations, this time of a terrestrial nature. "I feel that America is much in want of explanation," he said, sitting up in bed. His back creaked from disuse. He gestured toward his old trunk—abandoned on the Addison Street Bridge years before but returned by Chicagoans who could make no sense of what they discovered written inside. "I need paper," he explained.

With Alice's help, Loren Woodville began work that afternoon on a book that would explain to his countrymen how Buddy Easter's baseball cards had found their way into the jet stream and air currents high in the stratosphere. And why, when one of them still floats down to Earth, landing often in the most unlikely of places, one should not be much surprised.